RADIO FREE ALBEMUTH

BOOKS BY PHILIP K. DICK

The Exegesis of Philip K. Dick

NOVELS

The Broken Bubble
Clans of the Alphane Moon
Confessions of a Crap Artist
The Cosmic Puppets
Counter-Clock World
The Crack in Space
Deus Irae (with Roger Zelazny)
The Divine Invasion
Do Androids Dream of Electric Sheep?
Dr. Bloodmoney
Dr. Futurity
Eye in the Sky
Flow My Tears, the Policeman Said
Galactic Pot-Healer
The Game-Players of Titan
Gather Yourselves Together
Lies, Inc.
The Man in the High Castle
The Man Who Japed
Martian Time-Slip
Mary and the Giant
A Maze of Death
Nick and the Glimmung
Now Wait for Last Year
Our Friends from Frolix 8
The Penultimate Truth
A Scanner Darkly
The Simulacra
Solar Lottery
The Three Stigmata of Palmer Eldritch
Time Out of Joint
The Transmigration of Timothy Archer
Ubik
Ubik: The Screenplay
VALIS
Vulcan's Hammer
We Can Build You
The World Jones Made
The Zap Gun

PHILIP K. DICK

‡

RADIO FREE ALBEMUTH

MARINER BOOKS
HOUGHTON MIFFLIN HARCOURT
Boston   New York

First Mariner Books edition 2020

Copyright © 1985 by The Estate of Philip K. Dick

Published by arrangement with HarperCollins Publishers.

All rights reserved

For information about permission to reproduce selections from this book,
write to trade.permissions@hmhco.com or to Permissions,
Houghton Mifflin Harcourt Publishing Company,
3 Park Avenue, 19th Floor, New York, New York 10016.

hmhbooks.com

Library of Congress Cataloging-in-Publication Data
Names: Dick, Philip K, author.
Title: Radio Free Albemuth / Philip K Dick.
Description: First Mariner Books edition. | Boston :
Houghton Mifflin Harcourt, 2020. | "Mariner Books."
Identifiers: LCCN 2020023424 (print) | LCCN 2020023425 (ebook) |
ISBN 9780358449034 (trade paperback) | ISBN 9780358448891 (ebook)
Subjects: GSAFD: Science fiction.
Classification: LCC PS3554.I3 R3 2020 (print) | LCC PS3554.I3 (ebook) |
DDC 813/.54—dc23
LC record available at https://lccn.loc.gov/2020023424
LC ebook record available at https://lccn.loc.gov/2020023425

DOC 10 9 8 7 6 5 4 3 2 1

PROLOGUE

IN 1932 IN April a small boy and his mother and father waited on an Oakland, California, pier for the San Francisco ferry. The boy, who was almost four years old, noticed a blind beggar, huge and old with white hair and beard, standing with a tin cup. The little boy asked his father for a nickel, which the boy took over to the beggar and gave him. The beggar, in a surprisingly hearty voice, thanked him and gave him back a piece of paper, which the boy took to his father to see what it was.

"It tells about God," his father said.

The little boy did not know that the beggar was not actually a beggar but a supernatural entity visiting Earth to check up on people. Years later the little boy grew up and became a man. In the year 1974 that man found himself in terrible difficulties, facing disgrace, imprisonment, and possible death. There was no way for him to extricate himself. At that point the supernatural entity returned to Earth, loaned the man a part of his spirit, and saved him from his difficulties. The man never guessed why the supernatural entity came to rescue him. He had long ago forgotten the great bearded blind beggar and the nickel he had given him.

I speak now of these matters.

PART ONE

PHIL

PART ONE

PHIL

1

MY FRIEND NICHOLAS Brady, who in his own mind helped save the world, was born in Chicago in 1928 but then moved right to California. Most of his life was spent in the Bay Area, especially in Berkeley. He remembered the metal hitching posts in the shape of horses' heads in front of the old houses in the hilly part of the city, and the electric Red Trains that met the ferries, and, most of all, the fog. Later, by the forties, the fog had ceased to lie over Berkeley in the night.

Originally Berkeley, at the time of the Red Trains and the streetcars, was quiet and underpopulated except for the University, with its illustrious frat houses and fine football team. As a child Nicholas Brady took in a few football games with his father, but he never understood them. He could not even get the team song right. But he did like the Berkeley campus with the trees and quiet groves and Strawberry Creek; most of all he liked the sewer pipe through which the creek ran. The sewer pipe was the best thing on the campus. In summer, when the creek was low, he crawled up and down it. One time some people called him over and asked if he was a college student. He was eleven years old then.

I asked him once why he chose to live his life out in Berkeley, which by the forties had become overcrowded, noisy, and afflicted by angry students who fought it out at the Co-op market as if the stacks of canned food were barricades.

"Shit, Phil," Nicholas Brady said. "Berkeley is my home." People who gravitated to Berkeley believed that, even if they had only been there a week. They claimed no other place existed. This became particularly true when the coffeehouses opened up on Telegraph Avenue and the free speech movement started. One time Nicholas was standing in line at the Co-op on Grove and saw Mario Savio in line ahead of him. Savio was smiling and waving at admirers. Nicholas was on campus the day the PHUQUE sign was held up in the cafeteria, and the cops busted the guys holding it. However, he was in the bookstore, browsing, and missed the whole thing.

Although he lived in Berkeley for ever and ever, Nicholas attended the University for only two months, which made him different from everyone else. The others attended the University in perpetuity. Berkeley had an entire population of professional students who never graduated and who had no other goal in life. Nicholas's nemesis vis-à-vis the University was ROTC, which in his time was still going strong. As a child Nicholas had gone to a progressive or Communist-front nursery school. His mother, who had many friends in the Communist Party in Berkeley in the thirties, sent him there. Later he became a Quaker, and he and his mother sat around in Friends Meeting the way Quakers do, waiting for the Holy Spirit to move them to speak. Nicholas subsequently forgot all that, at least until he enrolled at Cal and found himself given an officer's uniform and an M-1 rifle. Thereupon his unconscious fought back, burdened by old memories; he damaged the gun and could not go through the manual of arms; he came to drill out of uniform; he got failing grades; he was informed that failing grades in ROTC meant automatic expulsion from Cal, to which Nicholas said, "What's right is right."

However, instead of letting them expel him, he quit. He was nineteen years old and his academic career was ruined. It had been his plan to become a paleontologist. The other big university in the Bay Area, which was Stanford, cost far too much for him. His mother held the minor post of clerk for the U.S. Department of Forestry, in a building on campus; she had no money. Nicholas faced going to work. He really hated the University and thought of not returning his uniform. He thought of showing up at drill with a broom and insisting it was his M-1 rifle. He never thought of firing the M-1 rifle at his superior officers, though; the firing pin was missing. Nicholas, in those days, was still in touch with reality.

The matter of returning his officer's uniform was solved when the University authorities opened his gym locker and took the uniform out of it, including both shirts. Nicholas had been formally severed from the military world; moral objections, more thoughts of brave demonstrations, vanished from his head, and in the fashion of students attending Cal he began roaming the streets of Berkeley, his hands stuck in the back pockets of his Levi's, gloom on his face, uncertainty in his heart, no money in his wallet, no definite future in his head. He still lived with his mother, who was tired of the arrangement. He had no skills, no plans, only inchoate anger. As he walked along he sang a left-wing marching song from the International Brigade of the Loyalist Army of Spain, a Communist brigade made up mostly of Germans. The song went:

> *Vor Madrid im Schützengraben,*
> *In der Stunde der Gefahr,*
> *Mit den eisernen Brigaden,*
> *Sein Herz voll Hass geladen,*
> *Stand Hans, der Kommissar.*

The line he liked best was "Sein Herz voll Hass geladen," which meant "His heart full of hate." Nicholas sang that over and over again as he strode along Berkeley Way, down to Shattuck, and then up Dwight Way back to Telegraph. Nobody noticed him because what he was doing was not unusual in Berkeley at that time. One often saw as many as ten students striding along in jeans singing left-wing songs and pushing people out of the way.

AT THE CORNER of Telegraph and Channing the woman behind the counter at University Music waved at him, because Nicholas often hung around there browsing through the records. So he went inside.

"You don't have your uniform on," the woman said.

"I've dropped out of the fascist university," Nicholas said, which certainly was true.

Pat excused herself to wait on a real customer, so he took an album of the Firebird Suite into a listening booth and put on the side where the giant egg cracks open. It fitted his mood, although he was not certain what came out of the egg. The picture on the album cover just showed the egg, and someone with a spear evidently going to break the egg.

Later on, Pat opened the door of the listening booth, and they talked about his situation.

"Maybe Herb would hire you here," Pat said. "You're in the store all the time, you know the stock, and you know a lot about classical music."

"I know where every record in the store is," Nicholas said, excited at the idea.

"You'd have to wear a suit and tie."

"I have a suit and tie," Nicholas said.

Going to work for University Music at nineteen was probably the greatest move of his life, because it froze him into a mold that never broke, an egg that never opened — or at least did not open for twenty-five more years, an awfully long time for someone who had really never done anything but play in the parks of Berkeley, go to the Berkeley public schools, and spend Saturday afternoons at the kiddies' matinee at the Oaks Theater on Solano Avenue, where they showed a newsreel, a selected short subject, and two cartoons before the regular subject, all for eleven cents.

Working for University Music on Telegraph Avenue made him part of the Berkeley scene for decades to come and shut off all possibilities of growth or knowledge of any other life, any larger world. Nicholas had grown up in Berkeley and he remained in Berkeley, learning how to sell records and later how to buy records, how to interest customers in new artists, how to refuse taking back defective records, how to change the toilet paper roll in the bathroom behind the number three listening booth — it became his whole world: Bing Crosby and Frank Sinatra and Ella Mae Morse, *Oklahoma,* and later *South Pacific,* and "Open the Door, Richard" and "If I'd Known You Were Coming I'd Have Baked a Cake." He was behind the counter when Columbia brought out LP records. He was opening cartons from the distributors when Mario Lanza appeared, and he was checking inventory and back orders when Mario Lanza died. He personally sold five thousand copies of Jan Peerce's "Bluebird of Happiness," hating each copy. He was there when Capitol Records went into the classical music line and when their classical music line folded. He was always glad he had gone into the retail record business, because he loved classical music and loved being around records all the time, selling them to customers he personally knew and buying them at discount for his own collection; but he also hated the fact that he had gone into the record business because he realized the first day he was told to sweep the floor that he would be a semi-janitor, semi-clerk the rest of his life — he had the same mixed attitude toward it he had had toward the university and toward his father. Also, he had the same mixed attitude toward Herb Jackman, his boss, who was married to Pat, an Irish girl. Pat was very pretty and a lot younger than Herb, and Nicholas had a heavy crush on her for years and years, up until the time they all became older and did a lot of drinking together at Hambone Kelley's, a cabaret in El Cerrito that featured Lu Watters and his Dixieland jazz band.

I met Nicholas for the first time in 1951, after Lu Watters's band had become Turk Murphy's band and signed up with Columbia Records. Nicholas often came into the bookstore where I worked during his lunch hour, to browse among the used copies of Proust and Joyce and Kafka, the used textbooks the students at the university sold us after their courses — and their interest in literature — ended. Cut off from the university, Nicholas Brady bought the used textbooks from the poly sci and literature classes that he could never attend; he had quite a knowledge of English lit, and it wasn't very long before we got to talking, became friends, and finally became roommates in an upstairs apartment in a brown shingle house on Bancroft Way, near his store and mine.

I had just sold my first science fiction story, to Tony Boucher at a magazine called *Fantasy and Science Fiction,* for $75, and was considering quitting my job as book clerk and becoming a full-time writer, something I subsequently did. Science fiction writing became my career.

2

THE FIRST OF Nicholas Brady's paranormal experiences occurred at the house on Francisco Street where he lived for years; he and his wife, Rachel, bought the house for $3,750 when they first got married in 1953. The house was very old — one of the original Berkeley farmhouses — on a lot only thirty feet wide, with no garage, on a mud sill, the only heat being from the oven in the kitchen. His monthly payments were $27.50, which is why he stayed there so long.

I used to ask Nicholas why he never painted or repaired the house; the roof leaked and in wintertime during the heavy rains he and Rachel put out empty coffee cans to catch the water dripping everywhere. The house was an ugly peeling yellow.

"It would defeat the purpose of having such an inexpensive house," Nicholas explained. He still spent most of his money on records. Rachel took courses at the University, in the political science department. I rarely found her home when I dropped by. Nicholas told me one time that his wife had a crush on a fellow student, who headed the youth group of the Socialist Workers Party just off campus. She resembled the other Berkeley girls I used to see: jeans, glasses, long dark hair, assertive loud voice, continually discussing politics. This, of course, was during the McCarthy period. Berkeley was becoming extremely political.

Nicholas had Wednesdays and Sundays off from work. On Wednesday be was home alone. On Sunday both he and Rachel were home.

One Wednesday—this is not the paranormal experience—when Nicholas was home listening to Beethoven's Eighth Symphony on his Magnavox phonograph, two FBI agents dropped by.

"Is Mrs. Brady home?" they asked. They wore business suits and carried bulging briefcases. Nicholas thought they were insurance salesmen.

"What do you want from her?" he demanded with hostility. He imagined they were trying to sell her something.

The two agents exchanged glances and then presented Nicholas with their identification. Nicholas was filled with rage and terror. He started telling the two FBI agents, in a stammering voice, a joke he had read in "Talk of the Town" in *The New Yorker* about two FBI agents who were checking up on a man, and, while interviewing a neighbor, the neighbor had said the man listened to symphonies, and the agents asked suspiciously what language the symphonies were in.

The two agents standing on Nicholas's front porch, on hearing his garbled version of the story, did not find it funny.

"That wasn't our office," one of them said.

"Why don't you talk to *me*?" Nicholas demanded, protecting his wife.

Again the two FBI agents exchanged glances, nodded, and entered the house. Nicholas, in a state of terror, sat facing them, trying to quell his shaking. "As you know," the agent with the greater double chin explained, "it is our job to protect the liberties of American citizens from totalitarian intrusion. We never investigate legitimate political parties such as the Democratic

or Republican parties, which are bona fide political parties under American law." He then began to talk about the Socialist
Workers Party, which, he explained to Nicholas, was not a legitimate political party but a Communist organization devoted to
violent revolution at the expense of American liberties.

Nicholas knew all that. He kept silent, however.

"And your wife," the other agent said, "could be of use to us,
since she belongs to the student corps of the SWP, in reporting
who attends their meetings and what is said there." Both agents
looked expectantly at Nicholas.

"I'll have to discuss this with Rachel," Nicholas said. "When
she comes home."

"Are you engaged in political activity, Mr. Brady?" the agent
with the greater double chin asked him. He had a notebook before him and a fountain pen. The two agents had propped one
of their briefcases between Nicholas and them; he saw a square
object bulging within it and knew he was being taped.

"No," Nicholas said, truthfully. All he did was listen to exotic
rare foreign vocal records, especially those of Tiana Lemnitz,
Erna Berger, and Gerhard Husch.

"Would you like to be?" the lesser agent asked.

"Um," Nicholas said.

"You're familiar with the International People's Party," the
greater agent said. "Had you ever considered attending meetings of it? They hold them about a block from here, on the other
side of San Pablo Avenue."

"We could use someone in there at the local group meeting,"
the lesser agent said. "Are you interested?"

"We can finance you," his colleague added.

Nicholas blinked, gulped, and then gave the first speech of
his life. The agents were not pleased, but they listened.

Later on that day, after the agents had left, Rachel arrived
home, loaded down with textbooks and looking cross.

"Guess who was here today looking for you," Nicholas said. He told her who.

"Bastards!" Rachel cried out. "Bastards!"

It was two nights later that Nicholas had his mystical experience.

He and Rachel lay in bed, asleep. Nicholas was on the left, nearer the door of their bedroom. Still disturbed by the recent visit of the FBI agents, he slept lightly, tossing a lot, having vague dreams of an unpleasant nature. Toward dawn, just when the first false white light was beginning to fill the room, he lay back on a nerve, awoke from the pain, and opened his eyes.

A figure stood silently beside the bed, gazing down at him. The figure and Nicholas regarded each other; Nicholas grunted in amazement and sat up. At once Rachel awoke and began to scream.

"Ich bin's!" Nicholas told her reassuringly (he had taken German in high school). What he meant to tell her was that the figure was himself, "Ich bin's" being the German idiom for that. However, in his excitement he did not realize he was speaking a foreign language, albeit one Mrs. Altecca had taught him in the twelfth grade. Rachel could not understand him. Nicholas began to pat her, but he kept on repeating himself in German. Rachel was confused and frightened. She kept on screaming. Meanwhile, the figure disappeared.

Later on, when she was fully awake, Rachel was uncertain whether or not she had seen the figure or just reacted to his start of surprise. It had all been so sudden.

"It was myself," Nicholas said, "standing beside the bed gazing down at me. I recognized myself."

"What was it doing there?" Rachel said.

"Guarding me," Nicholas said. He knew it. He could tell from having seen the expression on the figure's face. So there was nothing to be afraid of. He had the impression that the figure, himself, had come back from the future, perhaps from a point vastly far ahead, to make certain that he, his prior self, was doing okay at a critical time in his life. The impression was distinct and strong and he could not rid himself of it.

Going into the living room, he got his German dictionary and checked the idiom that he had used. Sure enough, it was correct. It meant, literally, "I am it."

He and Rachel sat together in the living room, drinking instant coffee, in their pajamas.

"I wish I was sure if I saw it," Rachel kept repeating. "*Something* sure scared me. Did you hear me scream? I didn't know I could scream like that. I don't think I ever screamed like that before in my life. I wonder if the neighbors heard. I hope they don't call the police. I'll bet I woke them up. What time is it? It's getting light; it must be dawn."

"I never had anything like that happen before in my life," Nicholas said. "Boy, was I surprised, opening my eyes like I did and seeing it — me — standing there. What a shock. I wonder if anybody else ever had that happen to them. Boy."

"We're so near the neighbors," Rachel said. "I hope I didn't wake them."

The next day Nicholas came around to my place to tell me about his mystical experience and get my opinion. He was not exactly candid about it, however; initially he told it to me not as a personal experience but as a science fiction idea for a story. That was so if it sounded nutty the onus wouldn't be on him.

"I thought," he said, "as a science fiction writer you could explain it. Was it time travel? Is there such a thing as time travel? Or maybe an alternate universe."

I told him it was himself from an alternate universe. The proof was that he recognized himself. Had it been a future self he would not have recognized it, since it would have been altered from the features he saw in the mirror. No one could ever recognize his own future self. I had written about that in a story, once. In the story the man's future self came back to warn him just as he, the protagonist, was about to do something foolish. The protagonist, not recognizing his future self, had killed it. I had yet to market the story, but my hopes were good. My agent, Scott Meredith, had sold everything else I had written.

"Can you use the idea?" Nicholas asked.

"No," I told him. "It's too ordinary."

"Ordinary!" He looked upset. "It didn't seem ordinary to me that night. I think it had a message for me, and it was beaming the message at me telepathically, but I woke up and that ended the transmission."

I explained to him that if you encountered your self from an alternate universe — or from the future, for that matter — you would hardly need to employ telepathy. That wasn't logical, since there would be no linguistic barrier. Telepathy was used when contact between members of different races, such as from other star systems, took place.

"Oh," Nicholas said, nodding.

"It was benign?" I asked.

"Sure it was; it was me. I'm benign. You know, Phil, in some ways my whole life is a waste. What am I doing at my age, working as a clerk in a record shop? Look what you're doing — you're a full-time writer. Why the hell can't I do something like that? Something meaningful. I'm a clerk! The lowest of the low! And Rachel is going to be a full professor some day, when she's through school. I should never have dropped out; I should have gotten my B.A."

I said, "You sacrificed your academic career for a noble cause, your opposition to war."

"I broke my gun. There was no cause; I was just inept the day we had to take apart our gun and put it back together. I lost the trigger down inside the works. That's all."

I explained to him how his subconscious was wiser than his conscious mind, and how he ought to take credit for its vision, its sense of higher values. After all, it was part of him.

"I'm not sure I believe that," Nicholas said. "I'm not sure what I believe any more. Not since those two FBI agents came by and rousted me. They wanted me to spy on my wife! I think that's what they were really after. They get people to spy on each other, like in 1984, and destroy the whole society. What does my life add up to, Phil, in comparison to yours, say? In comparison to anyone's? I'm going to Alaska. I was over the other day talking to the man at Southern Pacific; they have connections to Alaska through a yacht that goes up there three times a year. I could go on that. I think that's what my self from the future or an alternate universe was there to tell me, the other night, that my life doesn't add up to anything and I better do something drastic. I probably was about to find out what I was supposed to do, only I wrecked it all by waking up and opening my eyes. Actually it was Rachel who scared it off by screaming; that's when it left. If it wasn't for her I'd know how to organize my future, whereas as it stands I know nothing, I'm doing nothing, I have no hopes or prospects except checking in the goddamn Victor shipment that's up there at the shop waiting for me, forty big cartons — the whole fall line they pushed on us, that even Herb went for. Because of the ten percent discount." He lapsed into gloomy silence.

"What did the FBI agents look like?" I asked, never having seen one. Everybody in Berkeley was scared of just such a visit as Nicholas had received, myself included. It was the times.

"They have fat red necks and double chins. And little eyes, like two coals stuck into dough. And they watch you all the time. They never take their eyes off you. They had faint but detectable southern accents. They said they'd be back to talk to both of us. They'll probably be by to talk to you too. About your writing. Are your stories left-wing?"

I asked, "Haven't you read them?"

"I don't read science fiction," Nicholas said. "I just read serious writers like Proust and Joyce and Kafka. When science fiction has something serious to say, I'll read it." He began, then, to talk up the virtues of *Finnegans Wake,* in particular the final part, which he compared to the final part of *Ulysses.* It was his belief that no one but himself had either read it or understood it.

"Science fiction is the literature of the future," I told him, when he paused. "In a few decades they'll be visiting the moon."

"Oh, no," Nicholas said vigorously. "They'll never visit the moon. You're living in a fantasy world."

"Is that what your future self told you?" I said. "Or your self from another universe, whatever it was?"

IT SEEMED TO me that it was Nicholas who was living in a fantasy world, working in the record store as a clerk, meanwhile always lost in great literature of a sort divorced from his own reality. He had read so much James Joyce that Dublin was more real to him than Berkeley. And yet even to me Berkeley was not quite real but lost, as Nicholas was, in fantasy; all of Berkeley dreamed a political dream separate from the rest of America, a dream soon to be crushed, as reaction flowed deeper and deeper and spread out wider. A person like Nicholas Brady could never go to Alaska; he was a product of Berkeley and could only survive in the radical student milieu of Berkeley. What did he know of the rest of the United States? I had driven across the country; I had visited Kansas and Utah and Kentucky, and I knew the isolation of the Berkeley radicals. They might affect America a little with their views, but in the long run it would be solid conservative America, the Midwest, which would win out. And when Berkeley fell, Nicholas Brady would fall with it.

Of course this was a long time ago, before President Kennedy was assassinated, before President Ferris Fremont and the New American Way. Before the darkness closed over us completely.

3

BEING POLITICALLY ORIENTED, Nicholas had already noted the budding career of the junior senator from California, Ferris F. Fremont, who had issued forth in 1952 from Orange County, far to the south of us, an area so reactionary that to us in Berkeley it seemed a phantom land, made of the mists of dire nightmare, where apparitions spawned that were as terrible as they were real — more real than if they had been composed of solid reality. Orange County, which no one in Berkeley had ever actually seen, was the fantasy at the other end of the world, Berkeley's opposite; if Berkeley lay in the thrall of illusion, of detachment from reality, it was Orange County which had pushed it there. Within one universe the two could never coexist.

It was as if Ferris Fremont stood amid the deserts of Orange County and imagined, at the north end of the state, the unreal thralldom of Berkeley and shuddered and said to himself something on the order of *That must go.* If the two men, Nicholas Brady in the north and Ferris Fremont in the south, could have looked across the six-hundred-mile distance between them and confronted each other, both would have been appalled, Ferris Fremont as much so as Nicholas Brady, who was already appalled as he read in the *Berkeley Daily Gazette* about the rise to political power of the publisher from Oceanside who had gotten his chance in the Senate by defaming his Democratic rival, Margaret Burger Greyson, as a homosexual.

As a matter of record, Margaret Burger Greyson was a routine senator, but the defamatory charges had formed the basis of Fremont's victory, not her voting record. Fremont had used his newspaper in Oceanside to blast Mrs. Greyson, and, financed by unknown sources, he had plastered the southern part of the state with billboards darkly alluding to Mrs. Greyson's sex life.

CALIFORNIA NEEDS A STRAIGHT CANDIDATE!
DON'T YOU THINK THERE'S SOMETHING QUEER ABOUT GREYSON?

That kind of thing. It was based on a supposedly actual incident in Mrs. Greyson's life, but no one really knew. Mrs. Greyson fought back but never sued. After her defeat she vanished into obscurity, or maybe, as Republicans joked, into the gay bars of San Diego. Mrs. Greyson, needless to say, had been a liberal. In the McCarthy days there wasn't that much difference in the public's view between communism and homosexuality, so Fremont had little difficulty winning, once his smear campaign began.

At that time Fremont was a callow lout, fat-cheeked and sullen, with beetle brows and pasted-down black hair that looked greased into place; he wore a pinstripe suit and loud tie and two-tone shoes, and it was said that he had hair on his knuckles. He was frequently photographed at the target range, guns being his hobby. He liked to wear a Stetson hat. Mrs. Greyson's only rejoinder to him that ever received any favor was a bitter remark, made after the returns had come in, that Fremont certainly was no straight shooter, straight or not. Anyhow, Mrs. Greyson's political career was ended, Ferris F. Fremont's begun. He flew at once to Washington, D.C., in search of a house for himself, his wife, Candy, and their two bulbous sons, Amos and Don.

Now, you should have seen the effects in Berkeley of all this shit. Berkeley did not take it well. The radical student milieu resented a campaign's being won on such a basis, and they resented Fremont's showing up in Washington even more. They did not so much care for Mrs. Greyson as they resented the winner; for one thing, as Republicans pointed out, there were many gays in Berkeley, and there certainly were many pinkos. Berkeley was the pinko capital of the world.

The pinko capital of the world was not surprised when Senator Fremont was named to a committee investigating un-American activities. It wasn't surprised when the senator nailed several prominent liberals as Communist Party members. But it was surprised when Senator Fremont made the Aramchek accusation.

Nobody in Berkeley, including the Communist Party members living and working there, had ever heard of Aramchek. It mystified them. What was Aramchek? Senator Fremont claimed in his speech that a Communist Party member, an agent of the Politburo, had under pressure given him a document in which the CP-USA discussed the nature of Aramchek, and that from this document it was evident that the CP-USA, the Communist Party of America, was itself merely a front, one among many, cannon fodder as it were, to mask the real enemy, the real agency of treason, Aramchek. There was no membership roll in Aramchek; it did not function in any normal way. Its members espoused no particular philosophy, either publicly or privately. Yet it was Aramchek that was stealthily taking over these United States. You'd have thought someone in the pinko capital would have heard of it.

At that time I knew a girl who belonged to the Communist Party. She had always seemed strange, even before she joined, and after she joined she was insufferable. She wore bloomers and informed me that the sex act was an exploitation of women, and one time, in anger at my choice of friends, she dropped her cigarette in my cup of coffee at Larry Blake's restaurant on Telegraph Avenue. My friends were Trotskyists. I had introduced her to two of them in public, without telling her their political affiliations. You never did that in Berkeley. Liz came by my table the next day at Larry Blake's, not speaking; I think it got her in trouble with the Party. Anyhow one time kiddingly I asked her if she also belonged to Aramchek as well as to the Party.

"What a crock," she said. "What a fascist lie. There is no Aramchek. I would know."

"If it existed," I asked, "would you join it?"

"It would depend on what it does."

"It overthrows America," I said.

"Don't you think monopoly capitalism with its suppression of the working class and its financing of imperialist wars through puppet regimes should be overthrown?" Liz said.

"You'd join it," I said.

But even Liz couldn't join Aramchek if it didn't exist. I never saw her after she dropped her cigarette in my coffee at Larry Blake's; the Party had told her not to talk to me again, and she did what it said. Still, I don't believe she ever managed to rise high in the Communist Party; she was a typical low-echelon type, devoted to following orders but never really getting them right. Ever since, I've wondered what happened to her. I doubt if she ever wondered what happened to me; after the Party pronounced the ban on me I ceased to exist, as far as she was concerned.

One night I had dinner with Nicholas and Rachel where the topic of Aramchek came up. The Socialist Workers Party had passed a resolution denouncing both Senator Fremont and Aramchek: one the arm of U.S. imperialism, the other the arm of militant Moscow.

"That's covering both bases," Nicholas commented. "You SWP are certainly opportunists."

Rachel smiled the superior sneering smile of a Berkeley poly sci girl.

"Are you still seeing that guy?" Nicholas said, meaning the SWP organizer that his wife had a crush on.

"Are you still in love with your boss's wife?" Rachel demanded.

"Well," Nicholas muttered, fooling with his coffee cup.

"I think Fremont has a great concept there," I said. "Denouncing an organization that doesn't even exist — one Fremont made up and says it's taking over America. Obviously no one can destroy it. No one's safe from it. No one knows where it'll turn up next."

"In Berkeley," Nicholas said.

"In Kansas City," I said. "In the heartland. In Salt Lake City — anywhere. Fremont can form anti-Aramchek cadres, youth groups on the right dedicated to fighting it wherever it manifests itself, armed uniformed bands of kids ever vigilant. It'll get Fremont into the White House." I was kidding. But, as we all know, I turned out to be right. After the death of John Kennedy, and his brother's death, and the death of virtually every other major political figure in the United States, it took only a few years.

4

THE PURPOSE OF killing the leading political figures in the United States by violent assassination, allegedly by screwed-up loners, was to get Ferris F. Fremont elected. It was the only way. He could not effectively compete. Despite his aggressive campaigns, he bordered on the worthless. Some time ago one of his aides must have pointed that out to him. "If you're going to get into the White House, Ferris," the aide must have said, "you've got to kill everyone else first." Taking him literally, Ferris Fremont did so, starting in 1963 and working his way forward during the administration of Lyndon Johnson. By the time Lyndon Johnson had retired, the field was clear. The man who could not compete did not have to.

There is no point in dwelling on the ethics of Ferris Fremont. Time has already rendered its verdict, the verdict of the world — except for the Soviet Union, which still holds him in great respect. That Fremont was in fact closely tied to Soviet intrigue in the United States, backed in fact by Soviet interests and his strategy framed by Soviet planners, is in dispute but is nonetheless a fact. The Soviets backed him, the right-wingers backed him, and finally just about everyone, in the absence of any other candidate, backed him. When he took office, it was on the wave of a huge mandate. Who else could they vote for? When you consider that in effect Fremont was running against no one else, that the Democratic Party had been infiltrated by his people, spied on, wiretapped, reduced to shambles, it makes more sense. Fremont had the backing of the U.S. intelligence community, as they like to call themselves, and ex-agents played an effective role in decimating political opposition. In a one-party system there is always a landslide.

One asks, Why should such disparate groups as the Soviet Union and the U.S. intelligence community back the same man? I am no political theoretician, hut Nicholas one time said, "They both like figureheads who are corrupt. So they can govern from behind. The Soviets and the fuzz, they're all for shadow governments. They always will be, because basically each of them is the man with the gun. The pistol to the head."

No one had put a pistol to Ferris Fremont's head. He was the pistol itself, pointed at our head. Pointed at the people who had elected him. Behind him stood all the cops in the world, the left-wing cops in Russia, the right-wing cops in the United States. Cops are cops. There are only divisions of rank, into greater and lesser. The top cop is probably never seen.

However, Nicholas was no political theoretician either. In point of fact he had no idea how the coalition behind Fremont had formed; in fact he had no idea it existed. Like the rest of us over those years, he simply stood amazed as prominent politicians were murdered and Fremont rose rapidly to power. What was happening made no sense. No pattern could be discerned.

There is a Latin motto, when one is seeking to know who has committed a crime, that goes, *Look to see who gains.* When John Kennedy was murdered, and Dr. King, and Bobby Kennedy, and the others, when George Wallace was crippled, we should have asked, Who gains? All men in America lost by these dreadful senseless murders except one second-rate man whose way was now clear to the White House: clear to get in and clear to remain. Who otherwise would have had no chance.

We should forgive ourselves, though, for not figuring out who was doing it and why; after all, it had never happened in the United States before, although the history of other countries is full of it. The Russians know it well; so do the English — take Crookback Dick, as Shakespeare calls Richard III. There was the paradigm for this: Richard, who murdered his way to the throne, killing even children, and all with the excuse that nature had made him ugly. Nature had made Ferris Fremont ugly too, inside and out. Personally, it never entered my mind. We thought of a lot of possibilities, but not really that. The Tartar mind had never schemed for the American throne until then.

I do not, however, propose to write about how Ferris Fremont got to power. I propose to write about his downfall. The former story is known, but I doubt if anyone understands the way he was defeated. I intend to write about Nicholas Brady, and about Nick Brady's friends.

Even though I had quit my job at the bookstore to write full-time, I still liked to drop into University Music to listen to the new LPs and say hello to Nicholas, who now spent much of his time with the salesmen from the various distributors or up in the office doing paperwork. By 1953 for all intents and purposes he managed University Music; the owner, Herb Jackman, had another store in Kensington and spent his time there. It was nearer his home. Pat still worked in Berkeley, and she and Nicholas were together most days.

What I didn't know was that Herb had a heart condition. He had suffered one heart attack in 1951, and his doctor ordered him to retire. He was only forty-seven and he would not retire; instead he bought a very small store in Kensington, and puttered around in it. The only day it did any business was on Saturday, whereas University Music employed five clerks and was busy all the time.

Nicholas and Pat, of course, knew about Herb's heart condition. Sometimes on Saturday night Herb and his buddies got together in the office at University Music and played poker, at which times I occasionally joined them. All his buddies knew about his heart condition. They were a rough bunch, but they liked him a lot; most of them were small businessmen in the neighborhood, and they had common interests, such as all the dopers moving onto Telegraph Avenue. They could see what lay ahead. Nicholas used to say later on that what killed Herb was the drug scene on Telegraph. Before Herb died he had time to see spade pushers offering joints to passersby openly across the street down toward Dwight. To a straitlaced man from Oklahoma like Herb, that would do it.

I also played poker with Tony Boucher and his friends, at his house on Dana; they, like me, were all science fiction writers. Nicholas never played poker; he was too intellectual for that. Nicholas was your typical Berkeley intellectual, involved with books and records and the Avenue coffeehouses. He and Rachel, when they felt like going out, crossed the bay to San Francisco and headed straight for North Beach and the coffeehouses there, along Grant. Before that they stopped in Chinatown and ate dinner at exactly the same restaurant, the oldest one there, according to them: Yee Jun's, on Washington. You had to go downstairs to the basement, and the tables had marble tops. There was a short waiter there named Walter who, it was said, fed homeless students for free, the sort filling up San Francisco who would one day cease being the Beatniks, as Herb Caen termed them, and become the Haight-Ashbury hippies. Nicholas was never a Beatnik or a hippie — he was far too intellectual for that—but he resembled one, with his jeans and tennis shoes and his short beard and tousled hair.

The big problem for Nicholas was the prospect of remaining a record clerk all his life. Even managing University Music seemed to be that, and it was messing up his head, especially as his wife moved toward getting her degree. Instead of going to school he was putting his wife through school. He had the feeling that Rachel looked down on him. Berkeley being a college town, he felt that most people looked down on him. It was a difficult period for him. Obviously his boss would have another heart attack, at which point Pat, as the legal owner of University Music, would undoubtedly put him, Nicholas Brady, in charge of the store. He would be doing what Herb had been doing, which he was virtually doing already, and it came into his mind that probably he would wind up like Herb: dead from worry and overwork at a job that gave little back, dead at an early age, at his post from nine in the morning until midnight, Retail record selling, for the independent owner, was a losing proposition; the big chains were starting to come in, Music Box and the Wherehouse, the discount record stores.

At this time Nicholas had another paranormal experience. He told me about it the next day.

THIS ONE HAD to do with Mexico. He had never been to Mexico and knew little about it, and this was why the detail of the dream amazed him so: every car, every building, all the people on the sidewalks and in the restaurants were so sharply etched. And it was no return to a past life because he saw Yellow Cabs—it was truly modern, a big city such as Mexico City itself, very busy, very noisy, but with the sounds somehow muted and at a constant background level of murmuring. In the dream he never heard a single clear word. No one spoke to him; there were no characters, just cars, taxis, street signs, stores, restaurants. It was entirely scenic. And it rolled on and on for hours, in a strange vivid shiny color, the kind, Nicholas said, you find in acrylic paint.

The dream had come to him oddly: during the day. At about two in the afternoon, on his day off, he had gotten sleepy and had lain down on the living room couch. The dream began at once. He was at a taco stand buying a taco. But then the scene rolled open, as if doors had swung wide or lifted up; all at once he no longer stood before the taco stand but, instead, faced a panorama of Mexico itself. Romantic and thrilling it was, sparkling with color in the night, drawing him toward it with many hints and promises. It fanned out in all directions, a vast foreign landscape not known to him, not a part of the contents of his own mind, lovely, compelling, leading him on so that after a short time he was in the midst of it, with the rich life spilling by on all sides: the murmur of people, the swish of traffic, and all so real, so unmistakably real.

At one point he found himself moving with a small group through a museum of some sort, located at the edge of the ocean. He saw many exhibits and pictures he could not later recall, but that section alone evidently lasted for hours. The total elapsed time of the experience, in real time, was almost eight hours. He had noticed what time it was when he lay down, and when he rose he rechecked it. Eight hours of scenic Mexico, and for no cost!

Later he said to me, "It was as if another mind were trying to communicate with me. Life unlived, I think. Where I might have lived. What I might have experienced."

I couldn't argue with that. His constricted Berkeley life certainly cried out for such a vivid trip.

"Maybe it means you should move to Southern California," I said.

"No, it was Mexico — a foreign country."

"Have you ever thought of moving to LA?"

He did not find that funny. "A vast mind was talking to me! Across endless miles of space! From another star!"

"Why?" I asked.

"I believe it has seen my needs. I believe it intends to direct my life toward some great goal presently unglimpsed. I —" Nicholas got a sly, secretive look on his face. "I have a name for it: Valisystem A. It stands for Vast Active Living Intelligent System A. I call it 'A' because it may be only one out of many. It has all those characteristics; it is vast, it is active, it is intelligent, and it forms a coherent system."

"You know all that from its showing you Mexico?"

"I sensed it there. I intuited its nature. Sometimes I lie awake at night and try to commune with it. All this has resulted from my appeals over the years; I've appealed for this many times."

I thought over the word "appeal" and then realized that the word he meant was prayer. He had prayed for this, was what he intended to say, but no one in Berkeley ever used the word "prayer." There was no religion in Berkeley, except among the Okies who had migrated out during World War II to work in the Richmond shipyards. Nicholas wouldn't be caught dead using the word "prayer."

I guessed, then, that he had had other experiences with Valis, as he called him.

As a matter of fact he had had other experiences, which he later told me about: dreams of a peculiar repetitive nature, in which large open books were held up before his eyes, with printing like that of old Bibles. In each dream he either read or tried to read the printing, with meager results — at least to his conscious mind. There was no telling how much he absorbed unconsciously and repressed or forgot on awakening: probably a great deal. I had the impression, from what he said, that he was shown enough writing in his dreams to have taken the equivalent of a crash course — in what, neither he nor I could tell.

5

THIS WENT ON for some time. A year later when I ran into Nicholas he was still seeing written pages in his sleep, although not as frequently. One interesting thing he told me was that he had discovered, upon falling into and out of sleep, that the writing appeared in his dreams only between 3:00 and 4:00 a.m.

"That must mean something," I said.

The only words he had been able to read clearly had to do with him, although he was certain that his name appeared frequently in other texts. This passage ran:

A RECORD CLERK IN BERKELEY WILL HAVE
MANY TROUBLES, AND AT LAST HE WILL

No more; the rest had been forgotten or just plain blurred. In that dream the book was held by, of all people, me; I stood with the pages open and extended to him, inviting him to examine them, which he did.

"Are you sure it's not God talking to you?" I said.

That was an unpopular topic in Berkeley, when it was a topic at all; I said it just to needle him. But he himself had said that the great open pages, the large old-looking books, resembled Bibles he had seen. He had made the connection himself. How-

ever, he preferred his theory that an extraterrestrial intelligence from another star system was conversing with him, and
for this reason he kept me posted about his experiences. Had
he decided it was God, he undoubtedly would have ceased talking to me and consulted a minister or priest, so his theory was a
lucky break for me.

Lucky, that is, insofar as I was interested in what he had to
say. However, since he had seen me in his dream extending the
written page, I was involved somehow. But although I was a
professional science fiction writer, I could not really give credence to the idea that an extraterrestrial intelligence on another star system was communicating with him; I never took
such notions seriously, perhaps because I was a writer of such
things and was accustomed to dredging them up from my own
mind in purely fictional form. That such things could genuinely
occur was foreign to my way of thinking. I did not even believe
in flying saucers. It was a hoax and fiction to me. So perhaps of
all people he knew to confide in, Nicholas had picked the worst.

As far as I was concerned it was a chronic fantasy life that
Nicholas's mind had hit on to flesh out the little world in which
he lived. Communicating with Valis (as he called it) made life
bearable for him, which it otherwise would not be. Nicholas, I
decided, had begun to part company with reality, out of neces-
sity. Being a record clerk in a city of educated intellectuals was
too much for him to endure. This was a classic example of how
the human mind, lacking real solutions, managed its miseries.

I stuck to this theory about Valis for several years — up to the
day, in the late sixties, when I personally saw Valis heal Nicholas and Rachel's little son of a birth defect. But that came later.

There was a lot, it turned out, that Nicholas hadn't told me,
from the start. He tailored what he said. It was his intention
not to appear crazy, which is a desire indicating some residual
smarts, some vestigial grip on reality after most of it had fled. He

knew he shouldn't be experiencing what he was experiencing, and he knew that if indeed he was (which he was), he should not talk about it. He selected me to tell because I wrote science fiction and therefore, he presumed, I was more tolerant, more broad-minded in regard to contacts with nonhumans. That was one matter Nicholas was certain about. Valis was nonhuman.

Regarding all this, Rachel, his wife, took the crudest and most derisive attitude imaginable. Her Berkeley intellectual ferocity grew continually. Nicholas, if he tried to discuss Valis in front of her, was immediately subjected to sneers that beggared description. You would have thought that he had become a Jehovah's Witness, another area of boundless contempt on his overeducated wife's part. A Jehovah's Witness or a member of the Young Republicans—some abomination of such an absolute nature as that. Something that set him apart from reasonable man entirely. Which I guess the narrations about his experiences with Valis did. You could hardly blame her. Except, I always thought, the excessive harshness was unnecessary; she should simply have sent him over to California State Mental Hygiene for some group therapy.

I still thought Nicholas should move to Southern California, mainly to get him out of Berkeley. He did go, but just to visit Disneyland. Still, that was a trip of sorts. It meant he had to get his car fixed up, with new tires; he and Rachel piled their sleeping bags, tent, and Coleman stove into the back of their Plymouth and set out, with the intention of sleeping on the beaches in order to save money. Nicholas also had a secret mission, about which he did not tell his boss, Herb Jackman. According to Nicholas's official story, this was simply a vacation. In actuality (he confided to me, his best friend), he would be visiting Progressive Records in Burbank, where he knew someone: their West Coast representative, Carl Dondero. This little record outfit put out folk music records, which sold better in Berkeley than anywhere else, and since Nicholas was part of the Berkeley scene he spent a lot of time listening to such folk singers as Josh White and Richard Dyer-Bennet, owned as many Hudson Back Bay Ballad records as existed, and could tell you who revived the five-string banjo (Pete Seeger, Nicholas claimed, and then discoursed on the Almanac Singers, with whom Seeger had sung anonymously). The idea was that Nicholas, if he liked what he saw at Progressive Records and liked what he heard from the brass there, might go to work for them. I had met Carl Dondero once, and he and I both felt that Nicholas should get out of Berkeley. This was Dondero's way of accomplishing it.

What Carl Dondero had not thought out clearly is the ominous fact that Los Angeles is the nut capital of the world; that every religious, paranormal, and occult group originates there and draws its followers there; that Nicholas, were he to resettle in the southland, would be exposed to other people like himself and hence would probably worsen rather than mend. Nicholas would be moving to an area which ill defined the quality of sanity. What could we expect from Nicholas, if he were exposed to LA? Valis, most likely, would emerge into the open as Nicholas's meager contact with reality dwindled out of existence entirely.

Nicholas, however, did not in fact plan to move from Berkeley. He and it were too closely bonded. What he looked forward to was lunch with the brass from Artists and Repertoire at Progressive Records; they would woo him and wine him, and he could then triumphantly say no to them and return to Berkeley, having been given a viable alternative which he had turned down flat. For the rest of his life, as a record clerk on Telegraph Avenue, he could tell himself that he had chosen his life in preference to the disloyalty of moving to LA.

But when he got down to the LA area, in particular down to Orange County and Disneyland, and had had a chance to cruise around in his old Plymouth, he discovered something unexpected, although more or less in fun I had suggested it to him. Parts of that region resembled his Mexico dream. I had been right. Upon leaving the freeway near Anaheim — he took the wrong exit ramp and wound up in the town of Placentia — he discovered Mexican buildings, low-rider Mexican cars, Mexican cafes, and little wooden houses filled with Mexicans. He had stumbled onto a barrio for the first time in his life. The barrio looked like Mexico, except that there were Yellow Cabs. Nicholas had made actual contact with the world of his visionary dream. And this changed everything in regard to taking the job at Progressive Records.

He and Rachel returned to Berkeley, but not to stay. Now that he knew an actual world existed as depicted in his dream — as seen in his dream — Nicholas could not be stopped.

"I was right," he told me on returning to the Bay Area. "It wasn't a dream. Valis was showing me where I ought to be living. I have a destiny down there, Phil, that dwarfs anything you can imagine. It leads to the stars."

"Did Valis tell you what your destiny down there is?" I asked him.

"No." He shook his head. "I'll find that out when the time comes. It's the same principle as in the spy services; you're to know only what's necessary for you to know. If you understood the big picture it'd blow your head off. You'd go crazy."

"Nicholas," I said, "you'd quit your job and move down to Orange County because of a dream?"

"As soon as I saw the barrio in Placentia I recognized it," Nicholas said. "Every building and street, every car that passed — they were precisely as I dreamed them. The people walking along, the street signs, even. Down to the smallest detail. Valis intends for me to move down there."

"Ask him why before you do it. You have a right to know what you're getting into."

"I trust Valis."

"Suppose he's evil."

"Evil?" Nicholas stared at me. "He's the absolute force of good in the universe!"

"I'm not sure I'd trust him," I said, "if it were me and my life. I mean, you are talking about your life, Nick. Here you are giving up your house and your job and your friends because of a dream he shows you — a preview. Maybe it's just precognition on your part. Maybe you're a precog." I had written several stories about precogs, in fact a novel, *The World Jones Made*, and I tended to view precognition as a mixed blessing. In my stories, and especially in the novel, it placed the character in a closed loop, a victim of his own determinism; he was compelled, just as Nicholas seemed now, to enact later what he foresaw earlier, as if by previewing it he was destined to fall victim to it, rather than obtaining the capacity to escape it. Precognition did not lead to freedom but rather to a macabre fatalism, just as Nicholas now displayed: he *had* to move to Orange County because, a year ago, he had experienced a preview vision of it. Logically it made no sense. Couldn't he avoid going just precisely because he had suffered a premonition?

I was willing to admit that what Nicholas saw in his dream-vision was an accurate representation of the barrio down in the city of Placentia in Orange County. But I saw it more as a paranormal talent on Nicholas's part than a communication from an extraterrestrial entity in another solar system. One had to draw the line of common sense somewhere. Using Occam's Principle of Scientific Parsimony, the simplest theory was mine. One did not need to drag in another, more powerful mind.

However, Nicholas did not view it that way. "It's not a question of which theory is more economical; it's a question of what's true. I'm not in communication with myself. I have no way of knowing that my destiny lies down in Placentia. Only a greater mind, above human level, would know that."

"Maybe your destiny lies directly at the center of Disneyland. You could sleep under the Matterhorn ride and live on Coke and hot dogs, like they sell there. There're bathrooms. You'd have all you need."

Rachel, who was listening to all this, shot me a look of pure malice.

"Well, I'm just doing what you do," I said to her. "Making fun of him. You don't want to live in the LA area, do you, Rachel? Outside of Berkeley?"

"I'd never live in Orange County," Rachel said vehemently.

"There you are," I said to Nicholas.

Nicholas said, "We're thinking of splitting up. So she can continue on at the university and I can pursue my destiny down there."

That made it real. Divorce based on a dream. What strange grounds. Cause of divorce? I left my wife because I dreamed about a foreign land . . . which proved to be ten miles from Disneyland, near a lot of orange trees. Down in plastic-town U.S.A. It was unreal, and yet Nicholas meant it. And they had been married for years.

The resolution to this came three years later when Rachel discovered that she was pregnant. Those were the days of the diaphragm, which wasn't all that good. This ended her university career; after she had little Johnny she didn't care where they lived. She got fat and sloppy; her hair became a mess; she forgot all she had learned at school and instead watched daytime TV.

In the mid-sixties they moved to Orange County. In a few years, Ferris F. Fremont would become president of the United States.

6

HOW ARE YOU to treat a friend whose life is directed from beyond the stars? What attitude do you take? I saw Nicholas rarely after he and Rachel moved down to Orange County, but when I did see him, when they drove up for a prolonged stay in the Bay Area or I flew down to visit them and take in Disneyland, Nicholas always filled me in on what Valis was up to. After he moved to Orange County, Valis communicated with him a lot. So from his standpoint the move was worth it.

Also, the job at Progressive Records turned out to be a vast improvement over working as a record clerk. Retail record selling was a dead end and Nicholas had always known it, whereas the recording field itself was wide open. Rock had become big, now, although that did not affect Progressive Records, which signed only folk artists. Even so, Progressive Records was getting them up there on the sales charts; they had some of the best folk artists under contract, many from the old San Francisco scene: from the Hungry i and the Purple Onion. They almost signed Peter, Paul and Mary, and, according to them, they had turned down the Kingston Trio. I heard about this through Nicholas; being in Artists and Repertoire, he himself auditioned new vocal artists, instrumentalists, and groups, made tapes of them on location ... although he did not have the authority to sign them. He did have the authority to reject them, however, and he enjoyed exercising this. It beat changing the toilet paper roll behind listening booth three, back up in Berkeley.

At last Nicholas's natural ear for a good voice was paying off. His talent plus what he had learned from listening to rare vocal records at University Music late at night were now underwriting him financially. Carl Dondero hadn't erred; in doing Nicholas a favor he had done Progressive Records a favor as well.

"So you have a groovy job," I said, as he and I and Rachel sat around their apartment in Placentia.

"I'm driving to Huntington Beach to take in Uncle Dave Huggins and His Up-Front Electric Jugs," Nicholas said. "I think we should sign with them. Sign them up. It's folk rock, really. A little like the Grateful Dead does on some of their tracks." We were listening to an LP of the Jefferson Airplane at that moment, quite a jump from the classical music Nicholas had loved back in Berkeley. Grace Slick was singing "White Rabbit."

"What a groovy broad," Nicholas said.

"One of the best," I said. I had just become interested in rock. The Airplane was my favorite group; one time I had driven over to Marin County to the town of Bolinas to gaze at the house reputed to be Grace Slick's. It was up over the beach but back away from the people and noise. "Too bad you can't sign her," I said to Nicholas.

"Oh, I see plenty of groovy broads," Nicholas said. "A lot of folksingers, aspiring folksingers, are broads. Most of them are what we in the industry call strictly no-talent. They've maybe listened repeatedly to tracks by Baez and Collins and Mitchell and imitated them — nothing original."

"So now," I said, "you have power over people."

Nicholas was silent, fooling with his glass of Charles Krug wine.

"How does it feel?" I asked.

"Well, I —" Nicholas hesitated. "I hate to see the expression on their faces when I say no. It's —" He gestured. "They have such high hopes. They come to Hollywood from all over the country with such high hopes. Like in the song by the Mamas & Papas, 'Young Girls Are Coming to the Canyon.' There was one girl today . . . she hitchhiked from Kansas City, Kansas, with a fifteen-dollar Sears practice guitar . . . she knew perhaps five chords, and she had to read out of a songbook. We don't generally audition them unless they're booked somewhere already. I mean, we can't audition everybody." He looked sad as he said this.

"What's Valis have to say these days?" I asked. Perhaps with his new, more expanded life he was no longer hearing voices and seeing printed pages in his sleep.

Nicholas got a strange look on his face. For the first time since the topic came up he seemed reluctant to discuss it. "I've —" he began, and then he motioned me to go along with him, out of the living room of the apartment and into their bedroom. "Rachel has a rule now," he explained, shutting the door after us. "I'm not to ever mention it. Listen." He seated himself on the bed facing me. "I've discovered something. The clarity with which I can hear him — or her, or them; whichever it is — depends on the wind. When the wind is blowing — it blows in here from the desert to the east and north — I receive the communication better. I've been taking notes, Look at this." He opened a dresser drawer; there lay a stack of papers, typed on, about a hundred sheets. And in the corner of the bedroom stood a small typing table with a Royal portable on it. "There's a lot I haven't ever told you," he said, "about my contacts with them. I think it's them. They seem to be able to come together and form a single body or mind, like a plasmatic life form. I think they exist in the atmosphere."

"Goodness," I said.

Nicholas said earnestly, "To them, this is a polluted ocean we live in; I've had dream after dream from their viewpoint, and always they're looking down — I'm looking down — into a stagnant ocean or pond."

"The smog," I said.

"They hate it. They won't descend into it. You're a science fiction writer; could life forms exist unsuspected in Earth's atmosphere, highly evolved, highly intelligent life forms, which take an active interest in our welfare and can help us when they choose? You'd think there would have been reports over the ages. It doesn't make sense; someone would have discovered them long ago. Maybe — this is one of my theories — maybe they recently entered our atmosphere, possibly from another planet or plane. Another possibility I've considered is that they're from the future, come back here in time to assist us. They're very anxious to assist us. They seem to know everything. Christ, I guess they can go anywhere; they don't have material bodies, just the energetic plasmatic forms, like electromagnetic fields. They probably merge, pool their information, and then separate. Of course I'm just theorizing. I don't know. That's the impression of them I get."

I said, "How come you can hear them and no one else can?"

"I have no theory about that."

"Can't they tell you?"

Nicholas said, "I really don't understand much of what they say. I just get impressions of their presence. They did want me to move down here to Orange County; I was right about that. I think it's because they can contact me better, being near the desert with the Santa Ana wind blowing a lot of the time. I've bought a bunch of books to do research, like the *Britannica*."

"If they exist, somebody else would have —"

"I agree." Nicholas nodded. "Why me? Why wouldn't they talk to the President of the United States?"

"Ferris F. Fremont?"

He laughed. "Well, I guess so; I see what you mean. But there're so many really important people.... One time — listen to this." He began rummaging among the sheets of paper. "They showed me an engineering principle, a motor with two shafts turning in opposite directions. They explained the whole principle to me; I saw the damn thing, round and very heavy. With no centrifugal torque, because of the opposed shafts. The shafts worked through a gear train to a common drive, finally, I guess, but I couldn't see that; it was on the other side. In the dream I held the whole unit in my hands — it was painted red. I don't know what the power source was, probably electricity. And I remember this: it had a cam system, a chain with weights that was tossed from one spinning rotor to the other very rapidly, to act as a brake. They wanted me to write all this down when I woke up; they showed me a very sharp pencil and note pad. They said — and I'll never forget this — they told me, 'This principle was known in your time.' You see what that implies?" Nicholas had become very excited; his face was animated and flushed, and the words spilled out. "It tells me they're from the future."

"Not necessarily," I said. "It could just mean that in the future the motor you saw becomes well known. It may merely mean that they know our future."

Nicholas stared at me, his mouth working silently, in perplexity.

"See," I explained, "beings of that high order could have transcended the barrier of —"

"This is real," Nicholas said quietly.

"Pardon?" I said.

In a low, steady voice, Nicholas said, "This is not a story. I've got over twenty thousand words of notes I've taken on this. Theories, research; what I've seen, heard. What I know. You know what I know? This is moving toward something, but I can't see what. They don't want me to see what; I'll find out when the time comes, when they want me to. They're not telling me very much, not really; sometimes I think as little as they can. So don't screw around with spinning science fiction theories, Phil. You understand?"

There was silence. We faced each other.

"What am I supposed to say?" I asked finally.

"Just be serious about it," Nicholas said. "Just take it for what it is: a very serious, maybe a very grim, matter. I wish I knew. I sense that they're in deadly earnest, playing a deadly game, on a scale beyond me, beyond all of us. Here for a purpose that —" He broke off. "Christ," he said, "this whole thing is getting to me. I wish there was someone I could tell; that's what bothers me, that I can't tell anyone. They moved me from Berkeley to Orange County . . . I can't even tell *that*."

"Why can't you tell that?"

"I've tried." Nicholas did not elaborate.

"You seem more mature," I said.

"Well, I got out of Berkeley." He shrugged.

"You have real responsibilities now."

"I had real responsibilities then. I'm beginning to realize that it's not a game."

"Your job —"

"What I'm being told. When I'm asleep. Just because I don't remember it when I wake up means nothing. I've read enough to know it's remembered somewhere in the brain. It goes into the unconscious and is stored. Listen." He gazed at me intently. "Phil," he said, "I think I'm being programmed. I catch a phrase, a word; nothing more. Nothing I can go on either way. Just enough to make me think so. If I am being programmed, then it's inhibited, which is the way programming works, either in the brain or in electronic circuitry, and eventually I'll run into

the disinhibiting stimulus, and all the programming will fire, either correctly or not, depending on how well it's laid down." He
paused and then added remotely, "I've been reading about it. I'd
never know."

"Even when the disinhibiting stimulus is encountered?"

"No, it would all seem natural, what I'd say and do. I'd think
it was my idea. Like a posthypnotic suggestion; you incorporate
it into your world view as logical. No matter how bizarre, or
how destructive, or how —" Again he was silent, and this time
he did not resume speaking.

"You've changed," I said. "Besides being more mature, but
along those lines."

"Moving down here has changed me," Nicholas said, "and
the research I've done has changed me; now I have the financial
resources to get prime source material to go on. Herb Jackman
never paid me beans, Phil. I just floundered around."

"It's more than doing research," I said. "Berkeley is full of
people doing research. What sort of friends do you have down
here? Who've you met?"

"People at Progressive, mostly," Nicholas said. "Professional
people, in the music industry."

"Have you told them about Valis?"

"No."

"Have you talked to a psychiatrist?"

"Shit," Nicholas said wearily. "You know and I know this isn't
a matter for a psychiatrist. I might have thought that a long,
long time ago. Years ago and six hundred miles away, in a town
that was nuts. Orange County isn't nuts; it's very conservative
and very stable. The nuts are up north in LA County, not here. I
missed the nut belt by sixty-five miles; I overshot. Hell, I didn't
overshoot; I was deliberately shot down here, to central Orange
County. To get out of parochial towns like Berkeley. To a place

where I could think and introspect, get perspective and some kind of understanding. More confidence, really. That is what I think I've acquired, if anything."

"Maybe that's it."

Nicholas said, half to himself, "It all seemed sort of—like fun, back in Berkeley, these inner contacts with another mind, deep in the night, involuntarily, with me just lying there passive and having to hear whether I liked it or not. We were kids there in Berkeley; no one living in Berkeley ever really grows up. Perhaps that's why Ferris Fremont loathes Berkeley so."

"You're aware of him a lot," I said, "now that you're down here?"

"I'm aware of Ferris Fremont," Nicholas said cryptically. "Now that I'm down here, yes."

Because of an imaginary voice, Nicholas had become a whole person, rather than the partial person he had been in Berkeley. If he had remained in Berkeley he would have lived and died a partial person, never knowing completeness. What sort of an imaginary voice is that? I asked myself, Suppose Columbus had heard an imaginary voice telling him to sail west. And because of it he had discovered the New World and changed human history.... We would be hard put to defend the use of the term "imaginary" then, for that voice, since the consequences of its speaking came to affect us all. Which would have constituted greater reality, an "imaginary" voice telling him to sail west, or a "real" voice telling him the idea was hopeless?

Without Valis addressing him in his sleep, showing him visually a happier promise, speaking to him persuasively, Nicholas would have visited Disneyland and returned to Berkeley. I knew it and Nicholas knew it. Whether anyone else assessed it this way was unimportant; I knew him and I knew that on his own, unaided, he would have stayed in his rut forever. Something had intervened in Nicholas's life and destroyed the hold that bad karma had on him. Something had severed the iron chains.

This, I realized, is how a man becomes what he is not: by doing what he could never do — in Nicholas's case, the totally impossible act of moving from Berkeley to Southern California. All his compeers would still be up there; *I* was still up there. It was spectacular; here he was, raised in Berkeley, sitting in his modern apartment (Berkeley has no modern apartments) in Placentia, wearing a florid Southern California–style shirt and slacks and shoes; already he had become part of the lifestyle here. The days of blue jeans were gone.

7

THE IMAGINARY PRESENCE of Valis — whose name Nicholas had been forced to make up, for want of a real one — had made him into what he was not; had he gone to a psychiatrist he would still be what he was, and he would stay what he was. The psychiatrist would have focused his attention on the origin of the voice, not on its intentions or on the results. That very psychiatrist was probably still living in Berkeley. No nocturnal voices, no invisible presence sketching out a happier life, would have plagued him. How undisturbed, the sleep of the foolish.

"Okay, Nick," I said. "You win."

"Pardon?" He glanced at me, a little wearily. "Oh, I see. Yes, I guess I win. Phil, how could I have stayed in Berkeley so long? Why did it take someone else, another voice, not mine, to goad me into life? Why was that necessary?"

"Um," I said.

"The incredible part is not that I heard Valis, listened to Valis, and moved here, but that without him, or them, I wouldn't have contemplated it, let alone done it. Phil, the idea of leaving Berkeley, quitting my job with Herb Jackman — it wouldn't even have entered my mind."

"Yeah, that is the incredible part," I agreed. He was right. It said something about the normal trajectory of human existence, *Homo* unimpeded: allowed to trudge out his circular course, like a wedge of dead rock circling a dead sun, mindless and purposeless, deaf to the universe at large, as blind as it was cold. Something into which no new idea ever came. Barred forever from originality. It made you stop and reflect.

Nicholas said, "Whoever they are, Phil, I have no choice but to trust them. I'm going to be doing what they want anyhow."

"I think you'll know," I said, "when your programming fires." If indeed — sobering thought — he had been programmed.

"You suppose I'll notice? I'll be too busy to notice."

That chilled me: the thought of him in action all at once, blurring, as if possessing sixteen arms.

"They —" Nicholas continued.

"I wish you wouldn't call them 'they,'" I said, "It makes me nervous. I'd be a lot less nervous if you'd say 'he.'"

"It's the joke about the five-thousand-pound canary: where does it sleep?" Nicholas said.

"Anywhere it wants."

"I call them 'they,'" Nicholas said, "because I've seen more than one of them. A woman, a man. Two for openers, and two is they."

"What'd they look like?"

After a pause, Nicholas said, "Of course you realize these were dreams. And dreams are distorted. The conscious mind sets up a barrier."

"To protect itself," I finished.

Nicholas said, "They had three eyes. The normal two, and then one with a lens, not a pupil. Dead center in the forehead, That third eye witnessed everything. They could turn it on and off, and when it was off it was entirely gone. Invisible. And during that time" — he took a deep shuddering breath — "they looked just like us. We — never guessed." He became silent.

"Oh, good God," I said aloud.

"Yep," Nicholas said, stoically.

"Did they speak?"

"They were mute. And deaf. They were in round chambers like bathyspheres, with lots of wires running to them, like electronic booster equipment, communications equipment, phone-type wires. The wires and boosters were so they could communicate with us, so their thoughts would form words we could hear and understand, and so they could hear us back. It was difficult, a strain for them."

"I don't know if I want to hear this."

"Hell, you write about it all the time. I've been reading some of your novels, finally. You —"

"Writing fiction," I said. "It's all fiction."

"Their craniums were enlarged," Nicholas said.

"What?" I was having trouble following him; it was too much for me.

"To accommodate the third eye. Massive craniums. A wholly different skull shape from ours, very long. The Egyptian Pharaoh had it — Ikhnaton. And Ikhnaton's two daughters, but not his wife. It was hereditary on his side."

I open the bedroom door and walked back into the living room, where Rachel sat reading.

"He's crazy," Rachel said remotely, not looking up from her book.

"Right," I said. "Completely. Nothing left. Only thing is, I don't want to be here when his programming fires."

She said nothing; she turned a page.

Following me out of the bedroom, Nicholas approached the two of us; he held a piece of paper toward me, for me to see. "This is a sign they showed me several times, two intersecting arcs arranged — well, you can see. It's a little like the Christian fish sign, the side of the fish with the arcs forming its body. The interesting thing is, if an arc intersects once —"

From the design on the extended piece of paper a pinkish-purple beam of light, an inch in diameter, fired upward into Nicholas's face. He shut his eyes, grimaced with pain, dropped the sheet of paper, and swiftly put his hand to his forehead. "All of a sudden," he said thickly, "I have the most violent headache."

"Didn't you see that beam of light?" I said. Rachel had set down her book and was on her feet.

Nicholas removed his hand from his forehead, opened his eyes, and blinked. "I'm blind," he said.

Silence. The three of us stood there, unmoving.

"I can see phosphene activity now," he said presently. "An afterlight. No, I didn't see any beam of light. But I see a phosphene circle. It's pink. Now I can make out a few things."

Rachel moved toward him, took him by the shoulder. "You better sit down."

In an odd, even voice, almost mechanical in quality, Nicholas intoned, "Rachel, Johnny has a birth defect."

"The doctor said nothing at all is —"

"He has a right inguinal strangulated hernia. It's already gone down into the scrotal sac. The hydroseal is broken. Johnny needs immediate surgery; go to the phone, pick it up, and dial Dr. Evenston. Tell him you're bringing Johnny into the emergency room at St. Jude Hospital in Fullerton. Tell him to be there."

"Tonight?" Rachel said, appalled.

Nicholas intoned, "He is in imminent danger of death." With his eyes shut he then repeated it, word for word, exactly as he had said it; watching him, I got the impression, suddenly, that even though his eyes were shut he was seeing the words. He spoke as if reading them off a cue card, like a performer. It was not his tone of voice, his cadence; he was following words written out for him.

I ACCOMPANIED THEM TO the hospital. Rachel drove; Nicholas was still having trouble with his eyes, so he sat beside her holding the little boy. Their physician, Dr. Evenston, very irritable, met them at the emergency room. First he told them that he had examined Johnny several times for possible herniation and found nothing; then he took Johnny off; time passed; Dr. Evenston eventually returned and said noncommittally that there was indeed a right inguinal hernia, reducible but needing immediate surgery, since there was always the possibility of strangulation.

On the way back to the Placentia apartment, I said, "Who are these people?"

"Friends," Nicholas said.

"They certainly are interested in your welfare," I said. "And your baby's."

"Nothing wrong can happen," Nicholas said.

I said, "But such powers!"

"They transferred information to my head," Nicholas said, "but they didn't heal Johnny. They just—"

"They healed him," I said. Getting him to the doctor and calling the doctor's attention to the birth defect was healing him. Why exert supernatural powers when natural curative means lay at hand? I remembered something the Buddha said after he witnessed a supposed saint walk on water: "For a penny," the Buddha said, "I can board a ferry and do that." It was more practical, even for the Buddha, to cross the water normally. The normal and the supranormal were not antagonistic realms, after all. Nicholas had missed the point. But he seemed dazed; as Rachel drove through the darkness he continued to massage his forehead and eyes.

"The information was transferred simultaneously," Nicholas said. "Not sequentially. It's always that way. It's what's called analog, in computer science, in contrast to digital."

"You're sure they're friends?" Rachel said sharply.

"Anyone who saves my boy's life," Nicholas said, "is a friend."

I said, "If they could convey all that exact information directly to your head like that, in one burst of colored light, they could let you know any time they want who they are, where they are from, and what they intend. Any confusion on your part regarding any of those issues is deliberate withholding of knowledge on their part. They don't want you to know."

"If I knew, I'd tell people," Nicholas said. "They don't want to see —"

"Why not?" I said.

"It would defeat their purpose," Nicholas said, after a pause. "They're working against —" He ceased talking, then.

"There's a great deal you haven't told me," I said, "that you know about them."

"It's all in the written pages." He was silent for a few blocks and then said, "They're working against great odds. So it follows that they have to operate with great caution. Or it will fail." He did not elaborate. He probably didn't know any more. Most of what he believed probably consisted of shrewd guesses, hatched out over long months of pondering.

I had worked up a little speech to give; now I gave it. "There is a slight chance," I said, "admittedly a very slight one, that what you're dealing with is religious, that in fact you are being informed by the Holy Spirit, which is a manifestation of God. We're all from Berkeley, raised there and limited by the secular viewpoint of a college town; we're not inclined to theological speculation. But healing is a typical miracle of the Holy Spirit, or so I understand. You ought to know about that, Nicholas, from having been a Quaker."

"Yes." He nodded. "When the Holy Spirit takes you over it does heal."

"Heard any non-English languages in your head?" I asked him. "That you don't know?"

Presently he nodded. "Yes. In my dreams."

"Glossolalia," I said.

"Koine Greek. I wrote down a few words phonetically, what I could, when I woke up. Rachel took a year of Greek; she recognized them. We both looked them up in her dictionary: Koine Greek."

"Is that still —"

"It qualifies. In the book of Acts in the Bible, other races recognized what the apostles were saying, in their own tongues, at Pentecost, when the Spirit first descended on them. Glossolalia isn't nonsense; it's foreign tongues you never knew. The Spirit brings them to your head so you can preach the gospel to every nation. It's generally misunderstood. I thought it was gibberish until I researched it."

"You've been reading the Bible?" I asked. "During your research?"

"The New Testament. And the Prophetic Books."

Rachel said, "Nick never knew any Greek. He was sure they weren't real words." The cruel biting quality had left her voice; worry about Johnny, and shock, had done it. "Nick very cautiously told a couple of people interested in the occult about dreaming in Greek, and they said, 'It's a past life. You're the reincarnation of a Greek-speaking person.' But I don't think that's it."

"What do you think it is?" I asked her.

"I don't know. The Greek words were the first thing that signified anything to me, that I ever took seriously about this. And now tonight, his diagnosing Johnny ... and I saw that pinkish-purple spark of light beamed up at him for an instant. I just don't know, Phil; it doesn't fit anything I've ever heard of. Nick seems to be catching glimpses of benign supernatural manipulators of some kind we don't know about—just cryptic glimpses, what they want him to see. Not enough to extrapolate on. I get the impression they're very old—from the Koine Greek, which is two thousand years out of the past. If they lapse into that, maybe there's your one inadvertent clue."

In a hoarse voice Nicholas said abruptly, "Someone is waking up in me. After two thousand years, or almost that long. He's not awake yet, but his time is coming. He's been promised it . . . a long time ago, when he was alive like us."

"Is he human?" I said.

"Oh, yes." Nicholas nodded. "Or he was once. The programming they're giving me—it's to wake him. They're having trouble, or anyhow it's very difficult; it takes a lot of things to do it. This man, this person, is important to them. I don't know why, I don't know who the man is. I don't know what he'll do." He lapsed into brooding silence for a time and then said, mostly to himself, as if he had said it or thought it many times before, "I don't know what's going to become of me when it happens. Maybe there are no plans for me at all."

"Are you sure you're not throwing six different theories up into the air to see which lands first?" I said. "I can tell theories when I hear them—speculation. You don't know, do you?"

"No," Nicholas admitted.

"How long have you had this one?"

"I don't know. They're all written down."

"In order of descending merit?"

"In the order they came to me."

"And each one," I said to him, "seemed equally true to you at the time."

Nicholas said, "One of them has to be true. Finally I'll find it. I have to."

"You could go to your grave not knowing," Rachel said.

"I'll understand it eventually," Nicholas said doggedly.

Maybe not, I thought; maybe she is right. Nicholas could flounder around forever, his stack of typed papers constantly growing with theory after theory, each one more lurid than the last, more comprehensive, more daring. Finally the man slumbering within him whom they were attempting to arouse back into wakeful life could appear, take charge, and finish Nicholas's thesis for him. Nicholas could write, I wonder if it's ... it may be that ... I'm sure that ... it has to be; and then the ancient man could rise into life and write down, He was correct; it is. I am.

"The thing that has worried me," Rachel said, "whenever you talked like this, is, What will he be like to me and Johnny if they're able to waken him, and I guess tonight shows that he'll take care of Johnny."

"With more than I can," Nicholas said.

"You're not going to fight?" I said. "You're just going to let it take you over?"

Nicholas said, "I'm looking forward to it."

To Rachel, I said, "Are there any vacant apartments in your building?" I was thinking to myself that as a free-lance writer I could live anywhere. I didn't have to remain in the Bay Area.

Smiling a little, Rachel said, "You think you should be down here to help take care of him?"

"Something like that," I said.

8

THEY HAD BOTH evidently accepted the invasion of Nicholas by this entity; they seemed resigned and not afraid. That was more than I could manage; the whole thing seemed unnatural and terrifying to me, something to be fought with all one had at one's disposal. The supplanting of a human personality by — whatever it was. Assuming Nicholas's theories were correct. In point of fact he could be totally wrong. Even so, perhaps because of this, I wanted to be down here. Over the many years Nicholas had been my best friend; he still was, even though six hundred miles separated us. And, like him, I had begun to like the Placentia area. I liked the barrio. There was nothing like it in Berkeley.

"It's a nice gesture," Rachel said, "to be with your friend at a time like this."

"It's more than a gesture," I said.

"Before you move to Placentia," Rachel said, "there is something I found out the other day by accident, that I don't think either of you realize. I was driving along one of those little palm-lined streets, just driving at random, trying to get Johnny to calm down and go to sleep before we got back to the apartment, and I saw a green clapboard house with a sign on it. 'Birthplace

of Ferris F. Fremont,' it said. I asked the manager of our building, and he said, Yes, Ferris Fremont was born in Placentia."

"Well, he's not here now," Nicholas said. "He's in Washington
D.C., three thousand miles away."

"But how grotesque," Rachel said. "To be living in the town
where the tyrant was born. Like him, it's an ugly little house, a
dreadful color. I didn't get out of the car; I didn't want to go near
it, even though it seemed to be open, and people were walking
around inside it. Like it was a little museum, probably with exhibits of his schoolbooks and the bed he slept in, like one of
those California historical sites you see near the highway."

Nicholas turned to gaze at his wife enigmatically.

"And nobody mentioned this to you?" I said.

"I don't think they like to talk about it much," Rachel said,
"the people around here. I think they'd rather keep it secret.
Fremont probably paid for it to be made into a historical site
himself; I didn't see any official state marker."

"I'd like to go there," I said.

"Fremont," Nicholas ruminated. "The greatest liar in the history of the world. He probably wasn't actually born there; he
probably had a PR firm pick it out as the kind of place he *ought*
to have been born in. I'd like to see it. Drive by there now, Rachel; let's take a look at it."

She made a left turn; presently we were moving along very
narrow tree-lined streets, some of which weren't paved. This
was Oldtown; I had been driven through it before.

"It's on Santa Fe," Rachel said. "I remember noticing that
and thinking I'd like to ride Fremont out of town on a rail." She
pulled up to the curb and parked. "There it is, over there to the
right." She pointed. We could see only dim outlines of houses.
Somewhere a TV set played a Spanish program. A dog barked.
The air, as usual, was warm. There were no special lights put up

around the house where, allegedly, Ferris F. Fremont had been born. Nicholas and I got out of the car and walked over, while Rachel remained in the car, holding the sleeping baby.

"Well, there's not much to see, and we can't get inside to-night," I said to Nicholas.

"I want to determine if it's a place I foresaw in my vision," Nicholas said.

"You're going to have to do that tomorrow."

Together he and I walked slowly along the sidewalk; grass grew in the cracks, and once Nicholas stubbed his toe and swore. We arrived at last at the corner, where we halted.

Bending down, Nicholas examined a word incised in the ce-ment of the sidewalk, a very old word put there some time ago, when the sidewalk had been wet. It was professionally printed.

"Look!" Nicholas said.

I bent down and read the word.

ARAMCHEK

"That was the original name of this street," Nicholas said, "evidently. Before they changed it. So that's where Fremont got the name of that conspiratorial group: from his childhood. From finding it written on the sidewalk. He probably doesn't even remember now. He must have played here."

The idea of Ferris Fremont playing here as a little boy — the idea of Ferris Fremont as a little boy at all, anywhere — was too bizarre to be believed. He had rolled his tricycle by these very houses, skipped over the very cracks we had tripped on in the night; his mother had probably warned him about cars passing along this street. The little boy playing here and inventing fan-tasies in his head about people passing, about the mysterious word ARAMCHEK inscribed in the cement under his feet, con-jecturing over the weeks and months as to what it meant, discerning in a child's mind secret and occult purposes in it that were to blossom later on in adulthood. Into full-blown, florid, paranoid delusions about a vast conspiratorial organization with no fixed beliefs and no actual membership but somehow a titanic enemy of society, to be hunted out and destroyed wherever found. I wondered how much of this had come into his head while he was still a child. Maybe he had imagined the entire thing then. As an adult he had merely voiced it.

"Could be the contractor's name," I said, "rather than the original street name. They inscribe that too, sometimes, when they're done with a job."

"Maybe it means an inspector had gone by here and completed his job of checking all the arams," Nicholas said. "What's an aram? Or it could mean the spot where you check for arams. You stick a metal pole down through a little hole in the pavement and take a reading, like a water-meter reading." He laughed.

"It is mysterious," I said. "It doesn't sound like a street name. Probably, if it was, it was named after somebody."

"An early Slavic settler to Orange County. Originally from the Urals. Raised cattle and wheat. Maybe owned a big land-grant ranch, deeded to him from the Mexicans. I wonder what his brand would be. An aram and then a check mark."

"We're doing what Ferris did," I said.

"But along more reasonable lines. We're not nuts. How much can you get from a single word?"

"Maybe Ferris Fremont knows more than we do. Maybe he put investigators into it, after he grew up and had money; maybe that was a childhood dream fulfilled: to research the mysterious word ARAMCHEK and find out what it really meant and why they had thought to stick it into the sidewalk forever and ever."

"Too bad Ferris didn't ask someone what the word meant."

I said, "He probably did. And he's still asking. That's the

problem; he still wants to know. He wasn't satisfied with any of the answers he got — like, 'It's the old street name. It's a contractor.' That wasn't enough. It portended more."

"It doesn't portend anything to me," Nicholas said. "It's just a weird word stuck in the cement sidewalk that's been here God knows how many years. Let's go." He and I returned to the car and presently Rachel was driving us all back to the apartment.

9

SEVERAL YEARS AFTER Ferris F. Fremont had been elected President of the United States, I moved from the Bay Area to Southern California to be with my friend Nicholas Brady. I had been doing well in my writing career; in 1965 I had won the Hugo award for best science fiction novel of the year for my novel *The Man in the High Castle*. That book had to do with an imaginary alternate Earth in which Germany and Japan had won World War II and had divided the United States between them, with a buffer zone in the middle. I had written several other well received novels and was beginning to get solid critical comment, especially on my really insane novel *The Three Stigmata of Palmer Eldritch*, which had to do with long hallucinogenic trips by the characters under the influence of psychedelic drugs. It was my first work dealing with drugs, and it soon earned me the reputation of being involved with drugs myself. This notoriety paid off well in sales but came back later on to haunt me.

My real trouble concerning drugs came when Harlan Ellison in his anthology *Dangerous Visions* said in an introduction to a story of mine that it was "written under the influence of LSD," which of course was not correct. After that I had a really dreadful reputation as a doper, thanks to Harlan's desire for publicity.

Later on I was able to add a paragraph to the afterword of the story stating that Harlan had not told the truth, but the harm was done. The police began to become interested in me and in the people who visited me. This became particularly true when the tyrant became President in the spring of 1969 and the darkness of oppression closed over the United States.

In his inaugural statement, Ferris Fremont discussed the Vietnam War, in which the United States had been actively involved for a number of years, and declared it to be a two-front war: one front six thousand miles away and the other front here at home. He meant, he explained later, the internal war against Aramchek and all that it espoused. This was really one war fought in two areas of the world; and the more important battlefield, Fremont declared, consisted of the one here, for it was here that the survival of the United States would be decided. The gooks could not really invade us, he explained, and take us over; but Aramchek could. Aramchek had grown more and more during the last two administrations. Now that a Republican had been returned to office, Aramchek would be dealt with, after which the Vietnam War could finally be won. It could never be won, Fremont explained, so long as Aramchek operated at home, sapping the vitality and will of the American people, destroying their determination to fight. The antiwar sentiment in the United States, according to Fremont, derived from Aramchek and its efforts.

As soon as he had been sworn in as President, Ferris Fremont declared open war on the surface manifestations of Aramchek and fanned out from there in all directions.

The defensive operation at home was titled Mission Checkup, this term having obvious medical connotations. It had to do with the basic moral health of America, Fremont explained when he directed the intelligence community to get under way. The basic premise was that antiwar sentiment sprang from a vast and secret subversive organization. President Fremont proposed to heal America of its sickness; he would destroy "the tree of evil," as he termed Aramchek, by "rooting out its seed," a metaphor that didn't even mix, let alone wash. The "seeds of the tree of evil" were the antiwar dissidents, of whom I was one. Already in trouble with the authorities for my alleged drug involvement, I was doubly in hot water due to my antiwar stand, both in my published writings and in discussions and speeches. The drug element made me vulnerable; it was a terrible liability for someone who wanted to oppose the war. All the authorities needed to do was nail me on a drug charge and they would forever destroy my effectiveness as a political person. I knew they knew that, too. It did not make for restful nights.

However, I was not the only worried person in America. Because of his old left-wing days in Berkeley, Nicholas was beginning to wonder how safe he was now that Ferris F. Fremont had come to power and had launched Mission Checkup. After all, Nicholas occupied a high position at Progressive Records, a firm doing very well; it was the typical goal of Mission Checkup to discern people like Nicholas — "sleepers," Fremont deemed them — and expose them to the harsh light of day. For this purpose the government began to hire and employ what they called "Friends of the American People," agents out of uniform who went around and checked up on anyone suspected of being a threat to security, either for what he had once done, such as Nicholas, or what he was doing now, such as me, or for what he might do in the future, as was possible with all of us. Thus no one was entirely ruled out. The FAPers wore white armbands with a star-in-a-circle on it, and pretty soon they were seen everywhere in the United States, diligently investigating the moral state of hundreds of thousands of citizens.

In the flatlands of the Midwest the government had begun to build large detention facilities, for the restriction and housing of those brought in by the FAPers and other para-police agencies. These facilities would not be used, President Fremont explained in a televised speech, "unless and until necessary," meaning unless and until resistance to the war got significantly stronger. The message was clear to anyone contemplating opposition to the Vietnam War; he might find himself living in Nebraska and hoeing a collective turnip field. This therefore acted as a deterrent, and since the camps did not see actual use they were not subject to juridical review. As threat they were sufficient.

Personally, I had one nasty run-in with a FAP undercover agent, one without an armband. He wrote me on letterhead paper, pretending to represent a small student FM station near Irvine; he wanted, he said, to interview me because the Irvine students were interested in my work. I wrote him and agreed, but after he showed up it was evident, before he had asked three questions, that he was a plainclothes FAPer. After asking me if I had secretly written any porno novels, he suddenly began to shout wild accusatory questions at me. Did I take drugs? Was I the father of any illegitimate black science fiction writers? Was I God as well as the head of the Communist Party? And, of course, was Aramchek financing me? It was an upsetting experience; I had to physically evict him — I could hear him standing outside still shouting at me even after I shut and locked the door. After that I was very careful as to whom I let interview me.

More damaging to me than the FAPer posing as an interviewer from a student radio station was the break-in of my house in late 1971, in which my files were forcibly blown open with plastic military explosives and thoroughly burglarized. I returned home to find water and rubble all over the floor, the file in ruins, and most of my business papers and all of my canceled checks gone. The entire house had been ransacked; windows in the back had been broken in, and door locks smashed. The police performed only a perfunctory investigation, telling me slyly that they believed I had done it myself.

"Why?" I asked the police inspector in charge.

"Oh," he said, grinning, "to throw suspicion off yourself, probably."

No one was ever arrested, although the police admitted at one point that they knew who had done it and where my stolen possessions now were. What they did say, though, of a positive nature, was that although I would not get my things back, on the other hand I would not be arrested. Evidently they had found nothing sufficient to incriminate me. That experience greatly colored my life. It made me aware how far the abuses of power and the destruction of our constitutional liberties had gone under President Fremont. I told as many people as I could about the break-in and burglary of my house, but I discovered very quickly that most people did not want to know, even antiwar liberals. They showed either fear or apathy, and several hinted, as the police had, that most likely I had done it myself, in order to "throw off suspicion"; of what they did not say.

Of my friends who were genuinely sympathetic, Nicholas remained foremost. However, he thought my house had been hit and my papers stolen because of him. He imagined that he was the real target.

"They wanted to find out if you were going to write about me," he said. "You're the one who could publicize them, by putting them in a science fiction novel. Millions of people would read it. The secret would be out."

"What secret?" I asked.

"The fact that I represent an extraterrestrial authority greater than any human power, whose time is destined to come."

"Oh," I said. "Well, I think they were interested in me, since it was my house they hit and my papers they read or stole."

"They wanted to see if we formed an organization."

"They wanted to see who I know," I said. "And what organizations I belong to and give money to; that's why they took all my canceled checks, every last one of them, years, decades of them. That hardly suggests anything about you and your dreams."

"*Are* you writing about me?" Nicholas asked.

"No," I said.

"Just make sure you don't give my actual name. I have to protect myself."

"Christ," I said angrily, "nobody can protect themselves these days, with Mission Checkup going on and all those pimple-faced little FAPers creeping around peering through their Coke-bottle-bottom glasses. We're all going to wind up in the Nebraska camps and you fucking well know it, Nick. How can you expect to be spared? Look what happened to me — they took years of my notes for future books; they effectively wiped me out. Just the intimidation alone ... hell, every time I write a few pages I know I can come home from the store and find it all gone again, like I did that day. Nothing is safe, nothing and no one."

"You think there've been other burglaries like yours?" Nicholas asked.

"Yes."

"I haven't read about them in the papers."

I gazed at him for a long time.

"I guess they wouldn't be reported," he mumbled lamely.

"Not really, no," I said. "Mine wasn't. It was just listed under all the thefts for the week in the county. 'Six hundred dollars' worth of stereo reported stolen by Philip K. Dick of Placentia, on the night of November eighteenth, 1971.' No mention of papers stolen or canceled checks stolen or files blown open. As if it were an ordinary burglary by junkies for something they could sell. No mention of the wall beside the files burned black by the heat of the blast. No mention of the big heap of water-soaked towels and rugs piled in the bathroom, which they used to cover the file when they detonated the C-three; it creates such heat that if —"

"You certainly know a lot about it," Nicholas said.

"I've asked," I said shortly.

Nicholas said, "I wonder if my four hundred pages of notes are safe. Maybe I should put them in a safe deposit box in a bank somewhere."

"Subversive dreams," I said.

"They're not dreams."

"The dream-control police. Sniffing out subversive dreams."

"Are you sure it was the police who hit your house?" Nicholas said. "It could have been a private group, sore at you because, say — well, say because of the pro-drug stand in your books."

"There never has been and never will be any 'pro-drug stand' in my books," I said angrily. "I write about drugs and drug use, but that doesn't mean I'm pro-drug; other people write about crime and about criminals, but that doesn't make them pro-crime."

"Your books are hard to understand. They may have been misinterpreted, especially after Harlan Ellison wrote what he wrote about you. Your books are so — well, they're nuts."

"I guess so," I said.

Nicholas said, "Really, Phil, you write the strangest books of anybody in the U.S., really psychotic books, books about crazy people and people on drugs, freaks and misfits of every description; in fact, of the kind never before described. You can't blame the government for being curious about the kind of person who would write such books, can you? I mean, your main character is always outside the system, a loser who finally somehow —"

"*Et tu*, Nicholas," I said, with real outrage.

"Sorry, Phil, but — well, why can't you write about normal people, the way other authors do? Normal people with normal interests who do normal things. Instead, when your books open, there is this misfit holding down some miserable low job, and he takes drugs and his girlfriend is in a mental institution but he still loves her —"

"Okay!" I interrupted. "I know it was the authorities who broke into my house because the house behind me was evacuated. And the black family that lives there has ten children, so someone is always there, constantly. The night of the burglary I noticed the house behind me was completely empty, and it stayed empty an entire week. And the broken windows and doors of my house were all in the rear, adjoining it. No private burglars would evacuate a whole house. It was the authorities."

"They'll get you again, Phil," Nicholas said. "Probably they wanted to see what your next book is about. What is your next book about, anyhow?"

"Not you," I said. "I can tell you that."

"Did they find the MS?"

"The MS of my new book," I told him, "was in my attorney's safe. I transferred it there a month before the hit on my house."

"What's the book about?"

After a pause I said, "A police state in America modeled on the Soviet Gulag prison system. A police slave-labor state here. It's called *Flow My Tears, the Policeman Said.*"

"Why'd you put the manuscript in your lawyer's safe?"

I said, reluctantly, "Well, I — shit, Nick. To tell you the truth, I had a dream."

Silence for a time.

10

NICHOLAS HAD BEEN right to be apprehensive about the FAP interest in him. Not long thereafter, as he sat at his desk in his office at Progressive Records, listening to a tape of a new singer, two FAPers paid him a surprise visit. The two government agents had fat red necks and both wore modern single-breasted polyester suits and stylish ties. They were middle-aged and heavyset; they carried briefcases, which they placed on the desk between them and Nicholas. Nicholas was reminded of the two FBI agents who had visited him years ago in Berkeley, but this time he was not scared and angry; he was just scared.

"Are we putting out too many protest songs?" he said, thinking to himself that he could readily show it not to be his personal responsibility but that of the chief of A and R, Hugo Wentz.

The greater of the two FAP agents said, "No, as a matter of fact your firm has a three-check rating with us, which is quite good. If anything, we're here to compliment Progressive Records, at least in contrast to findings obtained throughout the record industry."

"It's pretty bad," the other agent chimed in. "As I'm sure you realize, Mr. Brady. A large number of Communist singers are being regularly recorded, and many protest songs are being aired these days, despite the general cooperation of the networks and major independent stations."

Nicholas knew it was not public policy for the radio stations to play protest songs; that was the reason Progressive Records didn't cut them. It was pointless; no DJ would air them. It was a matter of economics, not principle.

"We are here regarding the following spinoff of Mission Checkup," the greater of the agents said. "In the course of your work, Mr. Brady, you must come in contact with many singers and groups whom you do not sign, correct? For every one you sign to a contract there must be a hundred you don't."

Nicholas nodded.

"We also know what salary you draw here," the greater agent continued. "And we know you have a small son who needs major dental work, that you're in debt, that you'd very much like to move out of your apartment into a house, that Rachel is talking about leaving you if you don't put Johnny in a special school, because of his stammering ... am I correct? We've talked it over with our superiors in an effort to find a way to assist you, and we've come up with this: If you will provide the government with a copy of the lyrics of each artist whom you come in contact with who shows pro-Communist sympathies, we will pay you a flat hundred dollars per artist. It's our estimate that you could enhance your salary by up to two thousand dollars a month this way, and you would not have to report it to the IRS; it would be tax-free. Of course, the determination as to which artists you report are pro-Communist and which are not belongs to us; but even if we accept only half of the ones you pass on to us, you should be able to —"

"And we guarantee," the other FAP agent broke in, "that this will remain an arrangement known only to you and to us. No one else, either at Progressive or anywhere else, will find out.

You'll receive a code name under which you report, and everything, including payments, will be filed under that. The identity of the coded informant will be known only to the two of us sitting here and to you."

"But if these artists aren't signed," Nicholas said, "what harm can they do?"

"They can change the slant of their lyrics," the greater agent said, "so they're not pro-Communist, and get signed up somewhere else."

Nicholas said, "But if the lyrics aren't subversive anymore, what does it matter? Why do you care about them then?"

The greater agent said, "Once they make it big they can again begin to sneak subversive poisons into their lyrics. And by that time it's very difficult to eradicate them, once they're known to the public, you see; once they've made it big. That's potentially a very dangerous situation: someone who slips something controversial in with ordinary lyrics and then begins to further slant them later on. So you can see why we don't merely go on who's recorded and being played; we need to know the names of those who aren't."

"They in some ways are the most dangerous," the other agent said.

THAT NIGHT NICHOLAS told me about this interview with the two government agents. He was angry by then, angry and shaking.

"You going to take them up on it?" I asked.

"Hell, no," Nicholas said. But then he said, "You know, I can't really believe the government is concerned with those loser artists. I think it's my loyalty they're interested in. Those two FAPers; it was a ploy to test me. They knew all about me; obviously there's a file on me back in Washington."

"There's a file on all of us," I said.

"If they know about Johnny's overbite and what Rachel's been saying to me, they undoubtedly know about my contacts with Valis. I'd better burn my notes."

"What," I said, "would a file on Valis look like? A file on a superior life form in another star system. . . . I wonder how it'd be cross-indexed. I wonder if it'd have a special marking."

"They'll get at Valis through me," Nicholas said.

"Valis will protect you," I said.

"Then you don't think I should do it?"

"Hell, no," I said. I was amazed at him.

"But they'll think I'm disloyal if I say no. That's what they're after: proof of disloyalty. They'll have it!"

"Fuck 'em," I said. "Say no anyhow."

"Then they'll know. And I'll be in Nebraska."

I said, "They've got you, then. Either way."

"That's right," Nicholas said. "Ever since the two FBI agents closed in on me back in the fifties. I knew it would catch up with me, my disloyal past. My Berkeley days — the reason I left the university."

"You broke your gun."

"I disabled my gun! I was a war protestor even then, one of the first. I knew Fremont's minions would find me out; they only had to examine their files. The computers popped me up, the first antiwar activist in America. And now it's cooperate with them or be arrested."

"I was never arrested," I said, "and I've done a lot more antiwar stuff than you. In fact, you haven't done any since you left Berkeley. Since the FBI came by that day."

"That proves nothing. I'm a sleeper. They probably think it's Aramchek that contacts me in the night. Valis is my name for Radio Free Aramchek."

"Aramchek is a word on a sidewalk."

"Aramchek is anything that opposes Fremont. Listen, Phil." Nicholas inhaled a deep, ragged breath. "I think I'm going to have to play ball with them, or anyhow appear to."

"Why?"

"Because," Nicholas said, "look what happened to you. Your place broken into, half your papers gone — you haven't been able to write since, for psychological reasons, for practical reasons; good lord, look at you — your nerves are shot. I know you're not able to sleep anymore, expecting them to come back and do it again, or maybe arrest you. I can see what it's done to you; after all, I'm your best friend."

"I'll live," I said.

"You don't have a wife and little boy," Nicholas said quietly. "You live alone, Phil; you don't have any family. What if the night they broke all the back windows and smashed down the doors your little son had been home, alone? They might have —"

"They waited," I said, "until I was out of the house; they were outside for a week getting ready — I saw them. They waited until the house was empty."

Nicholas said, "The government hires ex-'Nam special forces veterans for commando raids like that. Search and seize, they call it. A military operation with military personnel using plastic military explosives — I saw the combat boot print they left in the closet of your study; you showed it to me. Phil, *those were armed soldiers who hit your house.* And I have Rachel and Johnny."

"You go along with them," I said, "and maybe your body lives, but your soul dies."

"I'll feed them names they can't use," Nicholas said. "Lurid rock lyrics that don't mean anything."

"And how'll you explain it to yourself when they arrest one of the loser artists you rat on?"

Nicholas gazed at me unhappily. In all the years I had known him I'd never seen such a wretched expression on his face.

"Because they will," I said. "And you know it. They may still arrest me. It's still hanging over my head."

"That's what I mean," Nicholas said. "And I don't want that hanging over my head, for Rachel's sake and for Johnny's sake. I want to be with my little son as he grows up; it's the most precious thing in my life. I don't want to be in a forced labor detention camp in the boondocks hoeing turnips."

"Ferris Fremont hasn't just taken over the country," I said. "He's also taken over human minds. And debased them."

"The Bible says don't judge," Nicholas said.

"The Bible says, 'My kingdom is not of this world,'" I answered angrily. "Which means there's a lot of explaining to do later on."

"I've got plenty of explaining to do right here."

"Not half of what comes later. Have you asked Valis what to do?"

"I don't ask Valis; he, they, tell me."

"Tell them to tell you not to cooperate."

"So far they've said nothing. If they say nothing then I go ahead as I normally would."

"You cooperate with Mission Fuck-Up," I said (this was what we all derisively called it), "and I'll bet you a buck Valis never communicates with you again."

"I will have to do what I have to do," Nicholas said.

"Are you going to report to them about me too?" I said. "About my writing?"

"They can read your writing; it's all published."

"You could clue them in about *Flow My Tears,* since it isn't out yet. You know what it's about."

"I'm sorry, Phil," Nicholas said. "But my wife and child come first."

"For this," I said bitterly, "I moved to Southern California."

"Phil, I can't afford for them to find out about Valis. I'm sorry, but that is too important. More important than you or me or anyone else."

I DIDN'T LIKE THE notion of a close friend of mine reporting regularly, for money, to the minions of Ferris Fremont. When I considered to myself that Nicholas knew everything there was to know about me, it became oppressively close and menacing in a very personal way. "If Valis exists," I said, "he'll protect you, as you told me a long time ago. And if he doesn't exist, then you have nothing to protect and therefore no motive for cooperating with them. Either way you should tell them to go shove it." In actuality I was thinking of my own self. I hadn't really done all that much antiwar activity, or contemplated that much yet to be done, but in the eyes of the FAPers it would be sufficient. And Nicholas had been informed of every iota of it.

It was the beginning of the first real rift in our friendship. Nicholas reluctantly agreed that he could hold out against the FAPers with their dossier on him, and still keep his family and job, but I could see that not only was he divided against me but against himself as well. The fact of the matter was that I could no longer trust my dearest friend Nicholas Brady, whom I had known and loved since the old days in Berkeley. The authorities had done their assigned job: they had driven another wedge between two men who had always trusted each other completely.

The destruction of our relationship was a mini-cosmos mirroring what was going on at all levels of American society under F.F.F. On the basis of what had happened to us I could infer that terrible tragedies were taking place everywhere. For instance, what about the young artists coming to Progressive Records to play and sing? The record company official who auditioned them was a paid cop, informing on them to higher police authorities. Undoubtedly this was taking place at all the other record companies as well. What about Nicholas's fellow employees? They now had — or potentially had — a paid informer in their midst, who augmented his salary at the expense of their safety and freedom. All this, so that little Johnny could go to the dentist. What a rationale.

The real motive, of course, was Nicholas's concern for his own freedom and safety. In effect it was a trade-off: he jeopardized, or proposed to jeopardize, the freedom and safety of others to secure his own. But the net effect of a lot of people doing this would be mutual hazard. For instance, suppose a couple of FAPers now approached me and asked me to report on Nicholas. I already knew that there was a fair chance he was reporting on me. What, then, would my reaction be? My ability to resist them would be substantially undermined.

The well-known police tactic of whiplashing would be coming into play; they would soon be saying to me, "You better report on Nicholas Brady before he reports on you," which meant, You had better get your friend before he gets you. We'd been put at each other's throats; the only winner would be Ferris F. Fremont. The police have been using the same tricks since the time of the Medes, and people are still falling for them. As soon as Nicholas reported on anyone, especially for money, he would be vulnerable to police blackmail forever. The police had laid a noose out before him, and Nicholas was obligingly placing his head in it. He was doing most of the work. Where was the man who had damaged his gun rather than submit to taking military training involuntarily as a price for his college degree? Gone down the drain of prosperity, evidently; now Nicholas had a cushy job and great prospects, not to mention power over other people. That was what had done it. Idealism had given way to more realistic motivations: safety and authority and the protection of a family. Time had worked a dismal magic on my friend;

he no longer strode along the pavement chanting old marching songs from the Spanish Civil War; in fact, if some young artist were to come to him with such lyrics, Nicholas would be in a position to pick up an easy hundred dollars.

"Here is what I will do," I told Nicholas, "if you spy for the government. First, I will phone the brass at Progressive and tell them. Second, I will park my car out front of your main entrance, and when I see young artists going up the walk with their guitars and high hopes and absolute trust in you, I will stop them and tell them you are a paid —"

"Shit," Nicholas said.

"I mean it," I said.

"Well, I guess I can't do it." He looked relieved.

"That's right," I said. "You can't do it."

"They'll destroy me. It's just like when the FBI men came by originally; it's me they're after. Do you know the possible consequences if they harm Valis?"

"Valis can take care of himself," I said.

"But I can't," Nicholas said.

"In that case you're no different from the rest of us," I said. "Because neither can I."

That appeared to be the end of the conversation. The moral of it, I could have pointed out to Nicholas, is that if you are contemplating informing on people you should tell no one. Telling me had been a mistake, since I had immediately been flooded by visions of his informing on me.

11

THAT NIGHT I MYSELF received a phone call from a cop, one whom I knew.

"A lot of people have access to your house, don't they?" he asked.

"Yeah, I guess so," I said.

"I have a tip I'm passing on to you. Someone is hiding dope in your house and the local FAP knows about it. If we're sent over to look for it and we find it we'll have to arrest you."

"Even though you know someone else is hiding it?"

"That's right," the cop said. "That's the law. Better find it and flush it before we're called to go over there."

I spent the rest of the night looking for it. In all I found five stashes of drugs in five separate places, one even inside the phone itself. I destroyed all of it, but for all I knew I missed some. There was no way I could be sure. And whoever it was could plant more.

The following day two FAPers came by to visit me. These were young: a slender youth in a white shirt, slacks, and tie, and with him a girl in a long skirt. They could have been Mormon missionaries, but both wore the FAP armband. It was the really young FAPers who were the worst, so I was not very happy to see these two people. The FAPer youth were the zealous spearheads.

"May we sit down?" the boy said brightly.

"Sure," I said, not moving. My friend the cop had warned me just in time.

The girl, seated on my couch with her hands folded, said, "We have mutual friends. Nicholas Brady."

"Oh," I said.

"Yes," the boy said. "We're friends of his. He's talked about you a great deal — you're a writer, aren't you?"

"Yep," I said.

"We're not interrupting your writing, are we?" the boy said. They were the epitome of grooming and politeness.

"Nope," I said.

"You've certainly written some important novels," the girl said. "*Ubik, Man in the Castle* —"

"*The Man in the High Castle*," I corrected her. Obviously they'd never read my work.

"You and Mr. Brady together," the girl said, "have certainly contributed a great deal to our popular culture, you with your stories and he selecting which artists are to be recorded. Is this why you're both living down in this area, the entertainment capital of the world?"

"Orange County?" I said.

"The Southland."

"Well, it makes it easy to meet people," I said vaguely.

"You and Mr. Brady have been friends for years, haven't you?" the boy said. "You lived together in Berkeley, as roommates."

"Yep," I said.

"And then he moved down here, and after a few years so did you."

"Yeah, well, we're good friends."

"Would you be willing to sign a notarized statement, under oath, as to his and his wife's political loyalty?"

Taken by surprise, I said, "What?"

"Or would you *not* be willing to?"

"Sure I would," I said.

"We would like you to draft such a statement during the next few days," the girl said. "We'll help in the preparation of the final draft down at our headquarters. And we will leave you several models to base yours on, as well as an instruction manual."

"What for?" I asked.

"To help your friend," the girl said.

"Why does he need help?" I said.

The boy said, "Nicholas Brady has a suspect background, from his Berkeley days. If he is to retain the position he now holds, he will need the support of his friends. You're willing to give that support, aren't you? You are his friend."

I said, "I'll give Nicholas any and all help I can." As I said it I knew instinctively that I had taken the bait; I was in some vague police trap.

"Good," the girl said, and smiled, whereupon both of them rose to leave. The boy placed a plastic package down on the coffee table.

"Your kit," he said. "Instructions, helpful hints, models; as an author you'll undoubtedly find this very easy. Along with your statement about your friend we'd like you to draft a short autobiographical sketch, so the person who reads your statement will know a little about you too."

"A sketch covering what?" I said, and now I was really afraid, really sure I had fallen into a trap.

"There's instructions covering that as well," the girl said, and both of them left. I was alone with the red-white-and-blue plastic kit. Seating myself, I opened the kit and began looking through the instruction booklet, which was printed on fine glossy paper. It bore the Presidential seal and the printed signature of F.F.F.

> Dear American:
>
> You have been invited to write a short article on the subject you know best: yourself! It is entirely up to you what matters you consider pertinent and what you feel should be left out. However, you will be graded not only on your inclusions but on what you omit.
>
> Perhaps you have been asked to do this by a delegation of your friends and neighbors, the Friends of the American People. Or perhaps you wrote for this kit on your own initiative. Or perhaps your local police suggested it to you as a way to . . .

I turned to the instruction booklet on the preparation of a notarized statement about a friend's loyalty.

> Dear American:
>
> You have been invited to write a short article on a subject well known to you: a close friend! It is entirely up to you what matters you consider pertinent and what you feel should be left out. However, you will benefit your friend by the greatest inclusion. What you write about him will, of course, be kept completely confidential; this article is for official use only.
>
> Perhaps you have been asked to do this by a delegation of your friends and neighbors, the Friends of . . .

I went to my typewriter, put paper in it, and began to compose the autobiographical sketch.

TO WHOM IT MAY CONCERN:

I, Philip K. Dick, being of sound mind and reasonably good health, wish to admit to being a high official for a period covering many years of the organization known to its enemies as Aramchek. In the course of my training for subversion and espionage, I have learned to lie and if not outright lie to distort so effectively that what I say is worthless to those who hold power in this our target nation, the U.S. of A. With these provisos in mind, I will now make a statement about my lifelong friend Nicholas Brady, who has, to my recollection, been a covert advocate and supporter of the policies of Aramchek for years, changing his mind as the official line of Aramchek continually changes in order that it be in accord with the policy of People's China and other Socialist powers, not excluding the U.S.S.R., one of our earliest acquisitions in the power struggle against man which we have waged since our inception in the Middle Ages.

Perhaps I should speak further of Aramchek, in order to better clarify my own situation. Aramchek, an offshoot of the Roman Catholic Church, is devoted to the principle that the means justify the end. We therefore employ the highest means possible, with no regard to the end, knowing that God will dispose of that which mere man has proposed. In connection with this we employ and have employed every artifice and strategy and resource available to us to thwart the goals of Ferris F. Fremont, current puppet tyrant of these the U.S. of A. During his childhood, to cite one example, we arranged to stencil an indentation of the name of our organization on the sidewalk down the street from the house in which he was born, for the purpose of spooking him in a most forceful way as to the fact that eventually WE WOULD GET HIM.

I signed this document and then sat back to consider the situation I was in. It wasn't good. I recognized this red-white-and-blue plastic kit; it was the notorious "voluntary information" kit, the first step in drawing a citizen into the active intelligence system of the government. Like an income tax audit, sooner or later every citizen got one. This was our lifestyle under F.F.F.

If I failed to turn over my autobiographical sketch and statement about Nicholas, the FAPers would be back, and next time they would be less polite. If I turned in an inadequate report on Nicholas and myself, they would politely request more material. It was a technique first employed by the North Koreans on captured American prisoners: you were given a piece of paper and a pencil and told to write down anything about yourself you felt like, with no suggestions from the jailers. It was amazing what revelations prisoners made about themselves, far surpassing what they would have confessed under suggestion. When it came time to inform, a man was his own worst adversary, his own ultimate rat. All I had to do was sit before my typewriter long enough and I would have told them everything there was about myself and Nicholas, and probably after I had told them the facts I would go on with fantastic inventions, all designed to nail the attention — and admiration — of my audience.

The human being has an unfortunate tendency to wish to please.

I was in effect exactly like those captured Americans: a prisoner of war. I had become that in November 1968 when F.F.F. got elected. So had we all; we now dwelt in a very large prison, without walls, bounded by Canada, Mexico, and two oceans. There were the jailers, the turnkeys, the informers, and somewhere in the Midwest the solitary confinement of the special internment camps. Most people did not appear to notice. Since there were no literal bars or barbed wire, since they had committed no crimes, had not been arrested or taken to court, they did not grasp the change, the dread transformation, of their situation. It was the classic case of a man kidnapped while standing still. Since they had been taken nowhere, and since they themselves had voted the new tyranny into power, they could see nothing wrong. Anyhow, a good third of them, had they known, would have thought it was a good idea. As F.F.F. told them, now the war in Vietnam could be brought to an honorable conclusion, and, at home, the mysterious organization Aramchek could be annihilated. The Loyal Americans could breathe freely again. Their freedom to do as they were told had been preserved.

I returned to the typewriter and drafted another statement. It was important to do a good job.

TO THE AUTHORITIES:

I, Philip K. Dick, have never liked you, and I know from the burglary on my house and the fact that you are busily at work hiding dope in the light sockets and telephone as I sit here that you don't care for me either. However, as much as I dislike you, and you me, there is someone whom I dislike even more, to wit: *Mr. Nicholas Brady*. I suggest that you dislike him too. Let me outline why.

First of all, *Mr. Nicholas Brady* is not a human being in the usual sense of the word. He has been taken over by (or more accurately will one of these days to the surprise of us all be taken over by) an alien life form emanating from another star. Far-ranging speculations can begin from this premise.

Perhaps, because my profession is that of a science fiction writer, you imagine that I am spinning a trial fantasy to see how you react. Not so, authorities. I only wish it were so.

I have myself with my own eyes seen *Mr. Nicholas Brady* demonstrate fantastic supernatural powers, bestowed on him by the alien suprahuman entity known as *Valisystem A*. I have seen *Mr. Nicholas Brady* walk through walls. I have seen him melt glass.

One afternoon, to demonstrate the staggering magnitude of his powers, *Mr. Nicholas Brady* caused Cleveland to materialize in the open pasture along the side of the 91 freeway and then disappear again with no one save ourselves the wiser. *Mr. Nicholas Brady* abolishes the bounds of space and time when the mood seizes him; he can return to the ancient past or leap ahead centuries into the future. He can, if he wishes, transport himself directly to Alpha Centauri or any other . . .

Fuck it, I thought, and ceased writing. It had been my intention to so thoroughly overstate the case in lurid hyperbole that the FAPers wouldn't give it an instant's credence.

I began, then, to think about the boy and girl who had brought me this plastic kit, this lethal thing. At the time I had hardly noticed them on a conscious basis, but the impression of their two faces had remained anyhow. The girl, I thought, hadn't been bad-looking: dark-haired, with green eyes, rather bright-looking, many years younger than me, but that hadn't bothered me before.

Picking up the red-white-and-blue kit I found a white card glued to it. On the card were their names and telephone numbers. Well, I thought to myself, maybe there is another way out of this. Other than complying. Maybe I should ask for further help in preparing these statements.

While I was getting my act together in regard to the black-haired FAP girl, the phone rang. It was Nicholas.

I told him what had happened that evening.

"Are you going to do it?" he asked. "Write a statement about me?"

"Well," I began.

Nicholas said, "It's not so easy when it's you, is it?"

"Shit, man," I said, "they've been hiding dope in my house; a cop tipped me off last night. I spent the whole night looking for it."

"They've got something on me too," Nicholas said. "They either have it or they arrange to have it, as in your case. Well, Phil, we're in the same boat. You better decide what to do. But if you inform on me —"

"All I'm being asked to do is write a statement of support," I said, but I knew he was right. They had us both, really, in the same grip. The pressures were the same.

Nicholas was right when he said, *It's not so easy when it's you.* "Fuck 'em," I had advised him. Well, so much for advice. The shoe was now on the other foot. And it hurt; it hurt deep into my soul, piercing and twisting and burning. And no solution lay at hand — none.

None except to call the FAP girl up and sweet-talk her. My freedom, my life, depended on it. And so did Nicholas's.

12

THE GIRL'S NAME was Vivian Kaplan. I waited an hour, to be sure she had arrived back home, and then dialed.

"Hello?"

I said hello, told her who I was, and then explained that I had tied myself up in knots trying to write my statement about Nicholas. "Maybe," I said, "it's because I know so much about him. More than anyone else does. It's hard to know what to put down and what not to. After all, I want a good grade." I figured that would get her.

"I'm certain you can do it," Vivian Kaplan said. "You are a professional writer; why, housewives and mechanics are getting the knack of it."

"Maybe it is precisely because I am a professional writer," I said.

"Meaning what?"

"Well, I am a *fiction* writer. I'm used to making things up."

Vivian said, "You're not to make anything up on these documents, Phil."

I said, "Some of the truth about Nicholas reads like the wildest fiction, so help me God."

That *did* gaff her. "Oh?"

"The disgrace," I said, "that forced him — the three of us — to leave Berkeley and migrate down here. Most of the secret he's still kept locked up in his heart."

"'Disgrace,'" Vivian echoed. "'Secret.'"

"He couldn't remain in Berkeley. Do you suppose you could come back here and we could talk about it?"

"For a little while," Vivian said. "But not for long."

"Just to help me get started," I said, pleased.

Half an hour later a small red Chevy II pulled up in my driveway. Vivian Kaplan got out, purse in hand, wearing a short imitation leather coat. I guided her into the house.

"I really appreciate this," I told her as I seated her in the living room. I took her coat and hung it in the closet.

Producing a small writing pad and pen from her purse, Vivian prepared to write. "What caused Mr. Brady's disgrace back in Berkeley? You dictate and I'll transcribe it."

From the kitchen I brought a bottle of wine, a five-year-old Louis Martini.

"None of that for me, please," Vivian said.

"Just a taste. It's a good year."

"Maybe a taste."

I poured us both wine. In the background I had music playing, and low lights. Vivian, however, did not seem to notice; she was waiting intently for what I had to say. She did not touch her wine.

"Nicholas," I said, "talks to God."

She stared at me, mouth agape.

"He started it in Berkeley. As a child he was a Quaker, you know. I'm sure you have that in your records. The Quakers believe that the Holy Spirit can come to you and talk to you. All his life Nicholas waited for God — which is the same as the Holy Spirit, especially if you are a trinitarian, which Nicholas and I are — to come to talk to him. A couple of years before we left Berkeley, in the early sixties it was, God first spoke to him."

Vivian, listening, had written nothing.

"Since then," I said, "Nicholas has maintained an intimate relationship with God. He speaks to him as you and I are speaking to each other now."

"Christ," Vivian said impatiently, "that isn't any good; I can't report that."

"Do you know anybody else who communes regularly with God?" I said. "Nicholas's whole life is built around it; speaking with God and hearing God speak back is everything to him. As well it might be. I envy his experience."

Vivian put her pen away. "Are you sure he isn't crazy? It sounds crazy to me."

"You should be writing this down," I said. "I'm going to reveal to you some of the things God has told him."

"I don't care about that!" Vivian said, with agitation. "It has no political bearing! What can we do with information like that?"

"God said," I told her, "that he is going to cause plagues to fall on this entire order of things and wash it away. Wet plagues, I'd guess, from the sound of it; something about water."

"Oh, balls," Vivian said.

"I believe he also said he would place a rainbow in the sky," I said. "Afterward, as a sign of peace between God and man."

Sharply, Vivian said, "Is this the best you can do?"

"I told you I was having trouble getting things down. This is why I wanted you to come over." I seated myself on the couch beside her and took her ballpoint pen from her. "I'll put down the opening sentence. 'Nicholas Brady—'"

"You got me over here for a religious thing? There's nothing we can do with a religious thing; there's nothing unpatriotic about God. God is not on our list. Can't you come up with anything else?"

"In Berkeley," I said, "talking to God is a disgrace. Nick was ruined there, when he confided it to people. They drove him off like an animal."

"That's Berkeley," Vivian said. "Where there's nothing but atheists and Commies. I'm not surprised. But this is Orange County. This is the real world."

"You mean down here it's okay?"

"Of course it's okay."

I breathed a sigh of relief. "Then Nicholas is safe at last."

"Phil," Vivian said, "there must be other things you know about Nicholas which would — you know what I mean — would offset this about God."

"It is not possible," I said, "to offset God. He is all-powerful and all-knowing."

"I mean in terms of the political file we're drawing up."

"Have some of the wine," I said, holding her glass toward her.

"No, I don't drink wine," Vivian said in agitation. "But I brought some good grass with me." She opened up her purse and rummaged inside,

I really wasn't surprised. It figured.

"I need a small box," she said, "to manicure it in. And a card such as a credit card. Here, this will do." She found a white business card in her wallet.

"Let me see that," I said, extending my hand. Vivian placed the lid of grass in it; I then carried the grass from the living room into the bathroom, where at once I locked the door behind me. In an instant I had dumped the marijuana into the toilet and had flushed it down; the contraband would not be found in my house, not this lid of it.

"What are you doing?" Vivian called sharply, from outside the locked door; she began to knock. "What did you do?"

I flushed the toilet once more, to be absolutely sure, and then leisurely unlocked the door.

"Did you flush it?" she demanded incredulously.

"Yes I did," I said.

"Why? Well, never mind; what's done is done. I have a little high-grade hash we can smoke. Fortunately I brought my hash pipe with me." She returned to the living room; I followed after her. It would be harder getting the hash away from her, I realized. No one voluntarily surrendered hash, especially after what I had just done. Vivian sat on the couch, her shoes off, legs drawn up, lighting the tiny cube of hash in her hash pipe. "Here." As smoke came from it she handed it to me. "This is the best hash I've had in months. It'll really get you off."

"I don't want drugs in my house," I said.

"No one can see in."

"I'm being set up," I said.

"Everyone thinks they're being set up. I've been turning on for two years and I've never been busted."

"Yes, but you're a FAPer."

"That makes it more dangerous for me," Vivian said. "Most FAPers are straight; it's very risky to be with FAP and to turn on at the same time. I have to wait until I'm around people like you before I can do it. That's one reason I was glad when they assigned me to cover you. That's why I came over here tonight when you called, so we could turn on together."

"I don't turn on," I said.

"Of course you do. Everyone knows you do. You're one of the biggest dopers in America. It's in your bio material published with your books—look what Harlan Ellison wrote in *Dangerous Visions*. We have that in triplicate. And all your friends say you turn on."

"That was made up," I said, "to sell books."

"You turn on," Vivian said. "Here, give me my hash pipe back. It's my turn for a hit."

I could scarcely flush her hash pipe down the toilet, so I returned it to her. Vivian inhaled deeply, her face flushed.

As she passed it back to me she said, coughing, "Hash makes me horny."

"Oh," I said, "Well."

"Does it make you horny?" She took another hit from her pipe, her eyes beginning to glaze over now, becoming unfocused; her whole body seemed limp, and at grateful ease.

"Let's go in the bedroom," I said.

"In a minute. When we're through with the hash." She continued to smoke, ritualistically now, in a lazy, blithe way. Her cares, her agitation about my political report, my dumping the lid of grass, had vanished.

The time had now come to turn the tables on the tyranny oppressing me. Once I had made little Vivian Kaplan my mistress, I could stop worrying about my political report. Taking her by the hand, I set her hash pipe down and lifted her to her feet. "Are you on the pill?" I asked her as I guided her down the hall toward my bedroom. I had to hold on to her to keep her from weaving into the wall.

"Of course I am," Vivian said. She was reflexively starting to unbutton her blouse as we approached the open bedroom door; humming and smiling from the hash, she entered the bedroom, and I kicked the door shut after us.

"Just a minute," I said as she sat on the edge of the bed removing her skirt. "I'll be right back." I returned to the living room where she had left her hash pipe. Placing it carefully back in her purse I closed the purse around it, thinking, this way if they break in and find the dope it'll obviously be hers. Despite her efforts, they won't be able to pin it on me.

"Hurry up," Vivian called from the bedroom. "I'm starting to crash." I hurried back down the hall to the bedroom and found her lying nude on the bed, her clothes in a pile on my typing chair. "Hash makes me sleepy sometimes," she said. "I have to get it on right away or I'm too out of it."

We made love. Toward the end Vivian did fall into a deep, untroubled sleep. Well, I said to myself as I padded down the hall to the bathroom to take a shower, I am now master — rather than victim — of the situation. This girl is not going to spy on me any longer. I have turned an enemy into something even better than a friend: a co-conspirator in sexuality.

After I had taken my shower I reentered the bedroom to find her asleep with the top sheet pulled over her. "Vivian," I said, touching her on the shoulder, "is there anything I can get you? Something to drink?"

"I'm hungry," Vivian murmured sleepily. "After I make out I'm always terribly hungry. When I first was making out I used to eat up everything in the refrigerator afterward. Half a chicken, a pizza, two hamburgers, and a quart of milk ... whatever I could find."

"I can fix you a frozen beef pie," I said.

"Got any soft drinks, like a Pepsi?"

I had a can of Coors beer, which I brought her. Vivian sat in her underwear on the bed, drinking the beer.

"What do you do," I asked her, "when you're not working for FAP? I mean, you can't run errands for FAP all the time."

"I go to school," Vivian said.

"Where? Cal State Fullerton? Santa Ana College?"

"Valentia High," Vivian said. "I'm a senior. I graduate this June."

"High school!" I said, stricken. "Vivian—" I could hardly speak; I was shaking with fear. "How old are you, for chrissakes?"

"Seventeen," Vivian said, sipping the beer. "I'll be eighteen this September."

Oh, my God, I realized. She's underage. It's statutory rape! A felony! As bad as the dope — in fact, worse. All she has to do is mention it to the police; arrest is automatic.

"Vivian," I grated, "it's illegal for you to go to bed with me. Don't you know that?" I began getting her clothes together. "You have to get right out of here!"

"Nobody knows I'm here," Vivian said calmly; she continued drinking the Coors beer. "Except Bill."

"Who the hell is 'Bill'?"

"The boy I was with earlier today, when we came as a team. I told him I'd call him when I got home, so he'd know I'm all right. We're engaged."

It was too much for me; I sank down on the chair facing her and just stared at her.

"He won't mind," Vivian said. "Just so long as you file your political response in time. That's all he cares about, racking up points at headquarters. We're on a quota system, but Bill, he always exceeds his quota and scores extra points. He's the most gung-ho FAPer among us. That's why I like him; he sort of offsets my own, you know, my indifferent attitude, as they call it. I don't really care about the quota or the points; I just enjoy meeting the people they assign us to."

And I had done it to myself. It had been my idea, my scheme, to lure the girl back to my house at night on a phony pretext, in order to go to bed with her. I had put my ass in the bed and my neck in the noose, all in the same move. Wonderful. Now what was I supposed to do? They really had me. I cooperated or I went to the Orange County Jail. And people died — were clubbed to death — at the Orange County Jail; it happened all the time. Especially political prisoners.

I'll be writing confessions the rest of my life, I said to myself. And articles on my friends. If they asked me to do a whole book on Nicholas I'd have to comply. Vivian Kaplan has me. I think I was set up, I thought suddenly. She got me to do this; that's why they send attractive young girls around, underage girls that don't look underage. Girls with dope and long legs and a welcoming innocent smile, who are glad to drive over to your house late at night, alone. Girls whose phone numbers are typed on the front of the goddamn informer kit, big as life. A veritable come-on.

"Now, about the God business," Vivian said, in a practical tone of voice. The hash had worn off; she was no longer mellow. "You can't use it, Phil; we're not interested in Nicholas Brady talking to God. What we'd like to know about are the Communist Party ties he still has left over from his old activist days at Berkeley. My superior feels that Brady got his job at Progressive Records so that he could very carefully slip aspiring new left-wing artists into the public eye. It's a common technique they use; meanwhile, of course, Brady remains personally inactive. But he must have links with the people who instruct him, even if it's just by mail. You're in a position to read his mail, aren't you? That's how the Party maintains control: by mail from New York, where the KGB operates. That connects the operator here with Moscow and the international planning network. We want to know which artists he's signed are crypto-Communists and who he gets his orders from; those are the twin prongs of—"

"Nicholas is just trying to make a buck," I said wearily. "So his kid can go to the dentist."

"He doesn't meet with anyone from New York? What about phone calls?"

"Tap his phone," I said, "for all I care."

"If you could get possession of his phone statement," Vivian continued, "and see if he's called New York; that would—"

"Vivian," I said, "I'm not going to do it."

"Not going to do what?"

"Spy on Nicholas. Or anyone else. You can fuck yourself. Take your kit back. I've had it."

After a pause Vivian said, "We have quite a bit on you, Phil. A lot of people know a lot about you."

"So what," I said, resigned and bitter at it all, ready to throw in the sponge, come what might. There was just so much they could do to me, just so much and no more.

Vivian said, "I've read the file on you."

"So?"

"So a case could be made against you that would stand up in court."

"You're wrong about that," I said, but it was I who was bluffing, not her. And we both knew it; I could see the sense of certitude on her face.

"Do you want us to go after you instead of Nicholas?" she asked.

I shrugged.

"It could be arranged. Really, we could get both of you together; your lives are intertwined. If one of you falls, the other falls automatically."

"Is that what your superior at FAP GHQ told you?" I said.

"We discussed it. A number of us."

"Then do your damnedest," I said. "I already know about the dope you've been hiding around here; I found it and destroyed it. I was tipped off."

"You couldn't have found it all," Vivian said.

"Is there an infinite amount?"

"No, but the person hiding it —" She broke off.

"If he can hide it," I said wearily, "I can find it. And if I can find it, that's the end of it. Like the lid of grass you brought. A FAPer smoking grass — it doesn't compute. You and your goddamn hash pipe — Christ, as soon as you brought out the grass I knew you were setting me up."

Vivian said, "Phil, you were set up a long time ago. What I did tonight is very little. Going to bed with me —"

"Let me take a look at your California driver's license." Suddenly something occurred to me. Maybe she wasn't underage after all. I hurried past her, out of the bedroom and down the hall in the direction of the living room; Vivian scuttled right behind me, trying to overtake me. It was no use; I wedged myself in the hallway and beat her to the living room and her purse.

"Get out of my purse!" she shrieked.

I grabbed up her purse, sprinted with it into the bathroom, locked the bathroom door after me. In an instant I had shaken the contents out onto the bathroom rug. The driver's license gave her age as nineteen. She was not underage.

That too had been a police trap, and an empty one. So much for that. But it showed me how close I was to the edge, how little separated me from a fall to oblivion.

I unlocked the bathroom door. Vivian was nowhere to be seen. Listening, straining, I heard her voice far off; she was on the phone in the bedroom.

When I entered the bedroom she hung up and stood facing me defiantly. "May I have my things back?" she said.

"Sure," I said. "They're on the bathroom rug. You can pick them up yourself." I accompanied her to the bathroom, where she knelt down and began to gather up her papers, cosmetics, wallet, and assorted possessions. "What did you do," I asked, "call FAP to tell them the plan didn't work?"

Vivian stuffed her possessions back into her purse, straightened up, returned to the bedroom silently to put on her shoes, walked down the hall to the living room, where she slid into her coat, and then, all her things gathered together, including her hash pipe, she opened the front door of the house and walked up the driveway to her parked car.

I went with her. The night was warm and pleasant. I felt good indeed; I had parried another police trap.

"I'll see you again, Phil," Vivian said.

"No, you won't," I said, opening her car door for her. "I have no wish to see you again. In bed or out of it."

"You'll see me again," Vivian said, getting in and starting up the motor.

I said, "You have nothing on me; I don't have to see you."

"Ask me what I did while you were taking your shower."

I looked down at her as she sat calmly behind the wheel of her car. "You did —"

"I hid it where you'll never find it," Vivian said; she began rapidly rolling up her window.

"Hid what?" I grabbed at the window, but it continued to roll up; I grabbed at the door handle, but she had locked it.

"Cocaine," Vivian said. Her window closed, she shifted into gear, the car suddenly roared off into the street and made a sharp right turn, its tires squealing. I stood impotently watching her go.

Bull, I said to myself. Another crock, like her being underage. But — how could I be sure? I had been in the shower at least fifteen minutes. Vivian Kaplan had had fifteen unobstructed free minutes to hide anything she wanted around my house — to hide stuff, to pry, to read, to see where things were ... anything she cared to do. Possibly, I thought, the whole going to bed with me had been only a ploy — designed to tie me up by distraction, so that I lost sight of the real issue. And what was the real issue? The fact that an admitted government agent, wearing an armband, openly identified as such, had obtained from me fifteen minutes of absolute privilege to come and go in my house, alone. She had been legally there. I had invited her over. And this, after my pal the friendly cop had warned me.

There is no use warning me, I said to myself with savage, helpless wrath. I am too fucking stupid. The warning is wasted; I just keep on truckin' anyhow. I invite them over; then I lock myself up in the shower for fifteen minutes, giving them the run of the house. She could have planted a gun and dope as well;

there I go, down the tubes, forever. Victim of a police trick carried off to perfection, in that I did most of the work myself.

And suppose it's another lie. Suppose she didn't hide any coke. Quantities of coke are minute; I could look for days, weeks, and never find it, and if there isn't any I could drive myself nuts, work myself into a paranoid psychotic frenzy and not find it — not find it and never know if it was an inch away or if it never existed. Meanwhile, every second of the night and day, waiting for the cops to come in on a tip and bust me — tear open a wall and find the coke right away: a ten-year sentence.

Suddenly chilled, I thought, Maybe her phone call was the tip. The tip the police were waiting for; not that the drugs are there, but that the drugs had been placed there successfully, that when they break in and examine the house they will find something.

Then my days — my hours — are numbered, I thought. There is no use searching. Better just to sit. Just walk back into the house and sit.

I did so. I closed the front door and seated myself on the couch; presently I got up to turn on the FM. Again I sat down. I listened to a performance of the Beethoven *Emperor* Concerto, sitting, listening, waiting, listening not to the familiar music but for the sounds of approaching cars. It was a hell of an experience. Time stretched out immeasurably. I had to go into the kitchen, finally, to look at the stove clock in order to obtain any idea of how late it was. One hour, two hours, passed. No one came: no cars, no pounding on the door, no pump shotguns and men in uniform. Just the radio playing and the house empty except for me.

I felt my forehead; it was hot and sweaty. Going into the bathroom I got the thermometer, shook it down, and took my temperature. It was 102 degrees: a fever from fear and tension.

My body made ill by the stress it was under, unfair and unjust stress, but very real. She was smart to shoot right out of here, I said to myself. After she told me that, whether it was true or not. Jammed down the gas pedal and laid rubber. If she shows up here again I'll murder her. She knows it; she'll stay away.

If I get out of this safe and alive, I said to myself, I will write a book about this. Somehow I will figure out a way to work it into a novel. So other people will know. Vivian Kaplan will go down in history for what she is, for what she does. That is my promise to myself, to keep myself going.

Never walk over a writer, I said to myself, unless you're positive he can't rise up behind you. If you're going to burn him, make sure he's dead. Because if he's alive, he will talk: talk in written form, on the printed, permanent page.

But am I alive? I asked myself.

Only time would tell. I felt at this moment as if a mortal blow had been delivered to me, a blade thrust deep; the pain was unbearable. But I might survive. I had survived the attack on my house; I had survived many things. Probably I would survive this. If I did, FAP was in trouble, Vivian Kaplan in particular.

I told myself that, but I didn't really believe it. What I believed was that FAP and its master Ferris Fremont had me. And I had sprung the trap myself — that was the worst part, the part that really hurt. My own cunning had betrayed me, had delivered me to the enemy. That was hard to bear.

13

THE COPS NEVER came; whatever Vivian Kaplan had been up to fizzled out, and I was able to relax. In the following days my temperature went down to normal, probably my blood pressure as well. I began to think more reasonably. However, I asked my lawyer what to do about them hiding dope in my house.

"Write a letter to Orange County Drug Abuse," he told me. "Tell them the situation."

"Will that—?"

"They may still bust you, but when they find the letter in their files they may be lenient."

Anyhow, nothing happened. I began to sleep at night again. Vivian evidently had been bluffing; I was beginning to notice a lot of bluffing going on. The police seemed fond of that tactic; it had to do with getting the suspect to perform the hard work himself, as I had demonstrated my willingness to.

They eat people like me for breakfast, I said to myself. My engineering a roll in the hay with Vivian had severely crippled my faith in my own tactics. I could not regain the conviction that in the end I, and people like me, would prevail. To prevail I would have to become a lot less stupid.

I of course told Nicholas the whole thing. He of course was incredulous.

"You did what?" he said. "You went to bed with an underage FAP girl who was carrying dope in her purse? My God; if they gave you a hacksaw in a cake you'd saw your way into jail. You want me to provide the cake? Rachel will be glad to bake it. Get your own saw."

"Vivian was working so many numbers on me at once that I got confused," I said.

"A seventeen-year-old girl puts an intelligent grown man in jail. Even when he's being super-cautious."

I said, truthfully, "It wouldn't be the first time."

"Stay away from her from now on," Nicholas said. "Entirely away. Spend your time with knotholes, if necessary. Anything but her."

"Okay!" I said irritably. But I knew I'd see Vivian Kaplan again. She would seek me out. There would be another round with the authorities — perhaps several. Until they had netted Nicholas and me to their satisfaction. Until we were harmless.

I wondered if the alleged protection which Valis supplied Nicholas extended to me. After all, we were in it together: two major stations in the network of pop culture, as the FAPers had put it. Kingpins, so to speak, in the vox populi.

Perhaps the only entity we could turn to for help in this tyrannical situation was Valis. Valis against F.F.F. The Prince of this World — Ferris Fremont — and his foe from another realm, a foe Fremont didn't even know existed. A product of Nicholas Brady's mind. The prognosis was not comforting. I would have preferred something or someone more tangible. Still, it was better than nothing; it provided a certain psychological comfort. Nicholas, in the privacy of our intimate rap sessions, could envision vast operations by Valis and his transcendent forces against the cruel bondage we were in. It certainly beat watching TV, which now consisted mostly of propaganda dramas extolling the police, authority in general, war, car crashes, and the

Old West, where simple virtues had prevailed. John Wayne had become the official folk hero of America.

And then there was the weekly "Conversation with the Man We Trust," Ferris F. Fremont speaking from a firelit alcove in the White House.

It was a real problem to get the masses to watch Ferris Fremont deliver his speeches, because he spoke in such a dull way. It was like sitting through an endless lecture on some obscure aspect of economics — exactly like that, since Fremont invariably gave a rundown of figures from all departments. Evidently, behind his nondescript figure a powerful White House staff lurked, never seen, who fed him an infinitude of typed information on every topic bearing on his rule. Fremont did not appear to regard all this as dull. "Iron production," he would stumble along, reading half the words off the cue card wrong, "is up three percent, giving rise to a justified optimism in agricultural quarters." I always had the feeling I was back in school, and the tests we had to fill out afterward reinforced this sensation.

This did not make Ferris Fremont a figurehead, however, fronting for the staff who fed his facts to him; on the contrary, when he departed from his prepared script the real savagery in him came out. He liked to depart when matters concerning America and its honor and destiny were mentioned. East Asia was a place where American boys were demonstrating that honor, and Fremont could not let a reference to that topic pass without an extempore comment, at which times his sallow face would furrow with intensity and he would stumble out words of grim determination to all who would challenge American might. We had a plethora of American might, to hear Fremont speak of it. Half his time was spent warning unmentioned enemies of that might. I usually assumed he meant the Chinese, although he seldom saw cause to mention them by name. Being from California, Fremont kept a special place in his heart for the Chinese; to hear him speak you would have thought they had overcharged us in their laying of railroad track — a matter he could not, and honor would not allow him to, forget.

Really, he was the worst speechmaker I had ever heard. I often wished the invisible White House staff who formed his compatriots would rise up, select one of their number who could talk, and delegate him to finish Fremont's prepared speech. Given the right pinstriped suit and loud tie, few people would notice.

These synthetic chats were carried by all networks in prime time, and it was a good idea to listen. You were supposed to do so with your front door open, so that roving bands of FAPers could make spot checks. They passed out little cards on which various simple-minded questions about the current speech were asked; you were to check the right answers and then drop the card in a mailbox. The enormous White House staff scrutinized your answers to make sure you understood what you were hearing. It was mandatory to put your social security number on the card; the authorities had taken to organizing all their files on the basis of social security numbers. Your mail-in cards went into your permanent file, for what reason no one knew. We calculated that these cards must be making the files very large. Maybe there were subtle trick questions, such as the K scale in the Minnesota MultiPhasic, the so-called "lying" scale.

Sometimes the questions did seem devious, with the high possibility of making an accidental incriminating answer. One went:

Russia is becoming (1) weaker; (2) stronger; (3) about the same in relationship to the Free World.

Naturally, Rachel and Nicholas and I, doing our cards in unison, marked (2). The ideology of the authorities always stressed Russia's increasing strength, and the need for the Free World to continually double its arms budget in order just to keep up.

However, a later question rendered this one suspect.

Russian technology is (1) very good; (2) adequate; (3) typically inept.

Well, if you marked (1) you seemed to be paying the Communists a compliment; (2) was probably the best bet, since it probably was true, but the way (3) was worded seemed to suggest that the right-thinking citizen would reflexively mark it. After all, what could one expect from captive Slavic minds? Certainly, typical ineptness. *We* were very good, not them.

But if their technology was typically inept, then how could (2) be the correct answer on the previous question? How did a nation with typically inept technology become stronger than ourselves? Nicholas and Rachel and I returned to the previous question and changed our answers to (1). That way it dovetailed with typically inept. The weekly questionnaire had many pitfalls. The U.S.S.R., like a Japanese wrestler, was both dumb and clever at the same time, strong and weak, likely to win and a sure bet to lose. All we in the Free World had to do was never falter. We managed this by turning in our cards regularly. It was the least we could do.

The answer to the above dilemma was imparted to us by Ferris Fremont the next week. How did a nation with typically inept technology become stronger than ourselves? Through subversion here at home, a sapping of the will of Americans through the guile of defeatism. There was a question on the next card about that:

The greatest enemy America faces is (1) Russia; (2) our high standard of living, highest the world has ever known; (3) secret infiltrators in our midst.

We knew to put (3). However, Nicholas that night was in a crazy mood; he wanted to check (2).

"It's our standard of living, Phil," he told me with a wink. "That's what's going to doom us. Let's all three of us check (2)."

"What's going to doom us is screwing around with these answer cards," I told him. "They take these answers seriously."

"They never read them," Rachel said. "It's just to make sure you listen to Fremont's weekly speech. How could they read all these cards? Two hundred million of them every week."

"Computer read," I said.

"I vote we mark (2) on that question," Nicholas said, and did so.

We filled out our cards, and then on Nicholas's suggestion he and I walked to the mailbox together, the three cards in the pre-franked envelope which the government provided.

"I want to talk to you," Nicholas said to me, as soon as we were outside.

"Okay," I said. I thought he meant about the cards. But it was not the cards he had on his mind. As soon as he began to talk I understood why he had behaved so erratically.

"I received the most compelling reception of Valis so far," he said in a low, very serious voice. "It completely shook me up. Nothing so far has — well, I'll tell you. What I saw visually was the woman again. She was seated in a modern living room, on the floor near a coffee table. A bunch of men were around on all sides of her, all wearing expensive Eastern-style suits, establishment suits. The men were young. They were deep in discussion. The woman suddenly, when they were aware of her, she —" He paused. "She turned on her third eye, the one with the lens instead of the pupil; she turned it on them, and, Phil — she read into their hearts. What they had done and weren't admitting, what they intended to do: everything about them. And she kept on smiling. They never guessed she had that eye with that all-seeing lens and was reading deep into them. There were no secrets left, nothing she didn't know. You know what she learned about them?"

"Tell me," I said.

"They were conspirators," Nicholas said. "They had plotted the murders of everyone who's been assassinated: Dr. King, the two Kennedys, Jim Pike, Malcolm X, George Lincoln Rockwell the Nazi Party leader . . . all of them. Phil, I tell you as God is my witness, she saw that. And as I looked at her I was made to understand what she was: the sibyl. The Roman sibyl who guards the republic. Our republic."

We had reached the mailbox. Nicholas stopped there, turned toward me, and placed his hand on my shoulder.

"She made me understand that she had seen them and she knew what they had done, and they would be brought to justice. The fact that she had seen them ensured that. There's no way they can escape paying for what they've done."

I said, "And they weren't conscious of her."

"They didn't even guess that their deeds are known, and known to her. It never entered their minds — they were still joking and laughing, like a bunch of pals, and there she was overseeing them with that third eye, that lensed eye, and she was smiling along with them. And then the eye and its lens disappeared and again she looked like an ordinary person. Same as anyone else."

"What is the purpose of the conspiracy?"

Nicholas said hoarsely, "They are all cronies of Ferris Fremont. Without exception. I was given to understand — I did understand — that the scene was in a Washington, D.C., hotel room, a lavish hotel."

"Jesus," I said. "Well, I see two separate pieces of information in that. Our situation is worse than we thought; that's one piece. The other piece is that we're going to be helped."

"Oh, she'll help us, all right," Nicholas said. "I tell you, man, I wouldn't want to be in their shoes. And they were still grinning, still shooting the bull back and forth. They think they have it made. They don't. They're doomed."

"I thought we were the ones who were doomed."

"No," Nicholas said. "It's them."

"Do we do anything?"

"I don't think you do," Nicholas said. "But —" He hesitated. "I think I'm going to have to. I think they're going to use me, when the time comes. When they begin to act."

I said, "They're already acting now; they told you, for one thing. If they tell enough people, that's it there. The truth about how our present regime got into power. Over a bunch of corpses, the corpses of some of the best men of our times."

"It's heavy," Nicholas said.

"Are you sure you didn't just dream this all up?" I said.

"It did come in a dream," Nicholas admitted. "There never was anything like this beamed at me before. Phil, you saw what happened that night about Johnny. When —"

"So Ferris Fremont arranged their deaths," I said.

"That's what the sibyl discovered, yes."

"Why you?" I said. Of all people to pass it on to.

"Phil," Nicholas said, "how long does it take to get a book out? From the time you start writing it?"

"Too long," I said. "A year and a half minimum."

"That is too long. She's not going to wait that long; I could tell. I could feel it."

"How long is she going to wait?"

Nicholas said, "I don't think she is going to wait. I think that for them to plan is the same as acting. They plan and act simultaneously; to think it is to do it. They are a form of absolute mentation, pure minds. She is an all-knowing mind from which nothing is hidden. It's scary."

"But this is very good news," I said.

"Good news for us anyhow," Nicholas said. "We won't be mailing in these damn cards much longer."

"What you ought to do," I said, "is write Ferris Fremont and tell him he and his henchmen have been seen by the Roman sibyl. What do you know about the Roman sibyl? Anything?"

"I researched her this morning in my *Britannica*," Nicholas said. "She's immortal. The original sibyl was in Greece; she was an oracle of the god Apollo. Then she guarded the Roman republic; she wrote a bunch of books which they used to open and read when the Republic was in danger." He added, "I'm thinking now of the great Bible-like books I saw held open to me originally, when my experiences began. You know, the sibyl became sacred to the Christians. They felt she was a prophet like the Hebrew prophets. Guarding God-fearing good men against harm."

It sounded like the exact thing we needed. Divine protection. The guardian of the Republic had answered from down the corridors of time, in her customary way. After all, was the United States not an extension through linear time of the Roman republic? In many ways it was. We had inherited the Roman sibyl; since she was immortal she had continued on after Rome vanished ... vanished but still existent in new forms, with new linguistic systems and new customs. But the heart of the Empire remained: one language, one legal system, one coinage, good roads — and Christianity, the later legal religion of the Roman Empire. After the Dark Ages we had built back up to what had been and even more. The prongs of imperialism had been extended all the way to Southeast Asia.

And, I thought, Ferris F. Fremont is our Nero.

"If it didn't take so long to produce a book," Nicholas was saying, "I'd think Valis told me so I could tell you and you could use it for a plot idea. But the time factor rules that out ... unless you've already done so." He eyed me hopefully.

"Nope," I said, in all candor. "Never used a thing you told me. Too fucked."

"You believe this, don't you?"

"I believe it all. As an FBI agent once said to me while shaking me down, 'You believe everything you hear.'"

"And — you can't use it?"

"It's for you, Nicholas," I said. "They want you, not me. So start truckin'."

"I'll 'start truckin'' on the signal," Nicholas said. "The disinhibiting signal." He was still waiting for that. The wait must have been hard, but certainly not as hard as having to choose what to do and when. All he had to do was wait until the signal came of its own accord and disinhibited the centuries-old entity slumbering within him.

"If Valis is going to throw Ferris Fremont out of office," I said, "I wonder how he's going to accomplish it."

"Maybe by giving his sons birth defects."

At that I laughed. "You know who that sounds like, don't you? Jehovah against the Egyptians."

Nicholas said nothing. We continued to walk.

"Are you positive it isn't Jehovah?" I asked him.

"It's hard to prove a negative, that it isn't something."

"But have you very seriously considered the possibility that it is? Because if it is, we can't lose; they can't win."

"They are doomed," Nicholas said.

"Do you know what they are going to get?" I said. "Blood clots, high blood pressure, heart trouble, cancer; their planes will crash; bugs will eat their gardens; their swimming pools in Florida will get lethal mold growing on the surface — do you know what it's like to try to stand against Jehovah?"

"Don't tell me," Nicholas said. "I'm not doing it. I wouldn't be caught dead doing it."

"You'd be better off caught dead," I said.

Suddenly Nicholas ducked his head, caught hold of my arm. "Phil — all I can see are dazzling pinwheels. How'm I going to get home?" His voice shook with fear. "Pinwheels of fire, like fireworks — my good God, I'm practically blind!"

It was the beginning of the transformation in him. How inauspiciously it had started: I had to lead him home, as if he were a child, to his wife and son. All the way he muttered in fear, cringing and hanging onto me. I had never seen him so frightened.

14

DURING THE NEXT week the fiery pinwheels remained, obscuring Nicholas's vision, but only at night; it was his night vision that had become impaired. A doctor who examined him told him that it resembled poisoning by alkaloids of belladonna; had he taken a lot of allergy medicine recently? No, Nicholas said. He had to stay home from work, after a few days; he was becoming dizzy, and when he tried to drive his car his hands shook and there was no sensation in his feet. His doctor suspected some form of poisoning or intoxicant, but he could not determine which one it was.

I checked up on Nicholas every day. One day when I showed up at his apartment I found him seated with several bottles of vitamins, including an enormous plastic container of vitamin C.

"What's all this about?" I asked him.

Seated there pale and worried, Nicholas explained that he was attempting in his own way to flush the toxin out of his system; water-soluble vitamins, he had learned from his reference books, acted on the system as a diuretic; he hoped, by taking enough of them, he could rid himself of the flashing wheels of jagged, colored fire that plagued him at night or when he blinked.

"Are you sleeping?" I asked him.

"No," he admitted. "Not at all." He had tried leaving his bed-side radio on to mild bubble-gum rock, but, he said, after a few hours the music assumed an ominous, menacing sound; the lyrics underwent a grotesque change, and he had to shut the radio off.

The doctor thought it might be blood pressure problems. He also alluded to the possibility of drugs. But Nicholas wasn't on anything; I was certain of that.

"And if I do get to sleep," Nicholas said shakily, "I have dread-ful nightmares."

He told me one of them. In the dream he was shut in a tiny cage under the Colosseum in ancient Rome; in the sky over-head, huge winged lizards were searching for him. All at once the flying lizards detected his presence under the Colosseum; they swept down and in an instant were tearing open the door of his cage. Trapped, with death at hand, all Nicholas could do was hiss at the lizards; evidently he was a small mammal of some kind. Rachel woke him from that dream, and, partially awake, he had extended his tongue and continued his hissing in a furious, inhuman way, even though, she told me, his eyes were wide open. After that he had come to and had told her a ram-bling story about walking toward the cave in which he lived, guided by his cat, Charley. Looking around their bedroom, Nicholas had begun to lament in fear that Charley was missing; how could he find his way, now, without the cat, seeing as how he was blind?

After that he kept the radio on playing bubble-gum rock. Un-til one night he heard the radio talking to him. Talking in a foul, malevolent way.

"Nick the prick," the radio was saying, in imitation of the voice of a popular vocalist whose latest record had just been featured. "Listen, Nick the prick. You're worthless and you're going to die. You misfit! You prick, Nick! Die, die, *die!!*"

He sat up, heard it while fully awake. Yes, the radio was saying "Nick the prick" all right, and the voice did resemble that of the well-known singer; but, he realized with horror, it was only an imitation. It was too cruel, too metallic, too artificial. It was a mechanical travesty of her voice, and anyhow she would not be saying that, and if she had said it the station would not have aired it. And it was addressed directly to him.

After that he never turned on the radio again.

During the day he took greater and greater quantities of the water-soluble vitamins, in particular C, and at night he lay wide awake, his thoughts racing in fear, the jagged, wildly colored buzz saws spinning before his eyes, completely obscuring the door. What if an emergency occurred at night? he asked himself. What if Johnny got sick? There was no way Nicholas could possibly drive him to the hospital; in fact, if the apartment building caught fire it was unlikely that Nicholas could even find his way out. One evening the girl across the hall had asked him downstairs to look at the master circuit-breaker box; he had accompanied her down the outside stairs all right but then later when she ran up again to answer the phone he had floundered around blindly in the dark, in overwhelming panic and confusion, until at last Rachel came down and rescued him.

Eventually he found his way to a psychiatrist, for the first time. The psychiatrist diagnosed him as manic and gave him a course of lithium carbonate to take. So now he was dropping tablets of lithium carbonate as well as his vitamins. Shaking and frightened, not knowing what was happening to him, he withdrew into his bedroom, not wishing — not able — to see anyone.

The next tragedy that struck was an abscessed and impacted wisdom tooth. Nicholas had no choice but to make an immediate appointment with Dr. Kosh, the best oral surgeon in central Orange County.

The Sodium Pentothal was a great relief to him; probably it was the first time in three weeks he had become completely unconscious. He returned home in good spirits — until the procaine wore off and pain flashed through his stitched-up jaw. The rest of the day he lay tossing and turning; all that night the pain was so great that he forgot the whirling buzz saws; the next day he phoned Dr. Kosh and pleaded for oral pain medication.

"Didn't I give you a prescription?" Dr. Kosh said, absentmindedly. "I'll phone the pharmacy and have them send it right out. I'm prescribing Darvon-N for you; that tooth had grown down into the jawbone; we had to sort of — well, crack the jawbone to get the pieces of tooth out."

Nicholas sat with a moist teabag between his jaws as he waited for the pharmacy delivery boy to ring the doorbell.

The doorbell rang at last.

Still woozy from the pain, Nicholas made his way to the door and opened it. A girl stood there with heavy black hair, hair so black that the coils of it seemed almost blue. She wore an absolutely white uniform. Around her neck he saw a gold necklace, with a gold fish suspended between links of golden chain. Fascinated, staring at the necklace in a hypnoidal twilight state, Nicholas could not speak.

"Eight forty-two," the girl said.

Nicholas, as he handed her a ten, said, "What — is that necklace?"

"An ancient sign," the girl said, raising her left hand to point to the golden fish. "Used by the early Christians."

He stood holding the bag of medication, watching her go. He was still there when Rachel came to tap him and rouse him to full consciousness.

The medication helped the pain, and in a few days Nicholas seemed okay. But he was, of course, under the weather from the oral surgery and stayed in bed resting. The buzz saws, mercifully, were now gone; he had not seen them since visiting Dr. Kosh.

"I have a favor to ask," he said to Rachel one day as she was getting ready to go shop at Alpha Beta. "Could you get me a few votive candles and a glass candleholder? The candleholder has to be white and the candles have to be white."

"What's a votive candle?" Rachel asked, puzzled.

"One of those little short fat candles," Nicholas said. "Like you see burning in Catholic churches."

"Why do you want them?"

Truthfully, Nicholas said, "I don't know. For — I guess healing. I need to get well." He was calmer these days, but very weak from the surgery. Anyhow, he seemed unfrightened; the fear and disorientation, the franticness we had seen on his face, was at last gone.

"How's your eyesight?" I asked him that night when I dropped over.

"Fine." Nicholas lay on his back in his bed, fully dressed; on the table beside him a white votive candle burned.

After I had shut the bedroom door Nicholas said, staring at the ceiling, "Phil, I really heard the radio saying that. 'Nick the prick, Nick the prick' over and over again." I was the only one he had told about it. "And I know," he said, "I know equally that it could not have been saying that. I can still hear the voice in my mind. Speaking very slowly, very insistently. Like when someone is trying to program you. You understand? Programming me to die. A demon voice. It wasn't human. I wonder how many times I've heard it in my sleep and not remembered it. If I hadn't had insomnia —"

"Like you say," I said, "it isn't possible."

"There are technical possibilities. They do exist. Such as electronic signal override, by a small gain transmitter located very nearby, say in the next apartment. That way it wouldn't affect any other receivers. Just mine. Or from a satellite passing overhead."

"A what?"

"There's a lot of illicit satellite override of U.S. radio and TV stations," Nicholas said. "Usually the material is subliminal. I must have somehow transliminated it, which I wasn't supposed to do. They fouled up somehow in their transmission. It sure as hell woke me thoroughly up, and that's exactly what it was *not* supposed to do."

"Who'd do that?"

Nicholas said, "I don't know. I have no theory. Some branch of the government, I suppose. Or the Soviets. There are a lot of secret Soviet transmitters overhead these days, beaming down to populated areas like this. Broadcasting filth and garbage and kinky suggestions, God knows what."

"But your name."

"Maybe everyone listening heard his own name," Nicholas said. "'Pete, you beat your meat.' Or, 'Mike, you're a dike.' I don't know. I'm exhausted from trying to figure it out." He pointed to the slightly flickering votive candle.

"So that's why you want that burning all the time," I said, understanding. "To drive—"

"To keep me sane," Nicholas interrupted.

"Nick," I said, "you're going to come out of this just fine. I have a theory. The whirling pinwheels of fire, they were due to poisons, toxins, from your infected wisdom tooth. So was what you heard on the radio. You were highly toxic without knowing it. Now that the oral surgery's done, you'll cease to be toxic and be okay. That's why you're better already."

"Except," he said, "what about the golden necklace the girl wore? And what she said?"

"How does that fit in?"

Nicholas said, "I've been expecting her at the door all my life. I recognized her when I saw her. There she was, and wearing what I knew she'd be wearing. I had to ask her what it was; there was no way I could keep from it. Phil, I was programmed to ask that question. It was my destiny."

"But that wasn't bad, like the buzz saws and what you heard from the radio."

"No," Nick agreed. "That was the most important experience I ever had, like a glimpse of—" He was silent for a time. "You don't know what it's like to wait year after year, wondering if it, if she, is ever going to show up, and at the same time knowing she is. Eventually. And then when you least expect it, but when you need it most—" He smiled up at me.

Most of his stress had departed, but, he told me, he still saw colors at night. Not the jagged pinwheels but rather vague patches, simply drifting. The colors seemed to change according to his thoughts; there was a direct connection. When he thought, in the long hypnagogic states preceding sleep, about erotic topics, the patches of foglike color turned red. Once he thought he saw Aphrodite, naked and lovely and huge-breasted. When he thought about holy topics, the colored patches turned pure pale white.

It reminded me of what I'd read in the *Tibetan Book of the Dead*, the Bardo Thodol existence after death occurs. The soul moves along encountering different-colored lights; each color represents a different kind of womb, a different type of rebirth. It is the job of the departed soul to avoid all bad wombs and come at last to the clear white light, I decided not to tell Nicholas this; he was screwed-up enough already.

"Phil," he said to me, "as I move along through these different-colored patches of light, I feel—it's very strange. I feel as if I'm dying. Maybe the oral surgery did something fatal to me. But I'm not scared. It seems . . . you know: natural."

It was anything but that.

"You are on strange trips, Nick," I said.

He nodded. "But something is happening. Something good. I think I'm past the worst part. The radio voice mocking me and insulting me in that gross way, and the whirling jagged buzz saws that were nearly blinding me — that was the worst part. I feel better with this candle." He pointed to the small narrow candle flame beside his bed. "It's strange . . . I wasn't even sure what the word 'votive' meant; I don't remember ever using it before. It just came to me, as the proper word. This was the kind of holy candle I wanted, and I knew how to ask for it."

"When are you going back to work?" I said.

"Monday. Officially I'm on leave, on my own time. Not on sick leave any longer. It was awful to be nearly blind, and so goddamn dizzy. I was afraid it would last forever. But when I saw the girl standing there, and the golden fish sign — you know, Phil, the Greek Orphic religion, around 600 B.C., they used to show the initiate a golden sign and they'd tell him, 'You are a son of earth and of starry heaven. Remember your birth.' It's interesting: 'Of starry heaven.'"

"And the person would remember?"

"He was supposed to. I don't know if it really worked. He was supposed to lose his amnesia and then start to recall his sacred origins. That was the purpose of the whole mystery ceremonies, as I understand it. Anamnesis, it was called: abolishment of amnesia, the block that keeps us from remembering. We all have that block. There's a Christian anamnesis, too: memory of Christ, of the Last Supper and the Crucifixion; in Christian anamnesis those events are remembered in the same way, as a real memory. It's the sacred inner miracle of Christian worship; it's what the bread and wine cause. 'Do this in remembrance of me,' and you do it, and you remember Jesus all at once. As if you had known him but had forgotten. The bread and wine, partaking of them, bring it back."

"Well," I said, "the girl told you the fish, the golden necklace sign, was an ancient Christian sign, so if you experience what you said — anamnesis, whatever — you'll remember Christ."

"Guess so."

"I have a feeling," I said, "a theory, actually, that you have seen that dark-haired girl with the fish necklace before. She was delivering medication from the pharmacy; don't you sometimes have them deliver? Couldn't she have come by before? Or you could have seen her at the pharmacy. Delivery people hang around a pharmacy when they aren't delivering; sometimes they even double as clerks. That would explain the shock of recognition, with you still half stoned from the Sodium Pentothal; déjà vu, I mean, occurring during great pain and under the lingering haze of the —"

"The pharmacy he called," Nicholas broke in, "is near his office, which is in Anaheim. I've never been there before; I never got anything from that pharmacy in my life. My pharmacy is in Fullerton, by my doctor's office."

Silence.

"Guess that shoots that," I said. "But you did fixate on what she wore because of the pain and stress and the residual haze of the Pentothal. It acted as a hypnotically fixating object, like a moving watch. Or like this candle flame." I pointed at the votive candle. "And the mention of 'early Christians' suggested to you to get a votive candle. You've been highly suggestive, almost in a hypnotic trance, since your surgery. It always happens."

"Are you sure?"

"Well, it seems logical."

Nicholas said, "I had the uncanny feeling, God help me — I had the incredible experience, Phil, for a few minutes after I saw her necklace, that I was back in early Rome, in the first century A.D. So help me. She said that, and all at once it was real, completely real. The present world — Placentia, Orange County, the U.S.A. — it was all gone. But then it returned."

"Hypnotic suggestion," I said.

After a pause, Nicholas said, "If I'm dying—"

"You're not dying," I said.

"If I die," Nicholas continued, "who or what is going to run my body for the next forty years? It's my mind that's dying, Phil, not my body. I'm leaving. Something has got to take my place. Something will; I'm sure of it."

Into the bedroom walked Nicholas's sheeplike cat, Pinky. The big tomcat hopped up onto the bed and kneaded with his paws, purring; he gazed affectionately at Nicholas.

"That's a strange-looking cat you have there," I said.

"You notice the change in him? He's beginning to change. I don't know why; I don't know in what direction."

Bending down I petted the cat. He seemed less wild than usual, more sheeplike, less catlike. The carnivore qualities seemed to be leaving him.

"Charley," I said, referring to Nicholas's dream.

"No, Charley is gone," Nicholas said, and then at once caught himself. "Charley never existed," he amended.

"Not for a while, anyhow," I said.

"Charley was very different from Pinky," Nicholas said. "But they both served as my guide. In different ways. Charley knew the forest. He was more like a totem cat, the kind an Indian would have." Half to himself, Nicholas murmured, "I really don't understand what's happening to Pinky. He won't eat meat any longer. When we feed him meat he starts trembling. As if there's something wrong about eating meat; as if he's been hit."

"Wasn't he gone for a while?"

"He recently came back," Nicholas said vaguely. He did not elaborate. "Phil," he said presently, "this cat began to change the same day I first saw the buzz saws and you had to lead me home. After you left I was lying on the couch with a towel over my eyes, and Pinky got up as if he understood there was something wrong with me. He began searching for it. He wanted to locate it and heal it, make me okay. He kept walking over me and on me and around me, searching and searching. I could sense it about him, his concern, his love. He never found it. Finally he lay down on my stomach, and he stayed there until I got up. Even with my eyes shut I could sense him there still trying to locate the problem. But with that small a brain . . . cats have really small brains."

Pinky had lain down on the bed near Nicholas's shoulder, purring, gazing at him intently.

"If they could talk," Nicholas murmured.

I said, "It looks as if he's trying to communicate with you."

To the cat, Nicholas said, "What is it? What do you want to say?"

The cat continued to gaze up into his face with the same intentness; I had never seen such an expression on an animal's face before, not even a dog's.

"He was never like this before," Nicholas said. "Before the change. The buzz saws, I mean; that day."

"That strange day," I said. The day, I thought, when everything began to become different for Nicholas, leaving him weak and passive, as he was now: ready to accept whatever came. "They say," I said, "that in the final days, in the Parousia, there will be a change in the animals. They'll all become tame."

"Who says that?"

"The Jehovah's Witnesses say it. I was shown a book they peddle; there was a picture, and it showed all the various wild animals lying around together, no longer wild. It reminds me of your cat here."

"'No longer wild,'" Nicholas murmured.

"You seem to be the same way yourself," I said. "As if all your fangs had been pulled.... Well, I guess there's a reason for that." I laughed.

"Earlier today," Nicholas said, "I fell into a half-sleep and I dreamed I was back in the past, on the Greek island of Lemnos. There was a gold and black vase on a three-legged table, and a lovely couch.... It was the year 842 B.C. What happened in the year 842? That was during the Mycenaean period, when Crete was such a great power."

"Eight forty-two," I said, "was the price you paid for your pain pills. It's a sum, not a date. Money."

He blinked. "Yes, there were gold coins too."

"The girl said to you, 'Eight forty-two.'" I was trying to get him to focus, to become alert again. "Remember?" To myself I thought, Come back, Nicholas. To this world. The present. From whatever other world you're drifting away to from pain and fear—fear of the authorities, fear of what lies ahead for all of us in this country. We've got to put up one last fight. "Nick," I said, "you've got to fight."

"What's happening to me is not bad. It's strange, and it started out terrible, but it isn't now. I think this is what I was expecting."

"They're sure putting you through the wringer," I said. "I'd resent it."

"Maybe it's the only way it can be done, What do we know about processes of this sort? Nothing at all. Who of us has ever seen one take place? I think they used to take place a long time ago, but not any more. Except for me."

I left him that evening feeling worried. Nicholas had decided to succumb and that was that. No one could tell him otherwise, including me. Like a boat launched without paddles into a current, he was moving along without control, going wherever it took him, into the indiscriminate darkness beyond.

I guess it was a way of getting away from the presence of Ferris F. Fremont and all he represented. Too bad I couldn't do likewise; then I could forget my worries about FAPers breaking down the door with warrants, dope hidden in my house, Vivian Kaplan going to the District Attorney on a trumped-up complaint of some sort.

WHEN NICHOLAS WENT to bed that night he found, as usual, that he could not sleep. His thoughts raced faster and faster, and with them the external patches of color projected by his head into the semigloom of his bedroom. Finally he got up and padded barefoot into the kitchen for some vitamin C.

That was when he made a discovery of importance. He had assumed from the start that the capsules in his great bottle were, as in the previous bottle, one hundred milligrams. However, these were time-release vitamin C, and each capsule contained not one hundred milligrams but five hundred. Nicholas was therefore taking five times the amount of vitamin C he had supposed. Making a quick tally he discovered that he was taking in excess of seven grams per day, plus the other vitamins. At first this scared him, but then he reasoned to himself that it meant nothing; since vitamin C was water-soluble, it was excreted from his system every twenty-four hours and so did not build up. However, seven grams a day certainly was a large quantity. Seven thousand milligrams or more! He had really saturated his system. Well, he said to himself, that ought to wash out everything bonded at a cellular level, including the lithium carbonate; it's going out as fast as it comes in.

He returned to bed, a little frightened now, lay on his back, and pulled the covers up. The votive candle burned on the table

to his right. As his eyes adjusted to the gloom he saw the floating patches of color, but they were receding from him faster
and faster as his thoughts — manic, the psychiatrist had said —
matched their velocity. They're escaping, he thought, and so is
my head; my mind is going along with them.

There was no sound. To his left, Rachel . . .

PART TWO
NICHOLAS

15

. . . SLEPT ON AND on, unaware that anything was happening. Pinky dozed, somewhere off in the living room, probably in his special place on the couch, and in his nursery Johnny was sound asleep in the single bed we had gotten him to replace his crib. The apartment was totally silent, except for the faint *whirr* of the refrigerator in the kitchen.

My God, I thought, the colors are receding faster and faster as if achieving escape velocity; as if they are being sucked out of the universe itself. They must have reached the edge of the world and are vanishing beyond. And my thoughts with them? The universe, I realized, was being turned inside out — reversed. It was an eerie feeling, and I felt terrible fear. Something was happening to me, and there was no one to tell it to.

For some reason it did not occur to me to wake up my wife. I simply continued to lie there, staring at the patches of foglike color.

And then, winking on abruptly, a square of particolors appeared directly above me. Violent phosphene activity, I realized; and now the idea came to me that somehow the immense doses of vitamin C I was taking had set this off. I was responsible for all this myself, in my efforts to heal myself.

The exaggerated particolored square shimmered and altered

at the direct center of my field of vision. It resembled a modern abstract painting; I could almost name the artist, but not quite. Rapidly, at the terrific rate of permutation which in the TV field they call flash-cutting, the frame of balanced, proportioned colors gave way to another frame, equally attractive. Within a few given seconds I had seen no less than twenty of them; as each frame, each abstract, appeared, it at once gave way to another. The overall effect was dazzling. Paul Klee, I said to myself excitedly. I am seeing a whole lot of Paul Klee prints — or, rather, the actual pictures themselves, an entire gallery display! It was, in many respects, the most wonderful and astonishing sight I had ever seen. Scared as I was, puzzled as I was to account for this, I made the decision to lie there and enjoy it. Certainly no such experience had ever come my way before; this was an extraordinary — in fact, unique — opportunity.

The dazzling presentation of modern abstract graphics continued all through the night, with Paul Klee giving way to Marc Chagall, and Chagall to Kandinsky, and Kandinsky to an artist whose style I did not recognize. There were literally tens of thousands of graphics by each master artist in turn ... which caused a peculiar thought to enter my mind after two hours had passed. These great artists had never produced so many works; it was patently impossible for them to have done so. Of the Klees alone I had now seen more than fifty thousand, although admittedly they had gone so rapidly that I had not been able to glimpse any distinct details, but rather only the general impression of fluctuating balance points in the various pictures, changing proportions of dark and light colors, adroit black strokes of the brush that gave harmony to what would otherwise have been less than high art.

I had the intense impression that this was a telepathic contact of some sort from a very remote point, that a TV camera was sweeping out the various displays of pictures in a museum somewhere; I recalled, presently, that the Leningrad Museum was said to possess an extraordinary collection of French abstracts, and it came to me that a Soviet TV crew was sweeping out the displays over and over again and then transmitting them at enormous velocity, six thousand miles across space, to me. But that was so unlikely I could not accept it. More likely, the Soviets were conducting a telepathic experiment, using their museum of modern abstracts as material to be sent to a target person somewhere, and for reasons unknown I was overhearing—whatever the verb—this experiment, tuning in on it by accident. The sender was not sending with me in mind; nonetheless, I was seeing this marvelous display of modern graphics, the entire collection at Leningrad.

All night I lay happily awake tuned in on this Soviet show or whatever it was; when the sun came up I was still flat on my back, fully awake, not frightened, not worried, having been bathed in the intense fluctuations of brilliant colors for over eight hours. Rachel got up, grumbling, to feed Johnny. I found, as I myself got out of bed, that I could see all right, except when I shut my eyes. When I shut my eyes I saw a perfectly stable, unchanging phosphene representation of what I had just been looking at: my bedroom, and then a moment later the living room with its bookcases and record cases, lamp, TV set, furniture. There was even a reverse-color Pinky, sound asleep in his special spot on the far end of the couch, next to a reverse-color *New Yorker* magazine.

I thought, I have a new kind of vision. A new sight. As if, up to now, I have been blind. But I don't understand it.

Usually I buttonholed my wife and narrated to her in great detail my nocturnal experiences, but not this time. It was too—puzzling. Where had the telepathic transmissions come from? Was there anything I should do in the way of response? Write to Leningrad somehow and say I'd received them?

Maybe the vitamin C affected the metabolism of my brain, I conjectured. After all, it's highly acid; such quantities in the system would produce a highly acid brain. Mentation, neural firing, improves under conditions of acidity. Perhaps the vivid phosphene activity, the multicolored graphics, had been projections of rapid synchronous neural firing along never-before-used circuits. In that case Leningrad had nothing to do with it; everything was a function and an activity within my head.

GABA fluid, I suddenly realized. What I saw was the effect of a vast drop in GABA fluid. There was new neural firing, along otherwise inhibited circuits. Good thing I haven't written Leningrad yet.

I wonder what kind of neural circuits they are, I asked myself. Probably I will find out, in time.

I stayed home from work that day. Toward noon the mail came; I walked unsteadily down the outside stairs to the row of metal mailboxes, retrieved the mail, and came back in.

As I laid the letters and ads out on the coffee table in the living room, an acute impression came over me and I said to Rachel, "A letter will be coming the day after tomorrow, from New York. It is highly dangerous. I want to be here to get it, as soon as it comes." I felt this overwhelmingly.

"A letter from who?" Rachel said.

"I don't know," I said.

"Will . . . you recognize it?"

"Yes," I said.

No mail at all came the next day. But the day after that seven letters arrived. Most of them were from aspiring young artists, the letters forwarded to me from Progressive. After I had glanced at the envelopes without opening them, I turned to one last remaining letter; my name and address were on it, but no return address at all.

"That's the one," I said to Rachel.

"Aren't you going to open it?"

"No," I said. I was trying to think what I was supposed to do with the letter.

"I'll open it," Rachel said, and did so. "It's just a printed ad," she said, laying the contents out on the coffee table; instinctively, for reasons not known to me, I turned my head so as not to see it. "For shoes," she said. "Mail-order shoes. Something called 'Real World Shoes.' With a special sole so that—"

"It's not an ad," I said. "Turn it over."

She did so. "Somebody's jotted their name and address on the back," she said. "A woman. Her name is—"

"Don't read it aloud," I said sharply. "I don't want to know her name; if you read it to me I'll remember it. It'll go into my memory banks."

"She must be the distributor," Rachel said. "But Nick, this isn't anything; it's just shoes."

"Get me a pen and about three sheets of typing paper," I said, "and I'll show you." Meanwhile I was still trying to introspect and come up with the answer as to what to do about this—with it and about it. Acute dread hung over me as I sat at the table with this shoe ad, as Rachel got the pen and paper.

I had to read it to decode it. Superimposed on the black type, in a liquid, bright red, I saw certain words of the ad as if embossed. Rapidly, I copied them onto a separate piece of paper and then, when I had finished, handed it to Rachel. "Read it," I said. "But just to yourself, not to me."

Rachel said falteringly, "It's a message to you. Your name is in it."

"What does it tell me to do?"

"Something about recording certain—it has to do with your job, Nick. Something about Party members who—I can't make sense out of it. Your handwriting is—"

"But it is to me," I said. "And it does have to do with Progressive and my job there, and recording Party members."

"How can it be?" Rachel said. "In a printed ad for shoes? I saw you with my own eyes get this message out of it, by picking words here and there ... the words are really in it; I can see them myself now, when I look at the ad. But how did you know which words to pick?"

"Different in color," I said. "They're in color and the other words are ordinary black, without color."

"*All* of the ad is black!" Rachel protested.

"Not to me," I said. I was still deep in heavy, fearful thought. "Code from the Party," I said. "Instructions, and the name of my — whatever she is — my boss; it's written in her hand on the back. My official contact."

"Nick," Rachel whispered, "this is awful. Are you —"

"I'm not a Communist," I said truthfully.

"But you knew this was coming. And you knew how to decode it. You were *waiting* for it." She stared at me wide-eyed.

I picked up the shoe ad, for the first time, turned it over, and as I did so a voice spoke inside my head. A transforming of my own thought processes, to confer on me a message.

"The authorities."

Just those two words — *the authorities* — as I held the piece of paper. This had not come from a KGB agent operating out of New York, as it appeared to have. It was not instructions from the Party. It was a forgery. The thing operated on three levels: on the surface, to Rachel's eyes, it was an ordinary ad. For some reason, unexplained, I had been able to penetrate to the encoded information within the meaningless data. Never mind why, I thought; all that matters is that I did, I had been able to, readily. On the third and deepest level it was a fake, a plant by the police. And here I sat with it in the living room of my own apartment: prime evidence of my treasonable activities. Enough to send me to jail for life and completely ruin me and my family.

I have to get rid of this, I realized. Burn it. But what good will that do? There will be more like this coming to me in the mail. Until they have me.

The voice inside my head spoke again. I identified it now. The sibyl's voice, as I had heard her in my visionary dreams.

"Phone FAP in LA. I will talk for you."

Getting the phone book I looked up the emergency number of the main FAP headquarters for Southern California, located in Los Angeles.

"What are you doing?" Rachel said apprehensively, following me. "You're going to call — FAP? But why? Good lord, Nick, you're going to destroy yourself. Burn the thing!"

I dialed.

"Friends of the American People."

Inside my mind the sibyl stirred, and at once I lost power over my own vocal apparatus; I was struck dumb. And then she began to speak for me, using my voice. Calmly, implacably, she spoke to the FAP agent on the other end of the line.

"I wish to report," my voice said, in a measured way not at all resembling my own cadences, "that I am being threatened by the Communist Party. For months they have been attempting to obtain my cooperation in a business matter and I have refused. They now are attempting to get their wish by coercion, force, and intimidation. Today I received a coded message from them in the mail, telling me what I must do for them. I will not do it, even if they murder me. I would like to turn this coded message over to you."

After a pause the FAP agent on the other end said, "Just a moment, please." A few clicks, then silence.

"Time is of the essence," I said to Rachel.

"Hello," a different voice said, older in sound. "Would you repeat what you just told the operator?"

"The Communist Party," I said, "is blackmailing me to force me to cooperate with them in a business matter. I've refused."

"What kind of business matter?"

"I'm an executive at a recording firm," I said. "We record folk artists. The Party wants to compel me to record pro-Communist singers so their message, including coded messages, will be played on American radios."

"Your name."

I gave him my name, address, and telephone number. Rachel, stricken, merely gazed mutely at me. She could not believe I was doing what I was doing. Neither could I.

"How are they blackmailing you, Mr. Brady?" the voice asked.

"I'm beginning to receive hit mail from them," I said.

"'Hit mail'?"

I said, "Mail designed to provoke a reaction out of fear of reprisal. In code. I can't read all the code, but—"

"We'll send someone over. Hang on to the written material you have in your possession. We will want to see it."

I said, or rather my voice uttered, "They've given me the name of someone back east to contact."

"Don't contact them. Don't leave your residence. Just wait until our representative comes by. You'll be instructed how to proceed. And thank you for contacting us, Mr. Brady. It was very patriotic." The man at the other end clicked off.

"I did it," I said to Rachel; I felt flooded with relief. "What I did," I said, "is I got out of the noose. This apartment would probably have been raided within the next hour. Certainly within the next day." Now it didn't matter even if they hit us; I had made the right call. The emergency was over, thanks not to me or any solution of mine but to the sibyl.

"But suppose," Rachel said frantically, "it turns out it is from the Party?"

"It's not from the Party. I don't know anyone in the Party; I'm not even sure there is a Party. If there is, they wouldn't be writing me, especially in code."

"It could be a mistake of some kind. They intended to write to someone else."

"Fuck 'em then," I said. Anyhow, I knew it was the authorities; or rather the sibyl knew. Valis knew. Valis, who had come through at the critical time and saved me.

Rachel said, "They'll think you're a Communist, from what you told them."

"No, they won't. No Communist would have phoned them in the first place, let alone said what I said. They'll know I am exactly what I am: a patriotic American. Fuck them and fuck the Party; they're one and the same, as far as I'm concerned. It's the Party that kills its political rivals in purges — Ferris Fremont is the Party, and the Party killed the Kennedys and Dr. King and Jim Pike to take power in America. We have one enemy and that's it. That's Comrade Ferris Fremont."

My wife stared at me dumbfounded.

"Sorry," I said, "but it's true. That's the great secret. That's what the people aren't supposed to know. But I know. I was told."

"Fremont isn't a Communist," Rachel said feebly, her face ashen. "He's a fascist."

"The U.S.S.R. turned fascist in Stalin's time," I said. "Now it's totally fascistic. America was the last stronghold of freedom and they took us over, internally, under fake names. We go too much on names — labels. Fremont is the first Communist Party president, and I'm going to get him out."

"Jesus Christ!" Rachel said.

"Right," I said.

"I've never seen you display such animosity, Nick."

"That letter today," I said savagely, "that alleged shoe ad — that's murder, murder aimed at me. I am going to get the sons-of-bitches for that — for sending that to me — if it's the last thing I do."

"But . . . you never showed such hate for the Party before. In Berkeley —"

"They never tried to kill me before," I said.

"Can . . ." She could scarcely talk; trembling, she seated herself on the arm of the couch, by Pinky. The cat still dozed. "Can FAP help you?"

"FAP the enemy," I said. "Finessed back onto itself. I will get it to do all the work; I already have."

"How many other people do you think know? About President Fremont, I mean?"

"Look at his foreign policy. Trade deals with Russia, grain sales at a loss to us; he gives them what they want. The U.S. is their supplier; it does what they say. If they're out of grain they get grain; if they're low on —"

"But our big military establishment."

"To keep our own people down. Not theirs."

Rachel said, "You didn't know this yesterday."

"I knew it when I saw the shoe ad," I said. "When I saw the message from the Communist Party that was also from FAP. They are working with the KGB in New York, not against it; how could it operate openly if FAP didn't let it? There is one intelligence community and one only. And we are all its victims, wherever we live."

"I need a drink," Rachel managed to say.

"Take heart," I said. "The beginning of the change has set in. The turning point has come. They will be exposed; they will stand in court, every one of them, and answer for the crimes they have committed."

"Because of you?" She gazed timidly at me.

"Because of Valis," I said.

Rachel said, "It's not you any longer, Nick. You're not the same person."

"That is right," I said.

"Who are you?"

I said, "Their adversary. Who is going to see them hunted down."

"You can't do it by —"

"I'll be given the names of others."

"Like yourself?"

I nodded.

"So that letter," Rachel said, "that shoe ad — it would never have gotten in the mail without the permission and cooperation of the American authorities."

"That's right," I said.

"What about Aramchek?"

I said nothing.

"Is Valis Aramchek?" Rachel asked hesitantly. "Or maybe you shouldn't tell me; maybe I'm not supposed to know."

"I'll tell you —" I began, but all I once I felt two great invisible hands grip me by the upper arms; they held so tightly that I grunted in pain. Rachel stared at me. I could not speak any further; all I could do was try to withstand the pressure of the invisible hands holding me. Then, at last, they released me. I was free.

"What happened?" Rachel asked.

"Nothing." I took in deep, unsteady breaths.

"The look on your face — something had hold of you, didn't it? You started to say something you shouldn't have." She patted me gently on the arm. "It's okay, Nick; you don't have to say. I don't want you to say."

"Maybe some other time," I said.

16

TOWARD THE END of the day two FAPers, both of them lean and alert young men, showed up at my door.

Silently, they examined the shoe ad I had received in the mail. I showed them the piece of paper on which I had written the encoded message that I had extracted.

"I am Agent Townsend," the first FAPer said. "And this is my teammate, Agent Snow. It was very alert of you to report this, Mr. Brady."

I said, truthfully, "I knew it would be coming. I even knew the day."

"I imagine," Agent Townsend said, "that the Communists would very much like to control someone in your position. You have power over a large number of recording artists, do you not?"

"Yes," I said.

"You can sign up and record whomever you wish?"

"I need the approval of two other executives," I said. "But usually they go along with me."

"They have come to respect your judgment?"

"Yes," I said.

"How has the Party contacted you before?" Agent Snow asked.

"They never before—"

"We realize they never turned the screws before. But did they contact you through mutual friends, or by phone, or mail? Or directly, through their agents?"

"I don't know," I said. "I know the contact, the pressure has been there, but it's been too devious and subtle up until now to put my finger on."

"No one person in particular."

"No," I said.

Agent Townsend said, "This is the first time they've come out overtly, then."

"Yes," I said.

"In your case," Agent Townsend said, "they made a mistake. We have a mail intercept on you, Mr. Brady; we intercepted this document and decoded it ourselves. We knew the hour of its arrival in your mailbox. You were watched as you took it upstairs to this apartment. You were timed as to how long it took you to react to it. And of course we were looking to see your reaction. Frankly, we didn't expect you to call us. We assumed you'd destroy it."

"My wife suggested I destroy it," I said. "But that could have been taken two ways."

"Oh, yes," Agent Townsend said. "Two ways easily. You read the encoded message and then burned it; that's a normal process for Party members; they wouldn't leave something like this lying around after they had assimilated its contents; it'd be incriminating."

The sibyl had directed me right. Inwardly, without any visible sign, I sighed with relief. Thank God for her, I said to myself; on my own, like Rachel, I most likely would have destroyed it, imagining that was enough. And thus incriminated myself forever.

Destroying it would have proved I had read it. That I knew

what it was. One does not carry a harmless shoe ad to the bathroom and set fire to it in the bathtub.

Studying the name and address written on the back of the document, Agent Townsend said to Agent Snow, "This looks like . . . you know, that girl's handwriting." To me he said, "Your friend Phil Dick knows a girl named Vivian Kaplan. Do you know her?"

"No," I said, "but he's mentioned her."

"You wouldn't have any samples of her handwriting around?" Agent Townsend asked.

"No," I said.

"Vivian is a rather far-out person," Agent Townsend said with a half smile. "She reported about you recently, Mr. Brady, that you hold prolonged conversations with God. Is that true?"

"No," I said.

"She got it from his friend," Agent Snow pointed out to Agent Townsend.

"What," Agent Townsend continued, "would possibly give rise to such an idea in her head? Can you think of anything?"

I said, "I never met the girl."

"She is reporting on you," Agent Townsend said.

"I know that," I said.

"What would your feelings toward her be," Agent Townsend said, "if evaluation of this shoe ad document showed that it emanated from her?"

"I would want nothing to do with her," I said.

"Well, we are not really sure," Agent Townsend said, "and in all likelihood it emanated from the KGB in New York, but until we are positive we have to consider the outside possibility that one of our own posts mailed it off to you."

I said nothing.

"What we'd like you to do," Agent Snow said, "is pass on to

us any further documents of this sort which you may receive, or any contacts with suspicious persons coming in any form whatever, phone or mail, or at your door. You realize, of course, that the Party may have decided to destroy you for your unwillingness to cooperate with them."

"Yes," I said. "I know that."

"I mean physically destroy. Kill."

I felt cold, hearing that, terribly cold.

"There is not much we can do to help you," Agent Snow said, "in that regard. If someone wants to kill a person they usually can."

"Could you assign anyone to stay with me?" I said.

The two FAP agents exchanged glances. "Afraid not," Agent Townsend said. "It exceeds our authority. And we don't have the manpower. You can if you wish buy a handgun. That might be a good idea, especially in view of the fact that you have a wife and small child."

"I'll do that," I said.

"We will okay it," Agent Townsend said.

"Then you don't think one of your own posts sent this," I said.

"Frankly, I doubt it very much," Agent Townsend said. "We'll conduct a routine inquiry. It would certainly simplify everything, from our standpoint. May I take this ad and the envelope?"

"Certainly," I said. I was glad to have it out of my hands.

THAT NIGHT I SAT out alone on the patio of our apartment, gazing up at the stars. By now I knew what had happened to me; for reasons I did not understand, I had become plugged into an intergalactic communications network, operating on a telepathic basis. Sitting there in the dark by myself I experienced the stars overhead and the enormous amount of traffic flowing between them. I was in touch with one station in the network, and I gazed up trying to locate it, although most likely locating it was impossible.

A star system with a name out of our own devising; I knew the star's name. It was Albemuth. But I could find no such star listed in our reference works, although the prefix Al was common to stars, since it signified the word "the" in Arabic.

There I sat, and there overhead twinkled and glowed the star Albemuth, and from its network came an infinitude of messages, in assorted unknown tongues. What had happened was that the AI operator of Albemuth's station, an artificial intelligence unit, had raised me at some prior time and was holding the contact open. Therefore information reached me from the communications network whether I liked it or not.

It was the voice of the AI unit which I saw in dreams as the "Roman sibyl." In point of fact it was not the Roman sibyl, not at all, and really not a woman; it was a totally synthetic entity. But I loved the sound of her voice — I still thought of the entity as her — since whenever I heard it, either in my head during a hypnagogic or hypnopompic state or in dreams, it meant that I would soon be informed of something. Beyond the AI voice, the synthetic female voice, lay Valis himself, the ultimate constituent link to the universe-wide communications network. Now that I had peaked in my rapport with it, enormous amounts of material were flooding across; ever since the phosphene activity they were evidently jamming it to me, feeding me as much as possible, in case, perhaps, the contact was broken.

They had never visited Earth — no actual extraterrestrials had landed ships and walked around here — but they had informed certain humans now and then throughout the ages, especially in ancient times. Since my contact came in most strongly between 3:00 and 4:00 a.m., I realized that probably a booster satellite, of alien origin, orbited Earth, a slave communications satellite that had been sent here thousands of years ago.

"What are you doing sitting out on the patio?" Rachel asked me.

"Listening," I said.

"To what?"

"To the voices of the stars," I said, although more accurately I meant the voices from the stars. But it was as if the stars themselves spoke, as I sat there in the chilly dark, alone except for my cat, who was out there out of custom anyhow; each night Pinky sat on the railing of the patio, communing as I was but over a longer period of time, over his entire adult life. Seeing him now I understood that he was picking up information in the night, from the night, from the pattern of blinks that came by starlight. He was hooked up with the universe as he sat here now, like myself, gazing upward silently.

The Fall of man, I further realized, represented a falling away from contact with this vast communications network and from the AI unit expressing the voice of Valis, which to the ancients would be the same as God. Originally, like the animal beside me, we had been integrated into this network and had been expressions of its identity and will operating through us. Something had gone wrong; the lights had gone out on Earth.

17

THESE REALIZATIONS CAME to me not as speculation or even as logical deduction, but as insights presented me by the sympathetic AI operator at work at my station. She was making me aware of that which man had ceased to understand: his role and place in the system of things. I saw on the inner screen of my mind an inferior agency creeping into our world, combating the wisdom of God; I saw it take over this planet with its own dreary plans and will, supplanting the benign will of God ... or Valis, as I still preferred to call him. Over the ages God had played a great game for the relief of this planet, but lifting the siege had still not been accomplished. Earth was still an unlit button on the exchange board of the intergalactic communications network. We had not yet begun to function as our first ancestors had, in communion with our creator and the lord of the universe. Such examples as me were random flukes — I had not achieved it; it had happened to me, due to a combination of circumstances. One of the deformed progeny had lifted the receiver of the long-abandoned telephone, so to speak, and was now hearing the sympathetic, informative voice that he and all his kind should have known by heart.

The new personality in me had not awakened from a sleep of two millennia; it had, more accurately speaking, been printed

out by the alien satellite, impressed on me afresh from outside.
It was an addition, not a substitution in place of me but a kind
of package identity based on the total knowledge of the satellite. It was to raise me to the highest level possible in my ability
to cope. The satellite, itself linked to higher life forms, was concerned with my capacity to live; it or they, the totality of them,
had seen me faltering under the oppression, and their response
was reflexive. It amounted to a rational attempt to give aid to
whoever was in touch with them, who was capable of assimi-
lating their printout. I had been selected for that reason alone.
Their concern was universal. They would have assisted anyone
they could reach.

The tragedy lay in their inability to reach the people of our
planet. It went back to the original invasion of our world by the
malign entity that did not wish to hear. It had contaminated
our world with its presence; it was not merely around us, it was
also in us. We bore its mark. Probably the maximum harm it
had done us was to sever us from the communications network.
Due to its opaqueness it probably was not even aware of what it
had done. Or if it understood, it did not consider it a loss.

It certainly was a loss as far as I was concerned, now that I
had heard the mild voice of the AI system as it relayed information to me and accepted questions in response. Were I never
to hear it again I would remember that sound the rest of my
life. It was far off; whenever I queried it, there was a measurable lag before it responded. I wondered how many stars away
it lay: deep in the heavens, perhaps, and perhaps serving many
worlds.

Already the AI voice had saved my life once, by taking over
and guiding me in the face of imminent police arrest. The only
fear I had now was loss of contact.

The AI voice, I soon understood, possessed the capacity to
educate and inform human beings on a subliminal level, dur-

ing times when they were relaxed in contemplation or in outright sleep. But this was not enough; on waking, the humans generally overrode these quiet promptings, which they correctly identified with the voice of conscience, and went their own way.

I asked the name of the opaque antagonist. The answer: it had no name. The messengers of the communications network continually baffled it by their wisdom, since it could not, as they could, see ahead in time; but it held out by its physical power, blind as it was.

The capacity to see ahead in time was now granted to me to a certain extent. Its first manifestation had come when I saw what I took to be the Roman sibyl expounding on the fate of the conspirators. This had been merely the precognitive statement of the AI monitor, transformed by my head to a visible entity familiar from Earth's history. She or it had merely stated what was coming, without interpretive comment. The forces that would unhinge the conspirators were as yet unstated; the monitor could foresee the consequences of certain acts without error, but either she could not see how those acts came about or she elected not to inform me. I believed it to be the latter. There was a great deal I still did not know.

Since I could question the AI unit, I asked her why the opaque adversary had not been removed a long time ago; obligingly, she furnished me with a diagram which showed the adversary drawn steadily deeper into the fulfillment of the general plan. Having materialized, the adversary was grist for the mill like everything else; I watched as the agency of creation simply incorporated the adversary and its projects along with whatever else its eyes fell on, making no distinction between what we would call good and what we would dismiss as bad. Instead of abolishing the blundering adversary, Valis had put it to work.

In all its activity of continually re-creating the universe, improving and shaping within the constant flow, the artisan employed the most economical means possible. Although it drew on everything, arranging it and most of all joining otherwise separate sections into totally new and unexpected entities, it took only what it absolutely needed. Thus its reshaping process took place within the universe, turning the universe into a kind of gigantic warehouse of parts, an almost infinite stockpile, in which the agency could find anything it desired.

The temporal process, it seemed to me, was a medium by which this proliferation of forms was capable of taking place, for the benefit ultimately of this shaping entity, which, I could see, moved backward through time from the far end of the universe. The plan by which the shaping entity worked seemed to be the form of the entity itself, as if it were transforming the sprawling, chaotic universe into a stupendous replica of its own eidos — form. But of this I couldn't be sure; the enormity of its creation made the distant outlines, both in terms of space and of time, beyond my scope. It was creating around me and right past me, as I sat there.

Once more the impression had begun to come over me by slow degrees that I was in Rome, not in Orange County, California. I sensed the Empire without seeing it, sensed a vast iron prison in which human slaves toiled. I saw as if superimposed on the black metal walls of this huge prison certain rapidly scurrying figures in gray robes: enemies of the Empire and its tyranny, a remnant opposed to it. And I knew, from a deep internal clock down within my own self, that the true time was A.D. 70, that the Savior had come and gone but would soon return. The gray-robed hurrying remnant, with a feeling of joy, awaited and prepared for his return.

Overwhelmed with this, I experienced, too, a barrage of foreign words flooding through my head, words I did not understand but whose impression was clear in any case: I was in deadly danger from the spies of Rome, from those angry armed men who moved everywhere, detecting anything opposed to the imperial glory. I had to be alert, watch what I said, guard with sealed lips the secret that was mine: my link to the inter-galactic communications network and Valis himself. Aware of this link, the Roman agents would kill me in an instant; it was Empire policy.

It was an ancient fight I was in, not a new one; it had been fought without cease for two thousand years. Names had changed, faces had changed, but the adversaries remained a permanent constant. The slave Empire against those who strug-gled for justice and truth — not freedom exactly, in the modern sense, but for virtues obscured today, buried under the bulk of an Empire that embraced both the United States and the Soviet Union as twin, equal manifestations. The U.S. and the U.S.S.R., I understood, were the two portions of the Empire as divided up by the Emperor Diocletian for purely administrative purposes; at heart it was a single entity, with a single value system. And its value system was the concept of the supremacy of the state. The individual counted in its scales as nothing, and individuals who turned against the state and generated their own values were the enemy.

We were the enemy, we who wore the gray robes and waited with eager anticipation for our King to return. I saw the Savior not as a martyr who had died for us but as our legitimate King, who would return, claim his kingdom, and rule with justice and truth over his own people. An Empire ruled subject people, but our King ruled only his own. We would not be enslaved by him, forced to adopt the customs of the Empire; we would share his customs as our own; they were our own. And where his people ended, his rule ended; that was a rightful kingship compared to the tyranny of Caesar.

It would be necessary to teach my wife certain codes, the use of meaningful terms to notify her when one of the Romans was in our midst. We constituted a voluntary secret community, who scratched cryptic signs in the dust; we had special handshakes to identify ourselves to each other; collectively, we waited for the coming event to free us. Outwardly we appeared the same as Caesar's people, and that was our strength. The question that gripped us was not, Would our King return? but, Would we be able to survive against the Romans — by stealth, since we held no worldly power — until he returned? Or would he return to find us gone or, worse, assimilated into the customs of the Empire, our own memory of what we actually were lost forever — or, perhaps, lost until, by his return, he could restore such memories? Reawaken in sleeping men a forgotten knowledge of who they were...?

I did not feel that it was a matter of my returning to a former life, of moving backward through time to some past existence. *Rome was here now;* it had invaded the landscape, rising up from within it, manifesting itself from its centuries-long place of inner concealment. Rather than me being back in the ancient world, Rome had revealed itself as the underlying reality of our present-day world; hidden still from the eyes of other Americans, it was nonetheless blatantly visible to me. The Empire had never died; it had only receded out of sight. My vision now enhanced by Valis, I saw Rome clearly as the landscape of our country; we had inherited it without realizing it. Stripped away were the mere accidental accretions; this was fundamental, what I saw now.

However much I hated Rome, I feared it more. My memory had become elongated, stretching out over a span of two thousand years, but what it encountered was a dreadful sameness: Rome lay spread out everywhere across the ages. What a giant entity it was, to extend that far in time. There lay no relief from it either in the past or the present, although in a sense I experienced no past, just a continual present of vast immensity.

So this was the antagonist ... or, rather, the physical manifestation of the antagonist. This was the corpus malus, the evil body; but within and behind it lay an evil spirit which had made the Empire what it was. Once it had been benign, but those days, when it had been a Republic — those had been swallowed up when free men had been swallowed up by the presence of oppression. How very much it weighed. Rome weighed down the world, armored as it was, huge with its black iron walls and cells and streets, its chains and rings of metal, its helmeted warriors. It seemed surprising that it had not sunk through the crust of the earth.

And now, in our midst at this latter time, the old battle continued on, the oppressor lying behind the iron body, striking at those who were not expressions of the Empire — ourselves, who served a King and walked other ways. We wore no armor, no metal, only the robes, sandals, and perhaps a golden fish in bracelet or necklace form. Our steps were lighter than those who complied with Roman customs, but we were vulnerable to death; we had no physical protection. Many of us had fallen already, to awaken later when the King returned. How soon would it be? Soon, but not yet. And when he returned he would not teach at the periphery of the Empire but would strike at its source, its heart; he would drive into its center and pull it down; this appearance of the King would be quite a surprise, quite a shock to the tyrant; quite different.

Before, the King had come quietly, at the margin of Roman affairs, simply to observe and to teach. He had not wished to be found by the Romans, cornered, tried, and murdered. That was the risk he had run and he had realized it. It was not his intention then to fight; he was King in identity, in spirit, but not in act. He had not died like Kings do but as criminals do, in disgrace. In the centuries since his dreadful murder he had lingered on, invisibly, with no body like ours, dancing outside our lives among the rows of newborn corn, dancing in the mists, pale and thin. People had seen him and mistaken him for a corn king, for the spirit of new life in the spring, the annual and permanent awakening after the death of winter. He had allowed them to imagine that he was nothing more; these were the centuries when knowledge of his real purpose was virtually lost. Mankind was acclimated to the idea of tyrannical rule. The King was visible only as mist itself, mist dancing in the mist, to bring the new crop to life; as if no men but only the corn now heard his voice.

But he had spoken to men originally, and he would speak to them again. He had promised his followers that they would hear his voice, and when they heard it they would recognize it. All promises he had made would be kept in time. He was stronger, now. It would not be much longer. The horn of freedom had begun to blow again, but, more important, the presence of the King was forming and strengthening; and this time he carried a sword.

The sword he carried was an instrument of judging. This time he would not be judged in a human court by human beings; he himself would judge.

I had already glimpsed him dancing toward me among the rows of new corn, with his large, expressive, dark eyes, his thin dark ragged beard, his hollow, rather sad face and small coronet, his linen robe and greaves. . . . But when he returned to judge, he would not appear as this gentle figure. He would breach through into our linear time, our world: mounted on a great white horse, he would ride into existence followed by his mounted host, all of them with swords and shields and glistening helmets. Colors would glow as banners waved, tassels bounced, helmets glinted. And the black iron walls of the prison would fall before him.

He could not lose. He could not be defeated or destroyed. He knew everything, and this time Valis had given him absolute power. The books would be unsealed and the records shown for the first time.

These were the large open books I had seen held up to me when my experiences began: the great volumes opened at last, as prophesied. It meant that the beginning of the end of time had arrived. The first stages had commenced.

For two thousand Earth years the clock of eternity had been stopped at A.D. 70. Now that clock showed a new time; its hands had at last moved forward. The King had chosen his battlefield. It was our world. Our portion of time, It was now.

He was in a sense still the corn king. Two thousand of our years ago he had come here, and had planted a crop, and then gone away. Now he had returned — or would soon — to harvest that crop. He knew that he would find his crop oppressed and stunted and stumbling and imprisoned away from the sun. He knew what had been done to it. And for that crop he held out an imperishable reward. Two thousand years would be wiped away. The destruction of the adversary would be complete; it never would have existed in the first place. The oppression never took place. Even the category of time was subject to his power and rule; he could abolish even that. When he was done, the memory of Rome's existence itself would be gone. And those who served the Empire would not have lived.

Those who had defied it, even to their deaths, would live forever.

Viewing this, receiving this panorama of information, I saw my relinkage to the information network less as an accident, a fluke. I saw it now in its rightful place: arranged for long in advance, even in my childhood, by Valis himself. So that I could be coached and educated in order to participate in the battle which lay ahead: in the throwing-down of Rome.

My experience was a phenomenon of the end time. And there undoubtedly were others like me. Re-creation, I thought, of the gray-robed messengers who hurried about the great iron walls, aiming to pull those walls into rubble; and filled, all the while, with the joy of welcoming their King back. What I was doing, born and created to do, was an act of — celebration.

I had been restored to life. After two thousand years.

Born again. A fresh, new entity entirely. Born again into completeness. With faculties and functions I had never had, which were lost, stripped away, in the original Fall. Stripped away, not from me as an individual; stripped away from our race.

18

I, NICHOLAS BRADY, understood that these primordial faculties and abilities had been restored to me only temporarily, that their existence in me depended on my relatedness to the communications web. Once I fell away from that again, the faculties and abilities would fall away too, and I would drop back down into the state of blindness in which I had lived up to now.

That was how I felt as I sat out on the patio, reading with intense satisfaction and joy the information visible in the light of the stars. I had been blind up until now, and I would be blind again. There was no way it could be made to last, not as long as the adversary continued to live on our planet. And the time had not yet come for his removal. The best we could hope for now was to roll him back a little — a small, defensive victory merely to stabilize our own situation.

Only when the King breached through linear time with his armed host, all riding their great horses into battle, would the change be permanent and for everyone. The veils would lift and we would see the world as it was. And ourselves as well.

The help we were being given now consisted of information only. We were being lent Valis's wisdom but not his power. The power would be given only to the rightful King; we could not be trusted with it — we would misuse it.

• • •

THAT NIGHT WHEN I went to bed I experienced one of the most vivid dreams so far, one which made a great impression on me.

I found myself watching an enormously powerful scientist at work named James-James; he had wild red hair and flashing eyes and was virtually godlike in the range and scope of his activities. James-James had constructed a machine which chug-chugged and flashed radioactive particles in showers from it as it operated; thousands of people sat about in chairs silently watching as the machine produced first an amorphous living slime and then a rough-cast baby; then, whirling and sparking and thumping, it cast up on the floor before us all a lovely young girl: pinnacle of perfection in the cosmic process of evolution.

Beside me in the dream, my wife, Rachel, rose from her seat, wishing to see better what James-James had accomplished. Immediately filled with rage at her audacity in standing up, James-James seized her and threw her to the floor, splintering her kneecaps and her elbows in his fury. At once I stood upright in protest; I moved down the stairs toward James-James, calling on the rows of silent people to complain. There then moved into this large assembly hall men in greenish-brown khaki uniforms, on motorcycles, carrying with them as they rapidly and smoothly advanced the emblems of Rommel's Afrika Korps: the sign of the palm tree.

To them I croaked in hoarse appeal, "We need medical assistance!" As the dream ended, the first scouts of the invading, rescuing Afrika Korps heard me and turned toward me, with fine, noble faces. They were dark-skinned men, rather small and delicate, a race apart from James-James, with his too-pale skin and bright red hair. Their eyes were large, gentle and expressive, dark; they were, I realized, the vanguard of the King.

Waking up from this disturbing dream, I sat by myself in

the living room; the time was about 3:00 a.m. and the apartment was totally silent. The dream suggested a limitation to what James-James — who was Valis — could do for us, or rather would do; that his power was in fact even dangerous to us if misused. It was to the rightful King that we would have to turn for ultimate help, expressed in the dream as "medical assistance," the thing we most needed in order to repair the damage done by the historical, evolutionary process that the original creator James-James had set in motion. The King was a correcting agent against the abuses of that temporal process; powerful and heroic as it was, it had claimed innocent victims. Those victims, at least eventually, would be healed by the legions of the rightful King; until he arrived, I realized, we would receive no such help.

Radioactive particles, I thought — remembering the rapid-fire emission of bits of light from James-James's cosmic machine — like you find in cobalt therapy. The double-edge sword of creation: radioactivity in the form of cobalt bombardment cures cancer, but radioactive emissions in themselves are cancer-producing. James-James's cosmic machine got out of hand and injured Rachel, who stepped out of line in the sense that she stood up. That was enough to enrage the cosmic lord of creation. We need a defender as well. An advocate on our side, who can intervene.

Cancer . . . the process of creation gone wild, I thought. And then, in an instant, the AI operator transferred an explanation to my mind; I saw James-James the creator as master of all prior or efficient causes, of the deterministic process moving forward up the manifold of linear time, from the first nanosecond of the universe to its last; but I also saw another creative being at the far end of the universe, at its point of completion, directing, accepting, shaping, and guiding the flow of change, so that it reached the proper conclusion. This creative entity, possessing absolute wisdom, guided rather than coerced, arranged rather than created; she or it was the architect of the plan and the controller of final or teleological causes. It was as if the original creator of the universe lobbed it like a great softball on a long blind trajectory, whereupon the receiving entity corrected its course and led it right into her glove. Without her, I realized, the great softball which was the universe — however well and hard it had been thrown — would have wandered out into left field somewhere and come to rest at some random, unpremeditated spot.

This dialectic structure of the change process of the universe was something I had never glimpsed before. We had an active creator and a wise receiver of what he created; this did not fit any cosmology or theology I had ever heard of. The creator, standing before the creation, his creation, had absolute power, but from my James-James dream I could see that in a very real sense he lacked a kind of knowledge, a certain vital foresight. This was supplied by his weak but absolutely wise counterplayer at the far end; together they performed in tandem, a god, perhaps, divided into two portions, split off from himself, so as to set up the dynamics of a kind of two-person game. Their goal was the same, however; no matter how much they might seem to conflict or work against each other, they commonly desired the successful outcome of their joint enterprise. I had no doubt, therefore, that these twin entities were manifestations of a single substance, projected to different points in time, with different attributes predominating. The first creator predominated in power, the final one in wisdom. And in addition there was the rightful King, who at any time could breach the temporal process at some point of his selection and, with his hosts, enter creation.

Like cancer cells, the original constituents of the universe proliferated without direction, a total panoply of newness.

Allowed to escape, they went wherever causal chains drove them. The architect who imposed form and order and deliberate shape was, in the cancer process, somehow missing. I had learned a great deal from my James-James dream; I could see that blind creation, not subjected to pattern, could destroy; it could be a steamroller that crushed the small and helpless in its eagerness to grow. More accurately, it was like one immense living organism which spread out into all the space available to it, without regard for the consequences; it was only impelled by the drive to expand and increase. What became of it largely depended on the wise receiver, who pruned and trimmed it as each step of the growth took place.

SEATED ON THE couch by myself I passed from a contemplation of this into a trancelike state, bordering on sleep but not quite sleep; I was still conscious enough to be aware of myself and, to a certain extent, to think. I found myself confronting a modern-looking teletype attached to wires that led into ultrasophisticated electronic assemblies far superior to anything we humans actually have.

IDENTIFY YOURSELF.

I watched the words print themselves out, and as they were printed I heard the same chug-chug made by James-James's radioactive cosmic machine of creation.

I said, "I am Nicholas Brady of Placentia, California."

After a measurable pause the teletype printed out: SADASSA SILVIA.

"What does that mean?" I asked.

Again a pause, and then again the chug-chug. But instead of seeing words printed out I saw a snapshot: a girl with Afro-natural hair, a small worried face, and glasses. The girl held a notebook and clipboard. Across the bottom of the snapshot the teletype printed out a phone number, but I could not see it clearly enough to read it; the figures blurred. I understood that I was supposed to remember it, but there was no way I could. The transmission was arriving from too distant a transmitter.

"Where are you?" I asked.

The teletype printed out: I DON'T KNOW. It seemed puzzled by the question; evidently it was a very low order of AI entity along the network.

"Look around you," I told it. "See if you can find something in the way of writing. An address."

Obligingly, the minor AI operator searched its environment; I could sense its local activity.

I HAVE FOUND AN ENVELOPE.

"What's the address on it?" I said. "Read it."

The ultramodern teletype printed out: F WALLOON, PORTU- GUESE STATES OF AMERICA.

That made no sense to me. Portuguese States of America? An alternate universe? I was as puzzled as it was; neither of us knew where the transmission came from.

And then contact broke. The teletype machine faded out and I could no longer sense its presence, Bewildered, I woke to full consciousness. Had this interchange signified anything? Or, de- spite my subjective impression of lucidity, had I been totally be- fuddled by a dream state, altered consciousness without true rationality? Perhaps "Portuguese States of America" merely symbolized a long distance away, another cosmos entirely. As far away as I could imagine: not to be taken literally.

I could still remember the face of the girl in the snapshot and the name Sadassa Silvia. Perhaps the low-order AI operator had reversed it; more likely it had been intended to read SILVIA SA- DASSA. The name meant nothing to me. I had never heard it be- fore. Nor had I ever seen the little worried face with its mouth turned down at the corner as if in weary depression. The phone number, plus any other data it had intended for me, was lost forever; that had not gotten through, at least not to my conscious mind. I wondered what the snapshot and name signified. No way to tell. Nothing, now, no meaning at all. Perhaps, in time, higher-placed operators in the AI spectrum, along the communications network, would eventually fill in the missing pieces of information and make it clear.

I had already noticed that, rather than arriving in linear fashion, network printouts tended to reach me in staggered clusters, placed at random, so that no pattern could be discerned until the final — and most important — cluster had been transmitted. That way the transmitter held the key segment in its possession until the last moment possible, reducing what it had previously given me to a cipher.

As I returned to the bedroom, Johnny called to me from his bed. "Daddy, can I have a drink?"

From the tap in the bathroom I got him a glass of water. And then, in a state of half-sleep, not fully recovered from the disquieting experience with the low-level AI unit, I took a piece of bread from the kitchen; carrying the bread and the water I entered Johnny's room. He was sitting up, reaching grumpily for the glass of water.

"Here is a game," I said. It had to be done stealthily and rapidly, because of the Romans, and it had to be done in such a manner that if they happened to see they would understand nothing and think only that I was giving my son bread and water. Bending down, I gave him the piece of bread, and then, before he took the water, I inclined the glass playfully, as if by accident, and managed to splash it on his hair and forehead. Then, wiping it off with the sleeve of my pajama, I traced with my finger a cross of water on his forehead and said very quietly, under my breath so that only he and I could hear, words in Greek that I did not know the meaning of. Then, at once, I gave him the glass of water to drink from, and as he handed it back I kissed him and hugged him, as if spontaneously. It was done in an instant, this ritual of ceremony, this series of actions, whatever it was, something ancient which I knew to do by instinct. As I let go of my son I said into his ear, for only him to hear: "Your secret name is Paul. Remember that."

Johnny gazed at me quizzically and then smiled. It was over. His real name had been given him, and under the correct circumstances.

"Good night," I said aloud, and left his bedroom; behind me he rubbed at his moist hair and, sleepily, lay back in his bed.

What was that all about? I asked myself. In the dream transmission something had been freighted across to me on an unconscious level, instructions rather than information, concerning the welfare of my son.

WHEN I RETURNED to bed I had another dream concerning Sadassa Silvia. I heard music as I lay in sleep, astonishingly lovely music, a woman singing, accompanied by an acoustic guitar. Gradually the guitar gave way to a small studio combo, and I heard, then, subtracks with backup vocals and the faint hint of an echo chamber. It was a professional production.

I thought, We should sign her up. She's good.

Presently I found myself in my office at Progressive Records. I could still hear the girl singing, again with the solo guitar. She sang:

> You have to put your slippers on
> To walk toward the dawn.

As I listened, I picked up a new album which we had mastered. A mock-up of the artwork and layout had already been prepared: inspecting it critically, I saw that the singer was Sadassa Silvia; there, in addition to her name on the album cover,

\

was her picture, the same Afro-natural hairstyle, the small worried face, the glasses. There was blurb material on the back, but I could not read it; the small letters blurred away.

That dream remained clear in my mind when I woke up the next morning. What a voice, I said to myself as I showered and shaved. In all my life I had never heard such a pure voice, so compelling; absolutely accurate in pitch, I realized critically. A soprano, something like Joan Baez; what we could do in the way of marketing a voice like that!

Thinking about Sadassa Silvia reawakened my concern about my job at Progressive. I had missed a lot of time; maybe I was ready now to go back. The dream was telling me that.

"Think you can make out okay alone?" I asked Rachel.

"Is your eyesight—"

"I can see well enough," I said. "I think it was all the vitamin C I was taking; it's finally flushed out of my system, taking everything else with it."

I spent one whole day walking around Placentia, enjoying myself immensely. There was a beauty in the trash of the alleys which I had never noticed before; my vision now seemed sharpened, rather than impaired. As I walked along it seemed to me that the flattened beer cans and papers and weeds and junk mail had been arranged by the wind into patterns; these patterns, when I scrutinized them, lay distributed so as to comprise a visual language. It resembled the trail signs which I understood American Indians used, and as I walked along I felt the invisible presence of a great spirit which had gone before me — walked here and moved the unwanted debris in these subtle, meaningful ways so as to spell out a greeting of comradeship to me, the smaller one who would follow.

You can almost read this stuff, I thought to myself. But I couldn't. All I could gather from the arrangements of trash was a participation in the passage of the great figure who had preceded me. He had left these discarded objects placed so that I would know he had been there, and in addition a golden illumination lay over them, a glow that told me something about his nature. He had brought the dust out of its obscurity into a kind of light; this was a good spirit indeed.

I had an acute feeling that the animals always saw this way, always were aware of who and what had passed along the alleys ahead of them. I was seeing with the hypervision associated with them. What a better world than our own, I reflected; it is so much more alive.

It was not so much that I had been exalted upward from my animal nature to the realm of the transcendent; actually I seemed closer to the animal world, more tuned to actual matter. Perhaps this was the first time I had really been at home in the world. I accepted all I saw and enjoyed it. I did not judge. And since I did not judge, there was nothing to reject.

I was ready to return to work. I felt cured. Having handled the shoe ad certainly helped. The crisis had come and gone. It did not disturb my tranquillity to know that in point of fact I had not dealt with the shoe ad, but, rather, that it had been handled for me, by unseen entities. What would have demoralized me would have been their absence: if they had let me fall, incompetent and confused, alone.

My incompetence had called these invisible friends forth. Had I been more gifted I would not now know of them. It was, in my mind, a good trade. Few people had the awareness I now possessed. Because of my limitations an entire new universe had revealed itself to me, a benign and living hyperenvironment endowed with absolute wisdom. Wow, I said to myself. You can't beat that. I had caught a glimpse of the Big People. It was a lifetime dream fulfilled. You'd have to go back to ancient times to find a comparable revelation. Things like this didn't happen in the modern world.

19

ONE WEEK AFTER I returned to Progressive Records, Mrs. Sadassa Silvia walked in and asked for a job. She did not want to be recorded by us, she informed us; she wanted a job such as I had: auditioning other artists. She stood before my desk, wearing pink bell-bottoms and a man's checkered shirt, her coat over her arm, her small face pale with fatigue. It looked as if she had walked a long way.

"I don't hire," I told her. "That's not my job."

"Yes, but you have the desk nearest the door," Mrs. Silvia said. "May I sit down?" Without waiting, she seated herself in a chair facing my desk. She had come into my office; I had left the door open. "Do you want to see my résumé?"

"I'm not personnel," I repeated.

Mrs. Silvia gazed at me through her rather thick glasses. She had a pretty, pert face, very much as it had appeared in the two dreams. I was amazed at her small size; she seemed unusually thin, and I had the impression that she was not physically strong, that in fact she was not well. "Well, can I just sit here a second and get my breath?" she said.

"Yes," I said, rising to my feet. "Can I get you anything? A glass of water?"

Mrs. Silvia said, "Do you have a cup of coffee?"

I fixed her coffee; she sat there gazing inertly ahead, slumped a little in the chair. She was well dressed, and in good taste, in a very modern way, a Southern California style. She had a little white hat on, down deep in her Afro-natural black hair.

"Thank you." She accepted the coffee from me and I noticed the beauty of her hands; she had long fingers and fastidiously manicured nails, lacquered but unpainted. This is a very classy girl, I said to myself. I judged her age as early twenties. When she spoke, her voice was cheerful and expressive, but her face remained impassive, without warmth. As if weighed down, I thought. As if she has had a good deal of trouble in her life.

"You want a job as what?" I said.

"I take shorthand and type and I have two years of college as a journalism major. I can copyedit your blurb copy for you; I worked on the school publications at Santa Ana College." She had the most perfect, lovely teeth I had ever seen, and rather sensuous lips — in contrast to the severity of her glasses. It was as if the lower half of her face had rebelled against an asceticism imposed on her by childhood training; I got the impression of an ample physical nature, checked by deliberate moral restraint. This girl, I decided, calculates everything she does. Calculates its worthiness before she does it. This is a highly controlled person, not given to spontaneity.

And, I decided, very bright.

"What kind of guitar do you own?" I asked.

"A Gibson. But I don't play professionally."

"Do you write songs?"

"Only poetry."

I quoted, "'You have to put your slippers on / To walk toward the dawn.'"

She laughed, a rich, throaty laugh. "Oh, yes. 'Ode to Empedocles.'"

"What?" I said uncertainly.

"You must have read it in my high school yearbook."

"How could I read it in your high school yearbook?"

Mrs. Silvia said, "When did you read it?"

"I forget," I said.

"A friend of mine wrote it under my picture. She meant I'm too idealistic, I guess. That I don't have my feet on the ground, but go charging off in all directions.... I get into different causes. She was very critical of me."

"You better go and see personnel," I told her.

Some aspects of the dream had been correct. In other regards it was completely off. As precognition, which is what Phil would have called it, faulty reception or faulty transduction and interpretation by my dreaming mind had badly disfigured the information. I could hardly record someone who took dictation. We wouldn't sell much of that. I could hardly act out the instructions of the dream, whether it came from Valis or not.

Still, it was amazing that this much was accurate. The dream had the name right, and she did look, in real life, as she had appeared in the snapshot and on the album cover. If nothing more, it proved the reality of dream precognition; nothing more, in all likelihood, in that it appeared to end here. If she got any kind of job with us it would be a miracle; as far as I knew we were overstaffed already.

Setting down her coffee cup, Mrs. Silvia rose and gave me a brief, spirited smile. "Maybe I'll be seeing you again." She departed from my office, walking in slow, almost unsteady steps; I noticed how thin her legs seemed, but it was hard to judge with the bell-bottoms.

After I shut my office door I discovered that she had left her résumé and her keys. Born in Orange County in the town of Yorba Linda, in 1951.... I couldn't help glancing over the résumé as I carried it out of my office and down the hall after her. Maiden name: Sadassa Aramchek.

I halted and stood holding the résumé. Father: Serge Aramchek. Mother: Galina Aramchek. Was this why the AI monitor had steered me to her?

As she emerged from the ladies' room I approached her, stopped her.

"Did you ever live in Placentia?" I asked her.

"I grew up there," Sadassa Silvia said.

"Did you know Ferris Fremont?"

"No," she said. "He had already moved to Oceanside when I was born."

"I live in Placentia," I said. "One night a friend and I found the name 'Aramchek' cut into the sidewalk."

"My little brother did that," Sadassa Silvia said with a smile. "He had a stencil and he went around doing that."

"It was down the block from the house where Ferris Fremont was born."

"I know," she said.

"Is there any connection between —"

"No," she said very firmly. "It's just a coincidence. I used to get asked that all the time when I used my real name."

"'Silvia' isn't your real name?"

"No; I've never been married. I had to start using another name because of Ferris Fremont. He made it impossible to live with the name 'Aramchek.' You can see that. I chose 'Silvia,' knowing that people would automatically turn it around and think I was named Silvia Sadassa." She smiled, showing her perfect, lovely teeth.

I said, "I'm supposed to sign you up to a recording contract."

"What doing? Playing my guitar?"

"Singing. You have a marvelous soprano voice; I've heard it."

Matter-of-factly, Sadassa Silvia said, "I have a soprano voice; I sing in the church choir. I'm an Episcopalian. But it's not a good voice; it's not really trained. The best I can do is when I get a little drunk and sing bawdy hymns in the elevator of my apartment building."

I said, "I can only tell you what I know." Evidently much of what I knew didn't add up. "Do you want me to go with you to personnel?" I asked. "And introduce you?"

"I talked to him."

"Already?"

"He was coming out of his office. He says you're not hiring. You're overstaffed."

"That's true," I said. We stood facing each other. "Why did you pick Progressive Records," I asked, "to try for a job?"

"You've got good artists. Performers I like. I guess it was just a wish-fulfillment fantasy, like all my ideas. It seemed more exciting than working for a lawyer or an oil-company executive."

I said, "What about your poems? Can I see some of them?"

"Sure," she said, nodding.

"And you don't sing when you play your guitar?"

"Just a little. I sort of hum."

"Can I buy you lunch?"

"It's three thirty."

"Can I buy you a drink?"

"I have to drive back to Orange County. My eyesight goes out entirely when I drink. I was totally blind when I was sick; I used to bump into walls."

"What were you sick with?"

"Cancer. Lymphoma."

"And you're okay now?"

Sadassa Silvia said, "I'm in remission. I had cobalt therapy and chemotherapy. I went into remission six months ago, before I finished my course of chemotherapy."

"That's very good," I said.

"They say if I live another year I probably could live five

years or even ten; there're people walking around who've been in remission that long."

It explained why her legs were so spindly and why she gave the impression of fatigue and weakness and ill health. "I'm sorry," I said.

"Oh, I learned a lot from it. I'd like to go into the priesthood. The Episcopal church may ordain women eventually. Right now it doesn't look so good, but by the time I finish college and seminary I think they will."

"I admire you," I said.

"When I was very sick last year I was deaf and blind. I still take medication to prevent seizures ... the cancer reached my spinal column and the fluid of my brain before I went into re-mission." After a pause she added in a neutral, contemplative tone, "The doctor says it's unknown for anyone who had it get into their brain to — survive. He says if I live another year he'll write me up."

"You really are quite a person," I said, impressed by her.

"Medically I am. Otherwise all I can do is type and take dic-tation."

"Do you know why you went into remission?"

"They never know that. It was prayer, I think. I used to tell people that God was healing me; that was when I couldn't see and I couldn't hear and I was having seizures — from the medi-cation — and I was all bloated up and my hair had" — she hesi-tated — "fallen out. I wore a wig, I still have it. In case."

"Please let me buy you something," I said.

"Want to buy me a fountain pen? I can't grip a regular ball-point pen; it's too small. I only have a little strength for gripping in my right hand; that whole side is still weak. But it's getting stronger."

"You can hold a big fountain pen okay?"

"Yes, and I can use an electric typewriter."

"I've never met anybody like you before," I said.

"You're probably lucky. My boyfriend says I'm boring. He always quotes Chuckles the Chipmunk from *A Thousand Clowns* in regard to me: 'Boring, boring, *boring*, boring, boring.'" She laughed.

"Are you sure he really loves you?" It didn't sound as if he did.

"Oh, I'm always running errands and making shopping lists and sewing; I spend half my time sewing. I make most of my own clothes. I made this blouse. It's so much cheaper; I save an awful lot of money."

"You don't have much money?"

"Just the Social Security for disability. It just pays my rent. I don't have very much left over for food."

"Christ," I said, "I'll buy you a ten-course meal."

"I don't eat very much. I don't have much of an appetite." She could see I was looking her up and down. "I weigh ninety-four pounds. My doctor says he wants me up to one-ten, my normal weight. I was always thin, though. I was premature. One of the smallest babies born in Orange County."

"You live in Orange County still?"

"In Santa Ana. Near my church, the Church of the Messiah. I'm a lay reader there. The priest there, Father Adams, is the finest person I have ever met. He was with me all the time I was sick."

It occurred to me that I had found someone with whom I could discuss Valis. But it would take a while to get to know her, especially considering that I was married. I took her to a stationery store, found her the right kind of fountain pen, and then said goodbye to her for the time being.

ACTUALLY I COULD discuss everything with my science fiction author friend, Phil Dick. That evening I told him about the AI teletype printing out "Portuguese States of America." It seemed to him a very important discovery.

"You know what I think?" he said, in agitation, sniffing reflexively at a tin of Dean Swift snuff. "Your help is reaching you from an alternate universe. Another Earth which took a different line of historical development from ours. It sounds like one in which there was no Protestant revolution, no Reformation; the world probably divided between Portugal and Spain, the first major Catholic powers. Their sciences would evolve as servants of religious goals, instead of secular goals as we have in our universe. You have all the constituents for this: help of an obviously religious sort, from a universe, an America, controlled by the first great Catholic sea power. It fits together."

"There probably are other alternate worlds then, too," I said.

"God and science working together," Phil said excitedly; he dove for more tins of snuff. "No wonder it sounds so far away when it talks to you. No wonder you dream about electronic booster equipment and people who are deaf and mute — they're distant relatives of ours who've evolved that way. It might make a good novel." This was the first time he had seen anything in my experience which might be used in a book, or anyhow had admitted to that.

"That would explain a dream I had which didn't make any sense," I said.

I had dreamed of a row of fish tanks, with the water in each stagnant and silted over. We were gazing down at the first one, only to see the life which lived at the bottom of the tank gasping and dying from the pollution. We — the great figures which looked down — turned to the next tank and found less pollution there; at least the little crustaceans and crabs were visible down in the murk. In the dream I suddenly realized that we were looking down at our own world. I was one of the small crabs living at the bottom, shyly concealed behind a boulder. "Look," the great but invisible person beside me said; he took a small shining object, a trinket of some sort, and held it down to the small crab in the tank which was me. The crab emerged cautiously, took the trinket in its claws, inspected it, and then retreated behind the boulder. I assumed the crab had made off with our trinket, but no; presently it was back with something to trade for the trinket. The great person beside me explained that this was an honest life form, that it did not take but made exchanges — barter, not theft. We both found ourselves admiring this humble life form, although at the same time I continued to understand that it was me, seen from his high vantage point, the vantage point of a superior life form.

Now we turned to a third tank which was not polluted at all. Creatures like helium-filled balloons waggled their way up to the surface from the mud, escaping the final end which befell the life forms in the previous tanks. This was a better one.

This one was a better universe, I now realized. Each of the fish tanks, with the life at the bottom, on the surface of the bottom in the mud and silt — each was an alternative universe or alternate Earth. We were in the worst.

"I guess," I said, "we're the only one in which Ferris F. Fremont came to power."

"The worst possibility," Phil agreed. "So those in one of the more advanced universes are assisting us. Breaking through from their world into ours."

"You see no transcendent religious power at work, then?"

"At work, yes, but in their world; theirs is a religious world, a Roman Catholic world with Christian sciences available to them. Obviously they've made a breakthrough in a scientific area we haven't, the ability to move between parallel worlds. We don't even admit the existence of parallel worlds, let alone know how to go from one to another."

"That's why it keeps seeming religious to me," I realized, "as well as technological."

"Sure thing," Phil said.

"It's interesting that the science in a religious world would be more advanced than ours."

"They never fought a Thirty Years War," Phil said. "That war set Europe back five hundred years ... the first great religious war, between Protestants and Catholics. Europe was reduced to barbarism—to cannibalism, in fact. Look what internecine religious warfare has done to us. Look at the deaths, the destruction."

"Yeah," I admitted. Maybe Phil was right. His explanation was purely secular, but it would account for the facts. The low-level AI operator had given me the one firm clue; "Portuguese States of America" could be nothing other than an alternate world. It was not the future helping, or the past, or extragalactic entities from another star—it was a parallel Earth, steeped in religiosity, coming to our aid. To assist what to them must have seemed a murked-over hell world where physical force ruled. Force, and the power of the Lie.

I thought, We finally have the explanation. It accounts for all the facts. We finally got the one good solid clue. The equivalent to the shift in the sun's apparent position during that eclipse, which verified Einstein's Theory of Relativity. Minute but absolutely accurate. The statement of a minor AI network operator, reading from an envelope it found, reading without understanding, merely doing it obligingly. Simply because it had been asked.

I now told Phil about the girl I had met, Sadassa Silvia. He did not react particularly until I came to the Aramchek part.

"Her real name," Phil said thoughtfully.

"That's why it was incised into the sidewalk," I said.

"If you have any more dreams about this girl," Phil said, "tell me. Anything."

"This is important, isn't it?" I said. "Them arranging for me to meet this girl."

"They just told you it was important."

I said, "They brought her into Progressive. They maneuvered both of us."

"You don't know that. All you know is the precog—"

"I knew you'd say that," I said. "'Precog,' shit—it's an arranging of both our lives by supratemporal forces."

"By a bunch of Portuguese scientists," Phil said.

"Bull. They brought us together. They didn't just tell me something; they did something." I couldn't prove it but I was certain of it.

I had not told Phil, or anyone else for that matter, about the shoe ad. All I had told him was that the personality of the telepathic sender had, recently, overpowered me completely for a limited and critical period of time. It did not seem to me a good idea to go into detail; it was a matter between me and my unseen friends. And, evidently, the FAPers. I tended anyhow to think of it as a past issue; Valis had settled it once and for all. Now we could get on to positive issues, such as Miss Silvia, Mrs. Silvia, or Miss Aramchek, whatever it was.

Phil was saying, "I'd like to know more about the sender overpowering you with his personality. What kind of personality was it? Does it fit with the alternate world theory?"

As a matter of fact it certainly did; the sender was highly religious in terms of executing the sacred rites of Christianity. I had, in stealth with Johnny, gone through three or four of the sacraments of the ancient liturgical church. And I had viewed the world, not as I customarily view it but from the eyes of a dedicated Christian. It was a different world entirely. Seeing what he saw, I knew what he knew; I understood the mysteries of the church.

I, who had grown up in Berkeley, singing Spanish Civil War marching songs in its radical streets!

A lot of the recent events remained known only to me; I had not told Phil and did not intend to. Perhaps I had made a mistake in admitting that the telepathic sender had taken possession of me; telling things like that might frighten people. . . . Well, the entire subject was inherently frightening, for that matter, and so I had restricted my audience to people such as Phil and a few professional people. These recent occurrences certainly should not be told, I had decided. They amounted to a description of a godlike power seizing me and turning me into its instrument, a benign power and benign instrument, but nonetheless those were the true dynamics of the situation, for better or worse.

If I accepted Phil's theory that it was a breaching through from an alternate parallel world, some of the eeriness was removed, but the awesome power remained, tremendous power and knowledge, of a sort unknown to our world. Perhaps ancient accounts of theolepsy — possession by a god, such as Dionysos or Apollo — described the identical event. Even so, it was not something to make public. This theory made it less threatening, but it did not defang it entirely. Nothing would. No words strung together could truly account for an experience of this magnitude, for an experience of such vast force. I would have to live with it to some degree unexplained. I doubted if any human theory, at least by the people I could tell, would completely subsume everything I had gone through and was still going through. For example, the precognition, the fact that they knew Sadassa Silvia was going to approach Progressive Records. Well, if they had covertly motivated her to come there, that would explain it; but it explained away one event by revealing another even more awesome one.

I was evidently not the sole human in their power, acting on their advice and authority. But that comforted me rather than frightened me. And it was to be expected. They would want to bring together those who acted as extensions of them. One could assess this as a "safety in numbers" situation. For one thing, it eased my worries about being wiped out. Suppose I were the only human on this planet they had established contact with. Too much would be riding on my shoulders. This way, with the appearance of Sadassa Silvia, I was relieved of that burden; they could work through any number of other people. And there was the black-haired girl with the fish necklace. I had already gone by the pharmacy to ask about her. They did not remember any such girl working for them; the pharmacist merely smiled. "They come and go," he had told me. "Those delivery girls." It was what I had more or less expected. But that made three people I knew of.

The tyranny of Ferris Fremont would be toppled by a number of extensions of the intergalactic communications web. It seemed evident that I would meet and get to know only those who would be working directly with me: those few and no more. If I went to FAP I could tell them only so much.

In fact, I had reflected that morning driving to work, what could I tell FAP anyhow — at least that they would believe? My experiences had taken, perhaps by design, a lunatic form; I would appear a religious nut, babbling about the Holy Spirit or a conversion to Christ or being born again, a mixture of ecstatic but irrational contacts with the Deity.... FAP and any other normal group would dismiss my witnessing upon first hearing. As a matter of fact, Phil had already informed FAP that I talked with God — much to their disappointment and disgust; as the FAP girl had said, We can't do anything with that.

"You going to answer me?" Phil was saying.

I said, "I think I've said enough. I don't really feel like finding all this in one of those dozens of paperback books you write for Ace and Berkley."

Phil flushed with anger at the jibe. "I've got enough already," he said. "And I can fill in the rest out of my own head. So tell me."

With reluctance I told him.

"Sufferin' succotash," Phil said, when I had finished. "A totally different human personality from yours. Taking over, acting and thinking. You know . . ." He rubbed the snuff from his nose, reflexively. "There's that business in the Bible: in Revelation, I think it is. The first fruits of the harvest, the first Christian dead coming back to life. That's where they get the figure of 144,000. They return to help create the new order, as the Bible calls it. Long before the others are resurrected."

We both pondered that.

"How does it say they'll return?" I asked. I had read it but couldn't remember; I had read so much.

"They will join the living," Phil said solemnly.

"Really?"

"Really. In a way not specified. I remember when I read that I wondered where they'd get their bodies from. Do you have a Bible here I can look it up in?"

"Sure." I gave him a copy of the Jerusalem Bible, and he soon had the passage.

"It doesn't say what I thought it said," Phil said. "But the rest is somewhere in the New Testament scattered about in different places. At the end times the first Christian dead will begin to return to life. When you consider how few of them there were in the apostolic age, ten or fifteen, then a hundred, I would think the first appearance of them — assuming this all has some relevance — would be like one here, another there, then maybe a fourth, fifth, and sixth. Scattered around the world. . . . But in what kind of bodies? Their bodies, the original ones, wouldn't be the ones they'd return in; Paul makes that clear. Those were corruptible bodies. *Sarx* was the Greek term he used."

"Well," I said, "the only other bodies around are ours."

"Right," Phil said, nodding. "Let me suggest the following to you. Suppose one of the first fruits returned to life, not outside in his own body, of whatever sort, but like the Holy Spirit does — manifests itself inside you. Tell me, how would this differ from what you've experienced?"

I had nothing to say; I just looked at him as he sat surrounded by his ubiquitous yellow tins and cans of snuff.

"You'd suddenly find an entity talking to you in Koine Greek," Phil said. "Ancient Greek. From inside your head. And it would view the world the way an early —"

"Okay," I said irritably. "I see your point."

"This 'telepathic sender who overpowered you with his personality' is in your own head. Broadcasting from the other side of your skull. From previously unused brain tissue."

"I thought you favored the alternate universe theory," I said, surprised.

"That was fifteen minutes ago," Phil said. "You know how I am with theories. Theories are like planes at LA International: a new one along every minute. Instead of another parallel universe, more likely it's a parallel hemisphere in your head."

"In any case," I said, "it's not me."

"Not unless you somehow learned ancient Greek as a child and have forgotten it consciously. And all the rest, like the information you suddenly had about Johnny's birth defect."

"I'm going to look up Sadassa Silvia," I told him. Rachel was not around to hear, fortunately.

"You mean look her up again."

"Yeah, well, I did buy her a fountain pen."

"Something to write with," Phil said meditatively. "An odd thing to buy a girl the first time. Not flowers or candy or theater tickets."

"I explained why—"

"Yes, you explained why. You buy someone a fountain pen so they can write. That's why. That's called final or teleological cause—the purpose of something. All this that you're involved with ultimately has to be judged in terms of its goal or purpose, not its origin. If a flock of philanthropic baboons decided to oust Ferris F. Fremont we should rejoice. Whereas if angels and archangels decided tyranny was nice we should groan our hearts out. Right?"

"Fortunately," I said, "we don't have that dichotomy to worry about."

"I'm just saying," Phil said, "that we shouldn't become too embroiled as to the identity of your mysterious friends; it's what they intend we should concern ourselves with."

I had to agree. The only thing I had to go on was the statement about the conspirators by the Roman sibyl, which is to say, the embodiment of the intergalactic communications network —I still saw it as that. For now, that had to be enough.

20

THAT NIGHT I RECEIVED, in my sleep, further information about Sadassa Silvia. In the dream, which shone in vivid sparkling lit-up colors, a great leather-bound book was held up to me. I saw its cover clearly. In gold leaf was stamped:

ARAMCHEK

The book was opened by invisible hands and then laid on a table. All at once, who should show up but Ferris F. Fremont, with his sullen face and heavy jowls; scowling, Ferris Fremont took a large red fountain pen and wrote his name in the book, which, I could see, was a lined ledger.

Now came an old lady with white hair tied up in a bun; she wore a white uniform such as nurses wear, and she peered through thick glasses, like Sadassa's. Smiling in a busy, efficient way, the old lady shut the ledger and hurried off with it under her arm. She resembled Sadassa. And, as I witnessed all this, a voice spoke, the familiar quasi-human AI voice I had come to recognize.

"Her mother."

That was all. One printed word, two spoken words—just

three words in all. But, instantly awake, I sat up in bed, then got up and left the bedroom, to fix myself a cup of coffee.

Aramchek was of course her mother's name. Aramchek — Sadassa's mother. Her mother signing up none other than Ferris F. Fremont, but signing him up to what? Aramchek, the ledger had said. Her name, the name of a covert subversive organization. A red fountain pen much like that I had bought Sadassa.

Red, subversive, signed up, Sadassa's old mother.

Jesus Christ! I said to myself as I sat in the living room waiting for the coffee water to boil.

It was not a dream; it was an information printout, clear, economical, and direct. It had pulled no punches; like a political cartoon, it had conveyed its message by graphic and verbal means: word and picture combined.

And in conjunction with the literal printout came a flood of auxiliary information, supplied by the same source. This was why my meeting Sadassa was so important: not Sadassa but her mother, who was now dead; I knew that, understood that. The scene I had witnessed happened years ago, when Ferris Fremont was young. He had been in his late teens; it was during World War II, before America got in. Mrs. Aramchek was an organizer for the Communist Party, and she had recruited the teenage boy Ferris Fremont; they both lived on the same block in Placentia. The Party had been active among the Mexican-Americans who picked crops in Orange County. Signing up the Fremont boy was an accidental spinoff.

It had not been a one-shot deal, a mere interlude in Ferris Fremont's youth. Because of his personality traits — unscrupulousness and deathless ambition to rise to power over other humans, lack of any fixed value system, an underlying nihilism — Ferris had proved to be exactly what Mrs. Aramchek was looking for. She had buried the facts of his Party membership and put him in a special category. Ferris Fremont would be her sleeper, to grow unannounced until the day came, if it could be manipulated into coming, when he held office on the American political scene.

This was grave and frightening, this awareness I now had. Sadassa knew that her mother had been an organizer for the California branch of the CP-USA. She had been a child, then, and automatically recruited — she had seen Ferris Fremont, and later, when he entered politics, after her mother's death, she had recognized him. She had never told anyone, however. She was afraid to.

No wonder she had changed her name.

I wished fervently that my invisible friends had not conferred this knowledge on me; it was too much. And not only this knowledge but acquaintanceship with Mrs. Aramchek's still-living daughter. What the hell was next?

Sadassa Aramchek, as she herself knew — as perhaps *only* she knew — was a living witness to the fact that the President of the United States was a sleeper for the Communist Party. That in fact, as the communications network continued to draw my thinking along the lines of truth, the CP in conjunction with Soviet political assassins, no doubt trained by the KGB, had taken over the United States in the name of anticommunism.

Sadassa Aramchek, who was in remission from lymphatic cancer, knew this; I knew this; the Party in the U.S.S.R. or at least members of it knew this; and Ferris Fremont knew this.

The shoe ad would have wiped me out; one less who knew it. A poisoned arrow from God knew who aimed at my heart a few days before I met Sadassa. Coincidence? Maybe. But no wonder Valis and his AI web operators had emerged to protect me overtly; I had been only hours away from falling victim to FAP on the eve of encountering the girl I was to link up with.

The antagonist had almost aborted us, powerful as my friends were. Only the omniscience of Valis had warded it off. How close, I thought, it had been.

And what was I supposed to do? Why had Valis selected me out of hundreds of millions of people? Why not an editor of a large newspaper, or a TV newsman, or a famous writer, or one of Ferris's political foes?

I remembered an earlier dream, then, starkly, and my heart slowed almost to a halt, thudding with discomfort. The dream of a record album of Sadassa Silvia. Which meant, graphically and obviously:

SADASSA SILVIA SINGS

That had been the title of the album; I remembered now, although at the time it seemed self-evident that the first LP by Sadassa Silvia should be called that. The other meaning of the verb "sing": to spill her story out.

As an executive of Progressive Records I could sign her up. And now I looked back, impressed and awed, at how I had been maneuvered to this valuable point, this position in a successful Burbank recording firm with many top folk artists under contract. Starting back years ago, the prevision of what I took to be Mexico. I would have been worth nothing as a record clerk in Berkeley; what could I have done then? Now I could do something. Sadassa played a guitar; she was good enough, despite what she said, to own and play a Gibson, the most expensive — and professional — acoustic guitar in the business. And she wrote lyrics. The fact that she could not or would not sing was not important; any singer could sing her lyrics. Progressive supplied material to its singers routinely. There were singers who couldn't write and writers who couldn't sing. We matched them up, when necessary; we were the master brokers. We were where it all came together.

And there was less FAP supervision of folk music than there was of the news media: TV, radio, news programs, and magazines. They looked only for songs protesting the Vietnam War. It was simple-minded censorship in the medium of pop music, because the messages were invariably simpleminded.

Sadassa Silvia was a smart, educated girl. I had a deep intuition that her lyrics were not obvious, at least not on the first go-round. Maybe on reflection, as the implications gradually sank in. . . .

Through our distributors we were in a position to market a new folk artist on radio stations, in record stores and drugstores and supermarkets, with ads, even concerts . . . across the entire United States simultaneously. And Progressive had a good reputation for keeping its nose clean. We had never gotten into trouble with FAP, as had some offbeat record firms. The closest FAP had come, to my knowledge, was their pitch to me to report on novice artists, and I had had the clout to throw that off.

Novice artists. Had the two fat-necked middle-aged FAPers who'd approached me been thinking specifically of Sadassa? Was she being watched? Surely Ferris Fremont would have her watched. But perhaps he didn't know she existed.

It showed how risky this all was, the visit by the two FAPers so recently. With Sadassa coming just now. First the two FAPers, then the shoe ad in the mail, now Sadassa. Valis had timed his intervention precisely; it could not have been delayed. Things were in motion, for me and for Phil; consider his visitors too. We were both being watched constantly . . . or at least I had been until I phoned FAP and gave them my pitch — Valis's pitch.

Perhaps I was temporarily free of supervision, Valis having arranged it with this in mind: my meeting with Sadassa.

Her lyrics, I reflected, set to sure-fire ballads, when repeated over and over again on AM rock stations would certainly get across to a large audience. And if her information were put in subliminal form the authorities might not—

Subliminal form. Now, for the first time, I comprehended the purpose of my nasty experience with the gross subliminal messages I had managed to transliminate. That, regrettably, had been necessary; I had to become consciously aware—in a manner I could never forget—of what could be done with subliminal cueing in popular music. People listening while half asleep, absorbing by night what they would soon think and believe the next day!

Okay, I said to Valis in my head. I forgive you for putting me through that ordeal. You made your point, all right. So it's fine. I guess there was no way to inform me of everything at once; it had to unfold in successive stages.

A further insight came to me, sharp and lucid. My friendship with Phil, him and his dozens of popular science fiction thrillers bought in drugstores and Greyhound bus stations, is a false lead. *That* is what the authorities are looking for: something showing up in those pulp novels. Those are winnowed thoroughly by the intelligence community, every single one. We, too, in the recording industry, are winnowed, but more for pro-dope subtracks, pro-dope and sexually suggestive stuff. It is in the field of science fiction that they look for political material.

At least, I thought, I hope so. I don't think we could get away with this as material stuck into a book, even subliminally. I think in pop tunes we have a better chance. And evidently that is what Valis feels too.

Of course, I realized, if we're caught they'll kill us. How will Sadassa feel about that? She's so young . . . and then I remembered the sad fact that she was in temporary remission from cancer; she could only expect to live a little while. It was a deeply sobering thought, but Sadassa did not have that much to lose. And probably she would see it that way. Before they could get her, the lymphoma would.

Perhaps this was the underlying reason why Sadassa had approached a recording firm for a job. An unconscious awareness that at a recording firm her story might be — but I was speculating now. The AI operators had not coached my thinking along these lines. Nor had they led me to wonder if Sadassa had been afflicted with cancer in order to push her to make public what she knew; it was my own individual mind conjecturing about that. I doubted it; more likely that was coincidence. And yet, I had heard it said that God brought good out of evil. The cancer was evil and Sadassa had it; wasn't this something good which Valis had managed to extricate from it?

21

THE NEXT DAY at work I stepped into the personnel office and had a chat with Allen Sheib, who had told Mrs. Silvia that we were overstaffed.

"Hire her," I told him.

"Doing what?"

"I need an assistant."

"I'll have to check with payroll and with Fleming and Tycher."

"Do it," I said. "And if you do, I owe you one. A favor."

"Business is business," Sheib said. "I'll do what I can. As a matter of fact, I think I owe you a favor. Anyhow, I'll try to swing it. What sort of wages?"

"That isn't important," I said. I could, after all, help finance her out of the funds I controlled — our under-the-table funds, so to speak: payoffs we did not report. In our confidential bookkeeping, Sadassa would be listed with a variety of local DJs. No one would be the wiser.

"You want me to interview her, see what she can do, so she thinks the job is legitimate?" Sheib asked.

"Fine," I said.

"You have her number?"

I did. I gave it to Sheib with instructions to say there was now a job opening and to come in to be interviewed. Just to make sure there was no foul-up I telephoned her myself.

"This is Nicholas Brady," I said when she answered. "At Progressive Records."

"Oh, did I leave something behind? I can't find my —"

"I think we have a job for you," I said.

"Oh. Well, I've decided I really don't want a job. I put in an application for a scholarship at Chapman College and since I talked to you they accepted my application, so I can now go back to school."

I was at a loss. "You won't come in?" I said. "And be interviewed?"

"Tell me what kind of job it is. Filing and typing?"

"As my assistant."

"What would I do?"

I said, "Go with me to audition new performers."

"Oh." She sounded interested.

"And possibly we could use your lyrics."

"Oh, really?" She perked up. "Maybe I could do both: go to school and that too."

I had a strange feeling that in her guileless, innocent way she had bumped us up ten notches in the kind of job she could expect from us. This interchange gave me a different impression of her. Perhaps coping with — and surviving — cancer had taught her lessons. A certain kind of grit, a certain tenacity. And she had, probably, only a short time left to fulfill her needs, to extract whatever she was going to extract from life.

"Please come in and talk to us about it," I said.

"Well, I could do that, I guess. I really should ... I had a dream about your record company."

"Tell me." I listened intently.

Sadassa said, "I dreamed I was watching a recording session through the soundproof glass. I was thinking how wonderful the singer was, and I was impressed by all the professional mix-ers and mikes. And then I saw the album jacket and it was me. *Sadassa Silvia Sings,* it was called. Honest." She laughed.

There wasn't much I could say.

"And I got the strong impression," Sadassa continued, "when I woke up, that I'd be working for you. That the dream was a good omen."

"Yeah," I said. "Most likely so."

"When should I come in?"

I told her at four o'clock today. That way, I figured, I could take her to dinner afterward.

"Have you had any other unusual dreams?" I asked, on impulse.

"That wasn't really unusual. What do you mean by unusual?"

"We can talk about it when you get here," I said.

SADASSA SILVIA SHOWED up at four o'clock wearing a light brown jumpsuit, a yellow sweater, hooped earrings to match her Afro-natural hair. She had a solemn expression on her face, as before.

Seated across from me in my office she said, "As I drove up here I asked myself why you might be interested in any unusual dreams I have had. I keep a notebook for my shrink in which every morning I'm supposed to write down my dreams before I forget them. I've been doing that as long as I've been seeing Ed, which is almost two years."

"Tell me," I said.

"Do you want to know? Do you really want to? All right; I've had the feeling for three weeks now — it began on a Thursday — that someone is talking to me in my sleep."

"Man? Or woman?"

Sadassa said, "In between. It's a very calm voice, modulated. I only retain an impression of it when I wake up . . . but it's a fa-

vorable impression. The voice is very lulling. I always feel better after I've heard it."

"You can't remember anything it says."

"Something about my cancer. That it won't come back."

"What time of night —"

"Exactly three thirty," Sadassa said. "I know because my boyfriend says I try to talk back to it; I mean, converse with it. I
wake him up by trying to talk, and he says it's always the same
time of night."

I had forgotten about her boyfriend. Oh, well, I said to myself; I have a wife and family.

"It's as if I'd left the radio on very low," Sadassa continued. "To a faraway station. Like you get on shortwave late at
night."

"Amazing," I said.

Sadassa said calmly, "I came to Progressive Records in the
first place because of a dream, very much like the one I had last
night. I was in a lovely green valley with very high grass, out in
the country, fresh and nice, and there was a mountain. I floated
along, not on the ground but weightlessly floating, and as I came
toward the mountain it turned into a building. On the building
they had put words, on a plaque over the entrance. Well, one
word: PROGRESSIVE. But in the dream I could tell it was Progressive Records because I could hear the most incredibly dul-
cet music. Not like any music I have ever heard in actuality."

"You did the right thing," I said, "to act on that dream."

"Did I come to the right place?" She studied my face intently.

"Yes," I said. "You interpreted the dream right."

"You seem sure."

"What do I know?" I said jokingly. "I'm just glad you're here.
I was afraid you wouldn't show up."

"I go to school — I will be going — during the day. Can we audition performers at night? I would expect so. We have to fit the job in around my school schedule."

"You don't want much," I said, a little nettled.

"I've got to go to school again; I lost so much time while I was sick."

"Okay," I said, feeling guilty now.

"Sometimes," Sadassa said, "I get the feeling that the government gave me cancer. Gave me a carcinogen to deliberately make me sick. It's only by a miracle that I survived."

"Good God," I said, jolted; I hadn't thought of that. Maybe it was so, everything considered. With her background. With what she knew, what she was. "Why would they want to do that?"

"I don't know; why *would* they? I'm paranoid, I realize that. But strange things happen these days. Two of my friends have disappeared. I think they're sticking 'em in those camps."

My phone rang. I picked it up and found myself talking to Rachel. Her voice shook with excitement. "Nick—"

"I'm with a client," I said.

"Have you seen today's *LA Times*?"

"No," I said.

"Go get it. You have to read it. Page three, the right-hand column."

"Tell me what it says," I said.

"You've got to read it. It explains the experiences you've been having. Please, Nick; go look at it. It really does!"

"Okay," I said. "Thanks." I hung up. "Excuse me," I said to Sadassa. "I have to go out front to the newspaper thing." I left my office, went down the hall to the big outside glass doors.

A moment later I had a copy of the *Times* and was carrying it back, reading it as I walked.

On page three in the right-hand column I found this article:

SOVIET ASTROPHYSICIST REPORTS RADIO
SIGNALS FROM INTELLIGENT LIFE

Not from outer space as expected but emanating close to
Earth.

Standing there in the hall, I read the article. The foremost
Soviet astrophysicist, Georgi Moyashka, using a collection of in-
terlinked radio telescopes, had picked up what he believed to be
deliberate signals from a sentient life form, these signals con-
taining the characteristics that Moyashka had anticipated finding. The big surprise, however, was their point of origin: within
our solar system, which no one, including Moyashka himself,
had anticipated. The U.S. space people had already gone on record as saying that the signals undoubtedly emanated from old
satellites put into space and then forgotten, but Moyashka was
certain that the signals were of alien origin. So far he and his
team had been unable to decode them.

The signals came in short bursts from a moving source that
seemed to be circling Earth, perhaps six thousand miles away;
they came on an unexpected ultrahigh frequency, rather than as
shortwave emissions with greater carrying distance. The transmitter appeared to be powerful. One odd point that Moyashka had noted which he could not account for was the fact that
the radio signals came only when the source was above Earth's
dark or night side; during the day the signals ceased. Moyashka
conjectured that the so-called Heaviside layer might be involved.

The signals, although short in duration, seemed "highly information rich" because of their sophistication and complexity.
Curiously, the frequency changed periodically, a phenomenon
found in transmissions seeking to avoid jamming, Moyashka
stated. Further, his team had discovered, entirely by accident,

that animals in their Pulkovo laboratory underwent slight but regular physical changes during the time of signal transmission. Their blood volume altered and their blood pressure readings increased. Provisionally, Moyashka conjectured that radiation accompanying the radio signals might account for it. The Soviets (the article finished) planned to launch a satellite of their own to intercept the orbit of this Earth-rotating transmitter to confirm their theory that it was a satellite not of terrestrial origin. They hoped to photograph it.

From the pay phone in the hall I called Rachel back. "I read it," I said. "But Phil and I already have a theory."

Bitingly, Rachel said, "This isn't a theory; this is a fact. I heard it on the noon news, too. It's real, even if we deny it, the U.S. denies it. I looked up Dr. Moyashka in your *Britannica;* there's an article on him. He discovered volcanic activity on the moon and some kind of thing on Mercury; I didn't understand it, but every time, people said he was wrong or crazy. Stalin had him in a forced labor camp for years. He's highly esteemed; he's a big wheel in the Russian space program, and the radio today says he heads their CETI Project—'Contacting Extra-Terrestrial Intelligence.' They're using telepathy and everything; they're really wild."

"Did the radio say how long they think the satellite's been transmitting?"

"The Russians just picked it up recently. They don't know anything about before that. But listen—short intense high-frequency bursts, always at night. Don't you receive your pictures and words around three a.m.? It fits, Nick! It does! You and Phil were thinking anyhow maybe it's a satellite orbiting Earth! I remember both of you talking about that!"

"Our new theory—" I began.

"The hell with your new theory," Rachel said. "This is the

biggest news in the history of the world! I'd think you'd be out of your mind with excitement!"

"I am," I said. "Catch you later." I hung up and returned to my office, where Sadassa Silvia sat, smoking a cigarette and reading a magazine.

"Sorry to keep you waiting," I said to her.

"The phone rang while you were out of the office," Sadassa said. "I didn't think I should answer it."

"It'll ring again," I said.

The phone rang. I picked it up and said hello. It was Phil; he had heard the news on the radio. Like Rachel, he was highly excited.

"I read about it in the *Times*," I informed him.

"Did the *Times* article mention that it broadcasts on the same frequencies our FM and TV sound travels on?" Phil said. "The scientist I heard commenting, from some U.S. space laboratory, says that virtually rules out the possibility that it's one of our own satellites, since ours don't broadcast on commercial frequencies. Listen, Nick; he said its signals would interfere with FM and TV reception so we might have to destroy it. But what I was thinking—remember when you heard that weird shit on your radio at night, as if it were talking to you? And we conjectured about a satellite override? Nick, this may be it! This thing when it transmits might very well override. And the scientist said, the one I heard commenting, that it doesn't broadcast in the strict sense of the word, that it's narrow tight beams, directed; 'broadcast' means in all directions, everywhere equally. This satellite's signals don't propagate in all—"

"Phil," I broke in, "I've got somebody with me right now. Can I get back to you tonight?"

"Sure," Phil said, mollified. "But you know, Nick, this could explain it; it really could. You're transducing these unusual alien signals."

"Catch you later, Phil," I said, and hung up. I did not want to discuss it in front of Sadassa Silvia. Or anyone else, for that matter. Although, I thought, I may be discussing it with Ms. Silvia one of these days, when the time is right; when I've sounded her out sufficiently beforehand.

Sadassa said, "Was it the article in the Times about 'prisons are a source of wealth'? That pitch for slave labor under the guise of psychological rehabilitation? 'Convicts need not be indoors, wasting years of their lives in idleness, rather, they could —' Let's see, how did they put it? 'Convicts could work out under the warm sun in labor groups rebuilding slums, contributing to urban renewal, and hippies could make their contribution to society, side by side with them and also the youth who can't get jobs. . . .' I felt like writing in to say, 'And when they die of overwork and starvation they can contribute their bodies in giant ovens, and we can melt them down into useful bars of soap.'"

"No," I said, "it wasn't that article."

"The alien satellite, then?"

Presently I nodded.

Sadassa said, "It's a fake. Or rather, it's one of ours and we won't admit it. It's a propaganda satellite we use to beam down subliminal material to the Soviet people. That's why it broadcasts on commercial FM and TV frequencies and alters its transmission frequency at random intervals. The Soviet people get eighth-of-a-second stills of happy Americans eating all the food they want, shit like that. The Russians know it and we know it. They beam down to us from unauthorized satellites and we do the same to them. They're going to shoot it down; that's what they're up to. I don't blame them."

It sounded convincing, except that it scarcely explained why the Soviet Union's foremost astrophysicist would make the announcement he had made — Moyashka had put his vast reputation on the line again, claiming the satellite to be extraterrestrial in origin. It seemed doubtful that a man of his probity would become embroiled in a strictly political matter.

"Do you really think a famous scientist like Georgi Moyashka would—" I began, but Sadassa, in her gentle but strict little voice, interrupted imperturbably.

"He does what they tell him. All Soviet scientists do and say what they're told. Ever since Topchiev purged the Soviet Academy of Sciences back in the fifties. He was the Party hatchetman in the Academy, then, its official secretary; he personally sent to prison hundreds of the U.S.S.R.'s top scientists. That's why their space program is so clunky, so far behind ours. They haven't even managed to miniaturize their components. They have no microcircuitry at all."

"Well," I said, nonplussed. "But in some areas—"

"Big booster rockets," Sadassa agreed. "They're still using tubes! The average stereo built in Japan is more advanced than the components used in a Soviet missile."

"Let's get down to the business of your job," I said.

"All right." She nodded sensibly.

"We can't pay you very much," I said. "But the work should be interesting."

"I don't need much," Sadassa said. "How much is much?"

I wrote down a figure and turned it to show her.

"That certainly isn't much," she said. "For how many hours a week?"

"Thirty hours," I said.

"I guess I could work that into my schedule."

Exasperated, I said, "I don't think you're being realistic. For that few hours it's good pay, and you're unskilled. This isn't typing and filing; this is creative work. I'd have to train you. I think it's a good deal. You should be glad to get it."

"What about publishing my lyrics? And using them?"

"We'll use them. If they're good enough."

"I brought some along." She opened her purse and brought out an envelope. "Here."

Opening the envelope I removed four pieces of paper on which she had written verses in blue fountain-pen ink. Her handwriting was legible but shaky, the aftereffects of her illness.

I read over the poems — they were poems, not lyrics — but my mind was on what she had just said. The Soviet Union was going to do what? Shoot the satellite down? What, then, would become of me? Where would my help come from?

"I'm sorry," I said, "I'm having trouble concentrating. They're very good." I said it reflexively, without conviction; maybe they were good, maybe not. All I could think of was the dreary, heartbreaking thing she had told me, her conjecture about Soviet intentions. It seemed obvious, now that she had uttered it. Of course they weren't merely going to photograph the alien satellite; of course they were going to shoot it down. They weren't going to allow an extraterrestrial vehicle, an intruder into our buttoned-down world, to beam split-second subliminal communications to our people, overriding our own managed TV and FM transmissions. Adding God-knew-what information we weren't supposed to know.

Radio Free Alpha Centauri, I said to myself bitterly. Radio Free Albemuth, as I had come to call it. How long are you going to last now that you've been found out? They can't get you with a missile; they will launch a satellite with an H-warhead and simply detonate you in the general blast. No more tight-beamed messages. And, I thought, no more dreams for me.

"Can I take these poems home?" I asked Sadassa. "And read them more leisurely?"

"Of course," she said. "Hey," she said suddenly, "what upset you? The poem about my lymphoma? Was that it? Most people are upset by that . . . I wrote it when I was so sick; you can tell by the content. I didn't expect to live."

"Yeah," I said. "That's what did it."

"I shouldn't have shown that to you."

"It's a very powerful poem," I said. "I'm not sure, frankly, how a poem about someone having cancer could be adapted to use as lyrics for a song. It certainly would be a first." We both tried to smile; neither of us made it.

"The others aren't so heavy," Sadassa said; she reached out and patted me on the hand. "Maybe you could use one of them."

"I'm sure we can," I said. What a charming, unhappy girl, I thought, struggling against such odds.

22

I CHANGED MY MIND and did not ask Sadassa Silvia out for dinner; instead I took off early and drove directly back down to Orange County and home. My mind remained on the new item, on what Sadassa had said — the whole situation frightened and appalled me.

Put very simply, I had come to regard Valis and the AI operators along the communications network as divine, which meant they were not subject to mortal death. One does not blow up God. Here, however, were my wife and my best friend nattering at me that the source of my divine help had been pinpointed: satellite orbiting Earth, beaming down information, and caught in the act now by the U.S.S.R.'s leading astrophysicist, their great scientific sleuth — Earth's cosmic cop, armed with radio telescopes, countersatellites with warheads, and God knew what else.

As thrilling as the thought was — that an extraterrestrial intelligence from another star system had put one of their vehicles into orbit around our planet and was beaming down covert information to us — it reduced something limitless to a finite reality, vulnerable to ordinary hazards. The entity I had assumed to be omniscient and omnipotent was about to be shot out of the sky. And with it, I realized, went the possibility of deposing

Ferris Fremont. When the Soviets, no doubt operating in conjunction with our more sophisticated tracking stations, brought down the ETI satellite, the hopes of free men in both nations died.

Unless, of course, there was no connection between the newly discovered satellite and my experiences. But, as both Rachel and Phil had already noticed, it was too much of a coincidence; it was too close.

God, I thought, I've been doing what it told me for years. Moving down to Southern California, going to work for Progressive Records — what am I going to do when they shoot it down? What'll my life be built around? But then I thought, Maybe Valis will install another satellite in its place. He could do that; with his foresight he would know the Soviet intentions long in advance — from the start, in fact. You cannot take him by surprise.

Or maybe you can.

It is possible, I said to myself as I tailgated a big truck in the right-hand lane, that the satellite has done its job. Already transmitted everything in its banks. But I'm used to hearing its voice, that lovely AI voice, informing me, comforting me, helping me . . . look what it did for Johnny; look what it had done for me. To be deprived of that . . .

What else have I got to live for? I asked myself. What else did I ever have to live for? My relationship with Rachel isn't all that much; I love my son, but I see him so rarely; my work is important but not that important. Something such as I have had, to hear that AI voice — it is worse to lose it than it was good ever to have had it. It hurts so much.

Pain of loss, I thought; the greatest pain in the world. My friend will one day soon cease talking with me. That day lies imminently ahead, as surely as the fact that right now the U.S.S.R. is preparing to launch an intercept satellite. The worldwide tyranny has spotted its enemy and now moves. The big blind engine is being cranked up.

When they blow that satellite out of the sky, I realized, they might as well blow me out of the sky as well. Being rescued from that shoe ad letter accomplishes nothing, now. All the help, all the knowledge and insight, all the coaching and guiding — down the rathole, for nothing: gone. And not just for me; for everybody who wanted a just society, who wanted to be free. For those who heard the AI voice and those who did not: our fate is the same. The one friend we had will one of these days be wiped away as if it never existed.

I felt the decay of the universe as I drove along the freeway: coldness and illness and final oblivion.

I suppose, I said to myself, I could rationalize it and say that because of Valis's help I have met a nice new girl, attractive and smart ... with a life expectancy measured in inches. We have been brought together just in time to go up in smoke. Plans, hopes, dreams — all reduced to smoke. Particles of a satellite which came here to be destroyed, the same as us: born to be blown up. The hell with it all, I thought wretchedly. Better not to have started this or tried. Better not to have even known help existed, to have imagined something happier for us in our lives.

When you attack a tyranny you must expect it to fight back. Why not? Why shouldn't it? How could I, with some idea of its nature, expect anything else? An H-warhead for the ETI satellite; cancer for Sadassa Silvia; if the shoe ad trap had worked, prison for me — prison or death.

Meditating about this I did not comprehend — or maybe I comprehended well enough and didn't care — that the truck ahead of me had slowed. Its brake lights came on; I didn't notice. I kept on going in my little VW bug, right on into the tail assembly, the huge iron rear bumper, of the truck.

I heard nothing and felt nothing, no concussion or shock. All

I saw was my windshield turn into a billion broken Coke bottle bottoms, a strange pattern like a giant spiderweb engulfing me. Fallen into the spiderweb, I remember thinking. To be eaten later. The spiderweb, but where is the spider? I thought. Gone away.

Liquid had spilled over my neck and chest. It was my own blood.

23

THE DIN AROUND me was terrible. Wheeled down a ramp, strapped flat; I tried to turn my head hut could not. Voices, movement; a face peered down at me, a woman's face, and I heard a woman's voice. She was flashing a light in my eyes and telling me to do something. I could not do it. Sorry, I thought.

"Are you in a health plan?" another voice asked insistently. "Do you have Blue Cross? Can you sign this form, if I hold it for you? Here's a pencil. You may sign it with your left hand if you wish."

The hell with you, I thought.

I could see two California Highway Patrolmen in their brown uniforms, standing off to one side with a clipboard, looking bored.

Wheelchairs, gurneys. Little young nurses in short skirts, and a crucifix on the wall.

Beside me a Highway Patrol officer bent down and said, "Don't let your insurance company fix up your car. It's leaking oil from the motor. The block is cracked."

"Okay," I managed to whisper. I felt nothing, thought nothing.

"I'm going to have to cite you, Mr. Brady," the Highway Patrol officer said. "For following too close and driving at an unsafe speed. I have your license; we're checking for warrants. You're going right into surgery, so I'll return your license to the personal property office of the hospital. It'll be with your other things, your wallet and keys and money."

"Thank you," I said.

The officer departed. I lay there alone, thinking to myself, What the hell, what the hell. They should call somebody, I thought. Rachel. They ought to notify her; I should tell them. Remind them. What do they care? I thought, I wonder what hospital this is. I was driving—where? Just into Orange County. I never made it back to Placentia, back home. Well, so much for that. I'll take his advice, I decided. Not let them fix the car. They can total it and auction it. What do I care what I get for it? What do I care about anything?

Two nurses took hold of my gurney and began to wheel it cheerfully. Bump, bump, roll. Stop for the elevator; they stood together, with smiles. I stared fixedly straight up. There was an IV bottle mounted above me. Five percent glucose, I read from the label. To keep a vein open, I decided.

Incredibly bright white lights beamed down on me. This was the operating room. They put a mask over the lower part of my face; I heard male voices, conferring. A needle stuck into my arm. It hurt. It was the first thing I had felt.

The bright white lights suddenly turned black, like dead coals.

I floated across a desert landscape which showed red and brown far below me. Far off, the outline of mesas. A great void in which I moved, suspended and effortless.

Someone approached me. Far off, beyond the dry mesas. Invisible presence, shining with love. It was Valis. I recognized his being; he was familiar: the concern, the understanding, the desire to help.

We exchanged no words. I heard no voice, no sound at all except a continual gentle roaring, like wind. The sounds of the wasteland, the desert, the great open places of the world. Wind and water rushing ... but they did not seem impersonal; they seemed alive, as if part of Valis. Expressions of him, as kind and warm and loving as he was; he animated the mesas.

Valis asked me, silently, if I thought he had forgotten me.

I said, What if they shoot down the satellite?

No matter. It is a pinpoint in the sky. Behind it lies only light. A sheet of light, not sky.

Did I cash in? I asked.

No response.

I'm coming here eventually, I said. I know that. I recognize this place; I have been here before.

You were born here. You have come back.

This is my homeland, I said.

I am your father, Valis said.

Where are you?

Above the stars, Valis said.

I came from above the stars?

Yes. Many times.

Then, I said, that was me? Who took over when the ad came in the mail?

That was yourself, remembering who you are.

Who am I? I said.

Everyone.

Amazed, I said, *Everyone?*

No response, only the pulsations of love.

What am I going to do? I asked.

You asked to be broken down, Valis answered. And healed. This is that breaking down and healing. You will be changed.

And go on? I asked.

The warmth of his love consumed me like an invisible cloud of light. He responded, And go on. Nothing is ever lost.

I can't be lost? I asked.

There is nowhere for anything to go. There is only here and us. For all time.

I realized then, that Valis and I had never been separated, that he had only fallen silent from time to time. I felt tired, now; I had drifted low over the mesas and I wanted to rest. There was a lessening sense of Valis's presence, as if he were withdrawing. Yet he still remained, like a lamp turned down, down but not off. Like a child, I had assumed that something no longer seen no longer existed. To an infant, when his parents leave the room they cease to be. But as he grows older he understands differently. They are there whether or not he can see them or touch them or hear their voices. It is an early lesson. But sometimes perhaps not completely learned.

So now I knew who Valis was; he was my father, my real father, from whose race I came repeatedly into this world, to leave again, to return again, to work toward some distant goal unseen, not as yet comprehended. The search, perhaps, was the goal. As I achieved a little motion toward it, I understood it. Overthrowing the tyranny of Ferris Fremont was a stop along the way, not a goal but a moment of decision, from which I then continued as before. Changed to some extent, but changed by my father, not by what I had done. For, I understood, Valis himself did it, through me. The virtue lay with him.

We are gloves, I realized, which our father puts on in order to achieve his objectives. What a pleasure to be that, to be of use. Part of a greater organism: its extensions into space and time, into the world of change. To influence that change — the greatest joy of all.

I can instruct you, Valis's thoughts came, without the satel-

lite. It is a thing to show them, a shiny toy. To make them understand. When it fired it did its task; it served to open your mind
and other minds. Those minds, opened once, will never close.
The contact is established and the circuit is in place. It will remain that way.

I am linked up then, I realized. For all time.

You have remembered. You know. There is now no forgetting. Be of good cheer.

Thank you, I said.

The reddish mesas, the level plain below me, faded; the sky
closed and the sound of rushing wind slowly diminished.

Valis was out of my sight now, his face turned away from me,
retractile in his cycle. I experienced this time no loss, as I always had before.

Son of Earth and starry heaven. The old rite, the disclosure
to the ancient initiate. I had undergone the Orphic ceremonies,
down in the dark caves, to emerge suddenly into the chamber
of light, to see the gold tablet that reminded me of my own nature and my past: trip across space from Albemuth, the far star,
migration to this world, to blend here in escape from our molelike enemy. That enemy had soon followed, and the garden we
built had been polluted and made toxic with his presence, with
his wastes. We sank into the silt; we became half blind; we forgot until reminded. Reminded by the rotating voice from the
nearby sky, placed there long ago in case a calamity occurred,
a break in the chain of continuity. Such a break did come. And,
presently, the voice automatically fired. And informed us, as
best as it could, of what we no longer knew.

If the Russians did photograph the ETI satellite, the invader,
they would find it old and pitted. I had been there thousands of
years. What a surprise that would be; they, too, might remember ... until the molelike adversary closed up their minds and

they forgot again. Were *made* to forget again, as the deformed landscape, clouded over by the poisoned atmosphere, occluded their senses and thoughts and they fell again, as before.

Recurrent cycles, I realized, of coming awake for a time, then falling back into sleep. I had, like the others, been asleep, but then I had woken up; or, rather, I had been awakened out of my sleep deliberately. The voice of a friend had called to me, as it moved among the rows of new corn, new life, and I had heard and recognized it. That voice was always calling, always attempting to wake us up, we who slept. Perhaps eventually we all would awaken. To communicate once again with our parent race beyond the stars . . . as if we had never left.

Albemuth. Our first home. We were wanderers, exiles, all of us, whether we knew it or not. Perhaps most of us wanted to forget. Memory — to be aware of our true condition, our identity — was too painful. We would make this place our home and we would recall nothing else. It was easier that way.

The simplicity of unawareness. The easier way. Deadly in its outcome: without memory we had fallen victim to our adversary. We had forgotten him, too, and been overtaken and surprised. That was the price we paid.

We paid it now.

24

WHEN I RETURNED to consciousness I found myself in the recovery room, with a nurse taking my pulse. My chest hurt; I had difficulty breathing. An oxygen mask covered my nose. And I was terribly hungry.

"My," the nurse said brightly. "We really ran our little car into a lot of trouble."

"What happened to me?" I managed to say.

"Dr. Wintaub will discuss your surgery with you," the nurse said. "After you're taken to your room."

"Did you notify . . . ?"

"Your wife is on the way here."

"What city is this?" I said.

"Downey."

"I'm a long way from home," I said.

HALF AN HOUR after I had been taken upstairs to a two-patient room, Dr. Wintaub entered to examine me.

"How do you feel?" he asked, taking my pulse.

"A bad headache," I said. I could not remember having had such a headache; it was equaled only by the pain I had experienced the night Valis had informed me of Johnny's birth defect. And my sight seemed impaired again, as well.

"You've been through a lot." Dr. Wintaub pulled the covers back, inspected my bandages. "Your lung was punctured by a broken rib," he said. "That was why we entered the chest cavity. You're going to be here, I'm afraid, for some time. The steering wheel of your car caught you head on and did most of the damage —" His voice abruptly come to a halt.

"What is it?" I said, afraid at what he had found.

"I'll be back in a minute, Mr. Brady." Dr. Wintaub departed from the room; I was left to wonder about it. Presently he returned with two male technicians. "I want his bandages removed," Wintaub said. "And the splints. I want to examine the wound."

They began removing the bandages, with extreme gentleness. Dr. Wintaub watched critically. I felt nothing, no discomfort, no pain. The headache remained; it was like a migraine headache, with a flashing grid of extraordinarily intense pink light in my right eye, a field of blurred color slowly moving from left to right.

"There, doctor." The technicians stepped back.

Dr. Wintaub came close; I felt his deft fingers touch my chest. "I performed this surgery," he murmured. "About two hours ago." He studied his wristwatch. "Two hours and ten minutes ago."

"Could you look at my eyes?" I said. "That's where the pain is."

Impatiently, Dr. Wintaub flashed a light in my eyes. "Follow the light," he murmured. "You're tracking okay." He returned to my chest. To the two technicians he said, "Take him down to X-ray and do a full chest series."

"All right to move him, doctor?" one of the technicians asked.

"Just be extremely careful," Wintaub said.

I was wheeled down to X-ray and chest plates were made,

several of them, and then I was returned to my room. While waiting at X-ray I managed to sit up enough to see my own chest.

A firm pink line crossed it. The incision had healed.

No wonder Dr. Wintaub wanted immediate X-rays; he had to know if the internal damage had mended as well.

Shortly, two unfamiliar doctors entered and began to examine me; with them they brought nurses and equipment. I lay silently, staring at the ceiling. My headache had begun to abate, for which I was thankful, and my vision was clearing, except for a residual pink phosphene color. From what I had seen of my chest, plus my knowledge of the meaning of the pink phosphene light, I understood the situation. Valis had handled my case, as he had handled Johnny's, in the most economical fashion possible: normal surgical procedure and then, under the influence of the satellite and its emissions, unnaturally rapid repair. Probably I was ready to leave the hospital.

The problem, however, lay with the doctors. They had never encountered such a thing.

"How soon do you think I'll be out of here?" I asked Dr. Wintaub when he appeared after dinnertime; I was sitting up eating a regular meal. I felt fine, now. The doctor could see this. It did not appear to please him.

"This is a teaching hospital," he said.

"You want the student doctors to see me," I said.

"That is correct."

"The chest cavity has repaired itself?"

"Completely so, as nearly as we can tell. But we'll need to keep you under observation; it may be superficial repair."

"Has my wife been called?" I asked.

"Yes, she's on her way. I told her the operation was successful. Mr. Brady, have you ever had surgery before?"

"Yes," I said.

"Did they note a highly accelerated rate of repair? Of tissue recovery?"

I said nothing.

Dr. Wintaub said, "Can you account for this, Mr. Brady?"

"Hormone production," I said.

"Not possible."

"I'd like to be discharged," I said. "So I can go home tonight with my wife."

"That is out of the question, Mr. Brady. After an operation of this severity —"

"I'll sign out AMA," I said. "Against medical advice. Bring me the forms."

"No way, Mr. Brady. I won't cooperate with you. We are going to study you until we know what has taken place in your body following surgery. When you came in here, one lung was almost —"

"Bring me my clothes," I said.

"No." Dr. Wintaub left the room; the door shut after him.

I GOT OUT OF bed and searched the closet and drawers. No clothes, except for a hospital gown. I put that on. If I had to I would leave that way. Neither Dr. Wintaub nor the hospital could hold me in view of my complete recovery.

There was no doubt of my recovery. I could feel it physically, and in my mind I was aware of it, as aware as I had been that night I comprehended Johnny's birth defect. The only problem I had was getting home. And that was a minor one.

I left the hospital room and walked down the hall, looking into rooms with open doors, until I saw a room with no one in it. The patients were out getting exercise after finishing dinner. Entering the room I opened the clothes closet. All I could find were a pair of fuzzy carpet slippers, a woman's bright print dress with plunging backline, and a turban made of pastel fabric. It would be better if I resembled a woman, I realized; they would be looking for a man. Fortunately, the woman whose clothes these were had an enormous build; I was able to get into all of them, and, after picking up a pair of dark glasses from a drawer, I set out into the hall again.

No one stopped me or interfered with me as I made my way down the corridor to a stairwell. Moments later I had reached the ground floor and had come out onto the parking lot. All that remained was to sit on a bench watching the incoming cars until I saw Rachel's Maverick.

I found a bench off to one side, seated myself, and waited.

An unspecified interval later — my watch was gone, either destroyed or in the patients' property safe — the green Maverick pulled hastily into a slot and Rachel and Johnny emerged, both distraught and disheveled.

As Rachel hurried up the walk past my bench I stood up and said, "Let's take off."

Halting, she stared at me in amazement.

"I wouldn't have recognized you," she said finally.

"They didn't want me to leave." I walked toward the car, motioning her to accompany me.

"Can you leave? I mean, are you well enough? The doctor said you'd undergone major surgery on your chest —"

"I'm fine," I said. "The satellite healed me."

"Then the satellite is what you've been experiencing."

"Yep," I said, getting into the car.

"You do seem physically okay . . . but you certainly look funny in those clothes."

"You can pick up my personal effects tomorrow," I said, slamming the car door after me. "Hi, Johnny," I said to my son. "Recognize Daddy?"

My son stared at me sourly and with suspicion.

"The satellite could have provided you with better clothes," Rachel said.

"I don't think it does that," I said. "You have to find your own. That's what I did."

"Maybe you should have waited until it thought of something," Rachel said. She shot me a glance as she drove from the hospital parking lot. "I'm glad you're all right."

As we found our way out onto the freeway, I thought to myself, I certainly got a printout while I was under the anesthetic. Did Valis engineer my accident so he could speak to me? No, Valis engineered my recovery so he could work through me. He took advantage of a bad situation and brought something out of it: the best colloquy we have had and probably will ever have. What I know now, I realized, is boundless. The major pieces are in place. The delight of finding each other, Valis and I. Father and son, together again. After millennia. The relationship restored.

But I understood something else which was not good. We really did not have a chance of toppling Fremont. Not really. Because of my position at Progressive Records we could do something; we could distribute what we knew in subliminal form on an LP, buried in subtracks and backup vocals, scrambled about in the sound-on-sound that our mixers provided us. Before the police got us we could pass on what we knew, Sadassa and I, to hundreds, thousands, or even millions of Americans. But Ferris Fremont would stay in power. The police would destroy us, would forge counterdocumentation and proof; we would go and the regime would survive.

Still, it was worth doing. I knew that absolutely; Valis had set this in motion and Valis could not err. He would not have brought Sadassa and me together, flooded me with help and information, if it wasn't worth it. To make it worth it, we did not have to win completely. We needed only a certain victory, one within reason. We could, perhaps, initiate a process that others more numerous and powerful would complete someday in the future.

Valis's will was not fully realized on Earth. This was the adversary's realm, the Prince of this world. Valis could only work within this world, work with a small remnant of men; he was the minority party, here, speaking as a still small voice to one man or a handful, from a hush, in sleep, during an operation. Eventually he would win. But not now. These were not the end times after all. The end times were always coming but never here, always nearby and influencing us but never realized.

Well, I decided, we would do the best we could. And know by faith that it was worth it.

As we drove along, I said to Rachel, "I have met this girl. I've got to work with her. You may not approve—no one may approve—but it has to be done. It may destroy us all."

Rachel, driving carefully, said, "Valis told you?"

"Yes," I said.

"Do what you have to do," Rachel said, in a low, tight voice.

"I will," I said.

25

I HAD NOT TALKED to Sadassa Silvia yet about her mother. As far as she knew I had no information about her past. That was the first step to be taken, to discuss Mrs. Aramchek. To get her to tell me openly what Valis and the intercommunications network had already transferred from their information banks to my mind. We could not work together otherwise.

The best place to talk to her, I decided, would be at a good quiet restaurant; that way we could avoid the possibility of being picked up by a government bug. I therefore phoned her from work and invited her out to dinner.

"I've never been to Del Rey's," she said. "But I've heard of it. They have a cuisine like the San Francisco restaurants. I'm free Thursday night."

On Thursday night I swung by her apartment, picked her up, and soon we were seated in a secluded booth in the main dining room at Del Rey's.

"What is it you want to tell me?" she said, as we ate our salads.

"I know about your mother," I said. "And Ferris Fremont."

"What do you mean?"

In a voice low enough for our safety, I said, "I know that your mother was an organizer for the Communist Party."

Sadassa's eyes flew open behind her thick glasses. She stared at me; she had stopped eating.

"I know further," I said quietly, "that she signed up Ferris Fremont when he was in his late teens. I know that she trained him as a sleeper, to go into politics with no sign of his real views or his real affiliations."

Still staring at me, Sadassa said, "You are really crazy."

"Your mother is dead," I said, "and so the Party — Ferris Fremont — thinks the secret is safe. But as a child you saw Fremont with your mother and you overheard enough. You're the only person outside the higher ranks of the Party who knows. That's why the government tried to kill you off with cancer. They found out you're alive despite your name change and that you know. Or they suspect you know. So you have to be killed."

Sadassa, frozen in one spot, fork half raised, continued to gaze at me in stricken silence.

"We are intended to work together," I said. "This information will go onto a record, a folk LP, in the form of subliminal bits of data distributed so that in repeated playings a person will unconsciously absorb the message. The record industry has techniques to accomplish that; it's done all the time, although the message has to be simple. 'Ferris Fremont is a Red.' Nothing elaborate. One word in one track, another in the next — maybe eight words maximum. Juxtaposed in the playback. Like code. I will see that the record saturates this country; we'll flood the market with it — a huge initial pressing. There will be only one pressing and one distribution, because as soon as people begin to transliminate the message the authorities will step in and destroy all —"

Sadassa found her voice. "My mother is alive. She's active in church work; she lives in Santa Ana. There's no truth in what you say. I never heard such garbage." Standing, she set down her fork, dabbed at her mouth; she seemed on the verge of tears.

"I'm going home. You're completely spaced; I heard about your accident on the freeway; it was in the *Register*. You must have gotten your marbles scrambled; you're crazy. Good night." She walked rapidly away from the booth, without glancing back.

I sat alone in silence.

All at once she was back, standing by me, bending over and speaking in a low, grim voice into my ear. "My mother is a down-to-earth Republican and has been all her life. She has never had anything to do with left-wing politics, certainly not the Communist Party. She never met Ferris Fremont, although she was present at a rally at Anaheim Stadium where he spoke — that's the closest she ever got to him. She is just an ordinary person, saddled with the name 'Aramchek,' which means nothing. The police have investigated her repeatedly because of it. Do you want to meet her?" Sadassa's voice had risen wildly. "I'll introduce you to her; you can ask her. It's saying crazy things like this that gets people into — oh, never mind." Again she strode off; this time she did not return.

I don't understand, I said to myself. Is she lying?

Shaken, I managed to finish my meal, hoping she would show up again, reseat herself, and take back what had been said. She did not. I paid the check, got in the Maverick, and slowly drove home.

WHEN I OPENED the apartment door, Rachel greeted me with one brittle sentence. "Your girlfriend called."

"What did she say?" I said.

"She's at the La Paz Bar in Fullerton. She told me to tell you she walked there from Del Rey's, that she doesn't have any money for cab fare, so she wants you to drive back to Fullerton, to the bar, and pick her up and take her home."

"Okay," I said.

"Do you think you and she can throw Ferris Fremont out of

office?" Rachel called after me sardonically. "You and she and Valis? That satellite?"

Pausing at the door, I answered, "No. I don't. Maybe some lesser tyranny in another universe. Some despotic ruler of America in an alternate world that's not so bad as this — but this world, this tyrant, no."

"I envy the people in that universe."

"Me too." I left the apartment and drove from Placentia to the La Paz Bar on Harbor Boulevard in Fullerton.

The La Paz Bar is extremely dark, and when I entered I could not see her anywhere. At last I made out her small figure; she sat alone at a small table in the rear, her purse in front of her beside an empty drink glass and a dish of corn chips.

Seating myself, I said, "I'm sorry I said those things."

"It's all right," Sadassa said. "You were supposed to say them. I just didn't know how to react — I had to get out of that restaurant. Too many people, too crowded. I had no instructions then as to what to say; you took me by surprise."

"Was it true, then? What I said? About your mother?"

"Basically, yes. I've received instructions since I saw you; I know what I'm supposed to say. You are to sit here until I've finished talking."

"Okay," I said.

Sadassa said, "What you told me came from the satellite. There is no other way you could have known it."

"That's right," I said.

"The information you told me introduced you to me as a member of our organization, a new one; that information is an initial step in understanding the situation, but it is not the full story. I'm to further initiate you into the organization by —"

"What organization?" I said.

"Aramchek," Sadassa said.

"Then Aramchek exists."

"Certainly it does. Why should Ferris Fremont spend half his time trying to stamp out a group that's imaginary? Aramchek includes hundreds, perhaps thousands of people, here and in the Soviet Union. I don't really know how many. The satellite reaches each of us directly and on an individual basis, so only the satellite knows who, how many, where, and what we are to do."

"What is Aramchek?" I said.

"I just told you. People here and there contacted and informed by the satellite. The satellite itself is called Aramchek; we get our name from it. You're a member of Aramchek, brought into it on the initiative of the satellite. It is always by the volition of the satellite that someone is brought in — exactly as you were: picked out, selected. We, you and I and the others, are the Aramchek people, exponents of a composite mind emanating from the satellite, which in turn receives its instructions by web from the planets of the Albemuth system.

"Albemuth is the correct name for the star we call Fomalhaut. We came from there originally, but the mind controlling the satellite is not like ours; rather, it is" — she paused — "much superior. The dominant life form on the planets of Albemuth. Whereas we were a less-evolved life form. We were given our freedom tens of thousands of years ago, and we migrated here to set up our own colony. When we fell into overwhelming difficulties, the satellite was dispatched to help us, to serve as a link back to the Albemuth system."

"I knew most of this already," I said.

Sadassa continued, "There is one thing you do not know, or rather do not realize. What has been happening is a transfer of plasmatic, highly evolved life forms from the Albemuth planets via the communications network to the satellite, and from there to the surface of this planet. Technically speaking, Earth is being invaded. That is what is really happening.

"The satellite has done it before — two thousand years ago, to be exact. It didn't work out that time. The receivers were eventually destroyed and the plasmatic life forms escaped into the atmosphere, taking the receivers' energy with them.

"You yourself personally were invaded by a plasmatic life form sent in energy form to take control of you and direct your actions. We, the members of the organization, are receptor sites for these plasmatic life forms from the home planets, a sort of collective brain — that's what we now consist of, to our own advantage. They are coming in a very small number, however, for the purpose of helping us; this is not a mass invasion but rather a small, highly selective one. It was with great deliberation that you were picked out as a receptor site; I was, too. Without this possession we could not succeed. We may not succeed anyhow."

"Succeed at what?"

"Dislodging Ferris Fremont."

"Then that is a major goal."

"Yes." She nodded. "A major goal here, in the limited terms of this planet. You have become a composite entity, part human and part — well, they have no name. Being energy, they merge together, split apart, and re-form into their composite form, as a band in the atmospheres of their home planets. They are highly evolved atmospheric spirits who once had material bodies. They are very old; this is why, when your theoleptic-like experience began, you had the impression of a very ancient person seizing possession of you, with ancient memories."

"Yes," I said.

"You thought it was a human being who had died," Sadassa said. "Didn't you? I thought so too when it happened to me. I imagined all sorts of things — I tried out every theory in the book. Valis let us —"

"I made up that word," I broke in.

"You were given that word; it was placed in your head. It is how we all refer to him. Of course it isn't his name; it is merely a label, an analysis of his properties. Valis allows us an interval in which to formulate theories acceptable to our own minds in order to minimize the shock. Eventually, when we are ready, we are given the truth. It is a hard blow to take, Nick, to discover that Earth is in the process of being selectively invaded; it conjures up horrific scenes of Martian insects, tall as buildings, landing and kicking over the Golden Gate Bridge. But this is not like that; this is for our benefit. It is selective, cautious, and considerate, and its only antagonist is our own antagonist."

"Will these plasmatic life forms leave after Fremont is destroyed?" I asked.

"Yes. They've come several times before in the past, given help and knowledge — medical knowledge in particular — and departed. They are our protectors, Nick; they come when we need them and then go away."

"It fits what I already know," I said. I found that my body was trembling, as if I were cold. "Can I have the waitress bring me a drink?" I asked Sadassa.

"Of course. If you have enough money, I'd like another. A margarita."

I ordered two margaritas.

"Well," I said as we sat sipping our drinks, "it's a lot easier for me now. I don't have to convince you."

"I already have the material written out," Sadassa said.

"What material?" I said, and then I understood. To be inserted as subliminal information on the record album. "Oh," I said, startled. "Can I see it?"

"I don't have it with me. I'll give it to you during the next few days. It's to go in an album you expect to sell well; you can have anyone record it, preferably one of your most popular artists. It should be, if at all possible, a hit record. This project has been building for years, Nick. For ten or twelve years. It must not misfire."

"What is the message like?" I asked.

"You'll see it. In time." She smiled. "It reads like nothing at all."

"But do you know what's really in it?"

"No," Sadassa said. "Not completely. It's a song about 'party time.' It goes something like, 'Come to the party.' It sounds of course like a fun party; you know. Then later the vocal line goes, '*Join* the party.' The singer says, 'Everybody join the party.' And a subtrack goes, 'Is everybody at the party? Is everybody present at the party?' Only if you listen carefully, they're saying, 'Is everybody *president* at the party?' and the singer is singing something about 'joining the party' at the same time the word 'president' is said — repeated, in fact, by an ensemble answer: 'President, president, president, join — joined — the party,' and so forth. I could make out that part. But the rest I couldn't."

"Wow," I said. It terrified me; I could see how the sound-on-sound would be dubbed in as voice override.

"But this record," Sadassa said, "which you at Progressive will create and release, contains only half the information. There is another record in production; I don't know who by or where, but Valis will synchronize its release with yours, and together the information bits on the two records will add up to the total message. For instance, a song on the other record might begin, 'In nineteen hundred and forty-one,' which was the year Fremont teamed up with the Communist Party. Alone, that figure means nothing; but the DJs will be playing a track on first the Progressive disc and then the other one, and eventually people will be hearing all the information run together as a single total message. Random chance will join the two halves together on station after station."

"We will wind up with people walking along humming, 'The president joined the Party in 1941?'" I said.

"Something like that, yes."

"Anything more?"

"'What a grand chick,'" Sadassa said.

"Beg pardon?"

"'What a grand chick.' Shortened in the song to 'Grand chick' or 'A grand chick.' Except that the backup vocals will occasionally change it from 'A grand chick' to 'Aramchek.' Consciously, people listening will continue to construe the words as 'A grand chick,' but on an unconscious level they will absorb the altered information. It goes back to the famous—"

"I know what it goes back to," I said. "The famous LP track still selling in the millions with the 'Smoke dope, smoke dope, everybody smoke dope' backup vocal subtrack."

She laughed her throaty laugh. "Right."

"Ferris Fremont knows about the satellite, does he?" I asked.

"They've guessed. Guessed right. They've been searching for it, and now of course Georgi Moyashka has located it, in cooperation with our own stations. Between the U.S. and the U.S.S.R., Aramchek—the satellite—has been pinpointed. The satellite that Moyashka is sending up is of course armed. It will 'accidentally' explode, taking the Aramchek satellite with it."

"Can another satellite be dispatched?" I asked. "From Albemuth?"

Sadassa said, "It takes thousands of years."

Stunned, I sat simply gazing at her. "And they haven't started one—"

"One is coming. It will arrive long after every human alive today on this planet is dead. The Aramchek satellite presently in our sky has been there since the time of the great Egyptian Empire, since the time of Moses. Remember the burning bush?"

I nodded. I knew the sensation of phosphene activity, blinding my vision: the manifestation of unending fire. We had been helped in our fight against slavery for a long time. But now the days of the satellite were numbered. The Russians could get a satellite up in — suddenly I realized: they've probably had one on the launch pad, waiting. As the final stage of a rocket, all in place. All they have to do is program its route.

"Liftoff," Sadassa said, as if reading my thoughts, "will be at the end of this week. And then the satellite dies. The help and information cease."

"How can you be so calm about it?" I said.

"I'm always calm," Sadassa said. "I taught myself to be calm. We've known it for months, that this was coming. We have the information we need — we have all we're going to get. It should be enough; the Aramchek satellite lasted until its work was done. There are enough of the plasmatic life forms here on Earth to —"

"I don't think we're going to be able to do it," I said.

"But we will make the record."

"Oh, yes," I said. "We can start tomorrow. Tonight, if you want. I have a couple of ideas who we can get to record it. Releases we were planning anyhow, good ones. Major ones we intended to promote."

"Fine," Sadassa said.

"Why did the satellite pick the Jews back in ancient times," I asked, "to speak to?"

"They were shepherds, out under the stars, not city dwellers cut off from the sky. There were two kingdoms, Israel and Judah; it was to Judah, the farmers and shepherds, that Valis spoke. Haven't you noticed that you hear the AI operator better when the wind is blowing in from the desert?"

"I wondered about that," I said.

"What we receive," Sadassa said, "is pararadio signals, a radiation enclosure of the radio beam, so that if the radio message is decoded it signifies nothing. That is why Dr. Moyashka has never been able to unscramble the instructions passing from the satellite to Earth; the radio signal alone is only half the total information. The violent phosphene activity you experience from time to time, especially when the plasmatic personality was beaming down, is stimulated by radiation, not the radio signal. That kind of radiation is unknown to us here. Except for the phosphene response it passes unnoticed, and only the receiving person experiences the phosphene response. Other organisms may experience changes in blood volume and pressure, but that is all."

I said, "That can't be the only reason the ancient Jews were selected, because they lived outdoors."

"No, that's not the only reason. That's why they were accessible to approach and contact. The position of ancient Judah to the tyrannical empires was the same as ours is to Ferris Fremont; they were an unassimilated remnant of mankind, unsullied by power and majesty. They always fought the empires, whatever they were; they always strove for independence and freedom and individuality; they were the spearhead of modern man, opposed to the crushing uniformity of Babylon, and Assyria, and most of all Rome. What they were to Rome then, we are to Rome now."

"But remember what happened in 70 A.D.," I said, "when they revolted against Rome. Complete massacre of their people, destruction of the temple, and dispersion forever."

Sadassa said, "And you're afraid of that happening now."

"Yes," I said.

"Ferris Fremont will destroy us whether we attack him or not. At the end of this week he will shoot the Aramchek satellite down, via Soviet technology. Meanwhile the FAPers are trying to locate all the tandem personalities created by the satellite — people like you and me, Nick. That's why the confession kits, that's why the growing police supervision. You didn't know what they were searching for when they came to you, but they did."

"Have they caught very many of us?"

"I don't know," Sadassa said. "Since we rarely have contact with one another ... such as you and I have as we sit here. But I've been told that half the organization has been discovered — on a person-by-person basis — and killed. We are killed, when we are found, not imprisoned. Often killed as they tried to kill me: by toxin. The government arsenals possess very potent toxins, as a weapon of domestic war. They leave no traces in the body; no coroner can ascertain the cause of death."

"But you lived on," I said.

"The fact that Valis healed me," Sadassa said, "was unexpected to them. Metastasizing cancer had riddled my body before he intervened and healed me. I was healed of it in a day; all the cancer cells, even in my spinal column and brain, disappeared. The doctors could find no trace."

"What happens to you when the satellite is destroyed?"

"I don't know, Nick," she said calmly. "I guess I succumb once more. Maybe not; maybe Valis's healing is permanent."

If it is not, I realized, then I regain my internal chest injuries from the auto accident. But I said nothing.

"What frightens you the most about this whole situation?" Sadassa asked. "The invasion? That was what —"

"The end of the satellite," I said.

"Then you're not frightened at what has happened to you. To each of us."

"No," I said. "Well, frightened in a good way because it was such a surprise. And I didn't understand it. But it saved me from the police."

"You got something in the mail."

"Yes," I said.

"They can detect the general area of a massive transmission print out. They knew the beam went to someone in your area. They probably mailed — the police cryptographers, I mean — probably mailed similar material to everyone near you. What did you do with it?"

"Phoned up FAP. But it wasn't me, it was —" I hesitated, not knowing how to refer to it.

"Firebright," Sadassa said.

"What?" I said.

"That's how I refer to the plasmatic entity in me; I call it 'firebright.' That's a description, not a name; he's like a little egg of pale, cold fire. Glowing with life up here." She touched her forehead. "It's strange to have him inside me, alive and unnoticed. Hidden in me, as he's hidden in you. Others can't see him. He's safe." She added, "Relatively safe."

"If I am killed," I said, "will he die with me?"

"He's immortal." She gazed at me for a time. "So are you now, Nicholas. Once firebright bonded to you, you became an immortal creature. As he goes on, you go on with him; when your body is destroyed and he leaves he will take you with him. They won't desert us. As you and I have housed and sheltered them, they will take us along, into eternity."

"A reward?" I asked.

"Yes. For what we've done, or tried to do. They value the effort, the attempt, as equal to the achievement. They judge by the heart. By intention. They know we can only do so much, that if we fail we fail. We can only try."

"You think we're going to fail too," I said.

Sadassa said nothing. She sipped her drink.

26

AT THE END of the week the Soviet Union announced that there had been a mysterious explosion aboard the intercept satellite which they had launched to photograph the ETI satellite. The force of the blast had destroyed both satellites. Cause of the mighty explosion was unknown, but presumed to be in the Soviet satellite's fuel supply. Dr. Moyashka had ordered a full inquiry.

Only two pictures of the ETI satellite had been transmitted before it was destroyed; surprisingly, they showed it to be pitted and evidently partially damaged from meteor showers. The implication, Dr. Moyashka said, was that the ETI satellite had crossed a great deal of interstellar space before reaching its position in orbit around Earth. The conclusion that it was a very old satellite, long in orbit, was rejected as unscientific and not in accord with Marxist-Leninist reasoning.

So much for that, I said to myself as I watched the news item on TV. They shot down God, or rather God's voice. Vox dei, I said to myself. Gone now from the world.

There must be many happy parties going on in Moscow.

Well, I thought glumly, a great epoch in the history of man has reached its end. Nothing will instruct us, nothing exists in our sky to cheer us when we are down, to lift us up and keep us alive, to heal our wounds. In Washington and Moscow they are saying, "Man has finally come of age; he doesn't need paternalistic help." Which is another way of saying, "We have abolished that help, and in its place we will rule," offering no help at all: taking but not giving, ruling but not obeying, telling but not listening, taking life and not giving it. The slayers govern now, without interference; the dreams of mankind have become empty.

THAT NIGHT AS Rachel, Johnny, and I, plus Pinky our cat, lay together on the big bed in our bedroom, a pale white light began to appear and fill the room.

Lying in my place on the bed I realized that no one could see the pale light but me; Pinky dozed, Rachel dozed, Johnny snored in his sleep. I alone, awake, saw the light grow, and I saw that it had no source, no location; it filled all spaces equally and made every object strikingly clear. What is this? I wondered, and a deep fear filled me. It was as if the presence of death had entered the room.

The light became so bright that I could make out every detail around me. The slumbering woman, the little boy, the dozing cat — they seemed etched or painted, unable to move, pitilessly revealed by the light. And in addition something looked down at us as we lay as if on a purely two-dimensional surface; something which traveled and made use of three dimensions studied us creatures limited to two. There was no place to hide; the light, the pitiless gaze, were everywhere.

We are being judged, I realized. The light has come on without warning to expose us, and now the judge examines each of us. What will his decision be? The sense of death, my own death, was profound; I felt as if I were inanimate, made of wood, a carved and painted toy . . . we were all carved toys to the judge who gazed down at us, and he could lift any — and all — of us off our painted surface whenever he wished.

I began to pray, silently. And then I prayed aloud. I prayed, strangely, in Latin — a Latin I did not know — phrases and whole sentences and always begging to be spared. That was what I wanted. That was what I asked for over and over again, in many languages now, in every language: for the judge to pass over me and let me go.

The pale, uniform light gradually faded out, and I thought to myself, it's because the satellite is gone. That's why. Death has flooded in to fill up the vacuum. Once life has been destroyed, that which remains is inert. I am seeing death return.

The next day Rachel noticed that Pinky seemed sick; he sat without moving, and once, as he sat, his head fell forward and struck the floor, as if from unbearable weariness. Seeing him, I understood that he was dying. Death had claimed him, not me.

I drove him to the Yorba Linda Veterinary Hospital, and the doctors there decided that he had a tumor. They operated while I drove back home. "We probably can save him," they told me as I left, seeing how disheartened I was, but I knew better. This was what had been ushered in, for all the world; the first victim was, of course, the smallest.

Half an hour after I got back to the apartment one of the veterinarians phoned. "It's cancer," she told me. "There is no renal function, no urine production. We can sew him back together and he'll live a week, but—"

"He's under the anesthetic still?" I said.

"Yes, he's still open."

"Let him drift away," I said. Beside me, Rachel began to cry. My guide, I thought. Dead now. Like Charley. Look at the forces in the world that are now unchecked.

"He must have had these malignant tumors growing for

some time," the vet was saying. "He's underweight and dehydrated, and —"

"He died last night," I said, and I thought, He was taken instead of me. Me or Johnny or Rachel. Maybe, I thought, he wanted it that way; he offered himself, knowing. "Thanks," I said. "I know you did what you could. I don't blame you."

The satellite had passed from our world and, with it, the healing rays, like those of an invisible sun, felt by creatures but unseen and unacknowledged. The sun with healing in its wings.

Better not to tell Sadassa, I decided. At least what Pinky died of.

That night, while I was brushing my teeth in the bathroom, I abruptly felt a firm, strong hand placed on my shoulder from behind: the grip of a friend. Thinking it was Rachel, I turned. And saw no one.

He has lost his animal form, I realized. He never was a cat. Supernatural beings mask themselves as ordinary creatures, to pass among us, to lead and guide us.

That night I dreamed that a symphony orchestra was playing a Brahms symphony, and I was reading the album notes. The words came to an end and there was the name:

HERBERT

My old boss, I thought. Who's been dead these years from his heart condition. Who taught me what devotion to duty meant. A message to me from him.

After the name there appeared a musical stave strung in catgut, indented into the soft paper as if by five claws. Pinky's signature; after all, Pinky could not write. I thought, My dead boss, who taught me so much and who is dead, reborn as Pinky? To lead me once again, and then go away, as before? When he couldn't stay any longer . . . a final note from him or them, whichever it was. From my friend. In any case, he guided me through many years; he helped form me; and then he died.

God be with him, I thought in my sleep, and I listened to the Brahms symphony, which was coming from a record booth at University Music — booth number three, behind which I had so often changed the toilet paper rolls in the bathroom, as part of my job, so many years ago. And yet he had been here just now, his firm hand gripping my shoulder with affection. In farewell.

AT PROGRESSIVE RECORDS we had begun taping sessions on the new LP — the catalog item into which Aramchek's subliminal information would be fed, track by track. I had gotten permission from the company brass to give my material to the Playthings to cut; the Playthings were our hottest new group. The only part that worried me was the possible reprisals to them, once the authorities became aware of the subliminal material. It would be necessary to set up machinery in advance to exonerate them. Them, and everyone else at Progressive.

I therefore made extensive memos showing that the decision regarding their material lay entirely in my hands, that I had obtained and prepared the lyrics, that the recording group itself lacked any authority to remove or alter the lyrics — it took me almost two weeks of precious time to ensure their safety, but this was essential; both Sadassa and I agreed. The reprisals, when they began, would be great. I hated to involve the Playthings at all; they were an amiable group, with malice toward none; but someone had to cut the LP tracks, someone who was a hot property. By the time I had completed the documentation, including signed letters from the Playthings protesting vigorously against the lyrics as not being suited to them, I was reasonably sure of their ultimate survival.

One day as I sat in my office listening to some preliminary

takes for the album — to be called *Let's Play!* — my intercom came to life.

"A young lady to see you, Mr. Brady."

Assuming it was a performer asking about an audition, I told the secretary in the front office to send her in.

A girl with short black hair and green eyes entered, smiling at me. "Hi," she said.

"Hi," I said, shutting off the takes of *Let's Play!* To the girl I said, "What can I do for you?"

"I'm Vivian Kaplan," the girl said, seating herself. I now noted the FAP armband and recognized her; this was the FAPer my friend Phil had told me about, the one who had wanted him to write a political loyalty report on me. What was she doing here? On my desk, on the portable Ampex tape recorder, was the reel of takes from *Let's Play!* in plain sight of the girl. But fortunately off.

Seating herself, Vivian Kaplan arranged her skirt, then brought out a note pad and pen. "You have a girlfriend named Sadassa Aramchek," she said. "There is also the subversive organization calling itself Aramchek. And the extraterrestrial slave satellite which the Soviets just blew up has sometimes been called the 'Aramchek satellite.'" She glanced at me, writing a few words with her pen. "Doesn't that seem to you an astonishing coincidence, Mr. Brady?"

I said nothing.

"Do you wish to make a voluntary statement?" Vivian Kaplan said.

"Am I under arrest?" I said.

"No, not at all. I tried without success to get a statement of political loyalty about you from your friends, but none of them cared enough about you to comply. In investigating you we came across this anomaly, the word 'Aramchek' showing up repeatedly in relation to you —"

"The only one that's related to me," I broke in, "is Sadassa's maiden name."

"You have no relationship to the organization Aramchek or the satellite?"

"No," I said.

"How did you happen to meet Ms. Aramchek?"

I said, "I don't have to answer these questions."

"Oh, yes, you do." From her purse Vivian Kaplan got a black flatpack of identification; I gazed at it, seeing that she was a bona fide police agent. "You can talk to me here in your office or you can come downtown with me. Which do you prefer?"

"Can I call my attorney?"

"No." Vivian Kaplan shook her head. "This is not that kind of investigation — yet. You haven't been charged with any crime. Please tell me how you met Sadassa Aramchek."

"She came here looking for a job."

"Why did you hire her?"

"I felt sorry for her, because of her recent bout with cancer."

Vivian Kaplan wrote that down. "Did you know her actual name to be Aramchek? She goes under the name Silvia."

"The name she gave me was Mrs. Silvia." That certainly was true.

"Would you have hired her if you knew her true name?"

"No," I said. "I don't think so; I'm not sure."

"Do you have a personal relationship with her as well as a business one?"

"No," I said. "I'm married and I have a child."

"You were seen together at Del Rey's Restaurant and at the La Paz Bar, both in Fullerton; once at Del Rey's and six times at the La Paz Bar, all recently."

"They serve the best margaritas in Orange County," I said.

"What do you two talk about when you go to the La Paz Bar?" Vivian Kaplan asked.

"Various things. Sadassa Silvia —"

"Aramchek."

"Sadassa is a devout Episcopalian. She's been trying to convert me into going to her church. She tells me all the church gossip, though, and that turns me off." This was true too.

"We taped your last conversation at the La Paz Bar," Vivian Kaplan said.

"Oh?" I said with fear, trying to remember what we had said.

Vivian Kaplan said, "What is this record you are going to be bringing out? There was a good deal of emphasis on it. A new LP by the Playthings."

"That's going to be our new hit record," I said; I could feel the sweat standing out on my forehead, and my pulse racing. "Everybody at Progressive is talking about it."

"You supplied the lyrics for the record?"

"No," I said. "Just supplementary material, not the basic lyrics."

Vivian Kaplan wrote all this down.

"It's going to be one hell of a record," I said.

"Yes, it sounds as if it would be. You're going to press how many copies?"

"We hope to sell two million," I said. "The initial pressing will be only fifty thousand, however. To see how it goes over." Actually, I planned to get them to press three times that number.

"When can you make a copy available to us?"

"It isn't even mastered yet," I said.

"A tape, then?"

"Yeah, we could get a tape to you sooner." It came into my mind that I could give her a tape which lacked the subliminal material; we would simply not add that layer of sound-on-sound.

"It is our opinion," Vivian Kaplan said, "after examining the evidence, that you are having a sexual affair with Ms. Aram-chek."

"Well," I said, "you can stick it up your ass."

Vivian Kaplan gazed at me for a time; then she wrote a few words with her pen.

"It's my business entirely," I said.

"What does your wife say?"

"She says fine."

"She knows, then?"

I could think of no answer to that. I had walked into a verbal trap, but one which meant nothing; they were on the wrong track entirely. I thought, They have the wrong ball; let them run it to the wrong goal line. Fine.

"As far as we can tell," Vivian Kaplan said, "you have completely severed your ties with your leftist Berkeley past. Is that so, Mr. Brady?"

"It is so," I said.

"Would you like to draw up a statement of political loyalty about Ms. Aramchek for our files? Since you know her and can speak reliably about her?"

"No," I said.

"We have great confidence in you, Mr. Brady, in terms of your patriotism."

"You should have," I said.

"Why would you turn this chance down to ratify your standing? This would virtually close your files."

"Nobody's file is ever closed," I said.

"Inactive, then."

"Sorry," I said. Ever since the displacement of my own will by the ETI helper I had found it difficult to lie. "I can't oblige you," I said. "What you want is evil and immoral; this is what is destroying the fabric of our society. Mutual spying by friend upon friend is the most insidious wickedness that Ferris Fremont has inflicted on a formerly free people. You can write that down, Miss Kaplan, and put it in my file; better yet, you can paste it on the outside of my file as my official statement to all of you."

Vivian Kaplan laughed. "You must feel you have a pretty good lawyer."

"I feel I have a pretty good grasp of the situation," I said. "Now if you're through, get out of my office. I have tapes to listen to."

Rising, Vivian Kaplan said, "When will you have the tape for us?"

"A month."

"It will be the tape you'll use to transfer onto the master?"

"More or less."

"'More or less' is not good enough, Mr. Brady. We want the exact master tape."

"Sure," I said. "Whatever."

Lingering for a moment, Vivian Kaplan said, "We got a telephone tip from one of your sound engineers. He said there's some very funny stuff in some of the subtracks."

"Hmmm," I said.

"It made him suspicious."

"Which sound engineer is that?"

"We protect the anonymity of our informants."

"You certainly should," I said.

"Mr. Brady," Vivian Kaplan said briskly, "I want to inform you at this time that you are terribly, terribly close to arrest, you and Ms. Aramchek, in fact your entire record firm and anyone connected intimately with you, your families, and friends."

"Why?"

"We have reason to believe that there will be subversive sentiments expressed in the *Let's Play!* album, put there probably by you and Ms. Aramchek and possibly others. We are giving you the benefit of the doubt, however; we will examine the record before its release and if we find nothing in it, you may release it on schedule and distribute as planned. But after analysis, if we find anything—"

"The curtain comes down," I said.

"Pardon?"

"The Iron Curtain," I said.

"What does that mean, Mr. Brady?"

"Nothing," I said. "I'm just tired of all the suspiciousness, all the spying and accusing. All the arrests and murders."

"What murders, Mr. Brady?"

"Mine," I said. "I'm thinking specifically of that."

She laughed. "You're highly neurotic, as your profile indicates. You worry too much. You know what is going to kill you, Mr. Brady, if anything does? Screwing around with that Aramchek girl at your age. The last time you had a physical exam you showed elevated blood pressure; that was when you were admitted to the hospital in Downey following—"

"The elevated blood pressure," I said, "was because—" I broke off.

"Yes?"

"Nothing."

Vivian Kaplan waited for an interval, and then she said in a low, quiet voice, "You don't have the satellite to help you any more, Mr. Brady. They got the satellite."

"I know," I said. "You mean the ETI one? Yes, the Russians blew that up; I saw that on TV."

"You're by yourself now."

"What do you mean?" I said.

"You understand what I mean."

"I don't," I managed to say; it was an effort to lie, a dreadful effort, an offense against myself. I could hardly do it. "I thought the official U.S. position on that satellite was that it — what crap did I hear? 'A discarded satellite of our own?' or something like that. Not from outer space; worthless. Our own obsolete signals coming back to us.

"That was before the Soviet Union photographed it."

"Oh," I said, nodding. "So now the line has changed."

"We know what that satellite was," Vivian Kaplan said.

"Then how could you destroy it? What kind of demented mind could give the signal to destroy it? I don't understand you. You don't understand me and I don't understand you. To me you are insane." I ceased; I had said too much.

"You want an alien entity ruling your mind? Telling you what to do? You want to be a slave to —"

"What the hell do you think you are, Ms. Kaplan?" I said. "That's what FAP is, a bunch of robots receiving their orders blindly and going out blindly to coerce everyone else who isn't already in the net into becoming a robot like them, all following the will of the leader. And what a leader!"

"Goodbye, Mr. Brady," Vivian Kaplan said, and my office door shut after her; she had gone.

I just put my head in the noose, I said to myself. Like Phil did with her; she seems to have an ability to get you to do it one way or another. Phil did it one way, I did it another. I hope they pay her a good salary, I said to myself. She deserves it. She could entrap anybody.

They have enough on me now, I realized, to execute a warrant any time they want. But they have always had enough. It makes no difference. They taped our conversation at the La Paz Bar; they have all they need. And due process, the constitutional guarantees, are no longer observed anyhow; the national security issue is always invoked in matters like this. So the hell with it. I'm glad I said it. I lost nothing I hadn't already lost.

There isn't much, I said to myself, that has not been lost. Now that the satellite is gone.

Within my mind, firebright stirred; I felt his presence. He was still alive, still there within me. Tucked away out of harm's way: safe.

I was not completely alone. Vivian was wrong.

27

I MET SADASSA IN the middle of an orange grove in Placentia; we walked together, holding hands, speaking in low voices. Perhaps they were picking up what we said, perhaps not. In any case we had to confer. I had to keep her informed.

First there was something I wanted to ask her about.

"The satellite is gone," I said as we walked, "but every now and then I still see something, superimposed and in color, as if it's a further satellite transmission to me." Everything I had ever been shown before had been comprehensible, at least with sufficient analysis; this, however, I could not fathom. "It has to do with —" I broke off; I had been about to mention Pinky.

What I was seeing now was a door, proportioned by the measure which the Greeks had called the Golden Rectangle, which they had considered the perfect geometric form. I repeatedly saw this door, marked with letters of the Greek alphabet, projected onto natural formations that resembled it: a dictionary stand, a basalt block, a speaker cabinet. And one time, astonishingly, I had seen Pinky pressing outward from beyond the door into our world, only not as he had been: much larger, more fierce, like a tiger, and, most of all, filled to bursting with life and health.

I now told Sadassa about my witnessing the outline of the

door, and she listened silently, nodding. At the end I told her what I glimpsed beyond the door: a static landscape, nocturnal, a quiet black sea, sky, the edge of an island, and, surprisingly, the unmoving figure of a nude woman standing on the sand at the edge of the water. I had recognized the woman; it was Aphrodite. I had seen photographs of Greek and Roman statues of her. The proportions, the beauty and sensuality, could not be mistaken.

"You are seeing," Sadassa said somberly, "the last receding image of love, moving away from you now that the satellite is gone. A kind of afterimage."

"My dead cat," I said, "is over there."

"It is the far shore," Sadassa said. "The other land, which we are now cut off from. You'll see it a few days longer and then it will be gone, and that will be the last; you won't see anything again." She laughed, but not happily. "It's like when you shut off your TV set; the picture dwindles before it fades out entirely. A residual charge."

"It's very beautiful," I said. "Perfect balance." I remembered, then, the original abstract graphics, the phosphene activity that had initiated the satellite's overwhelming of my human mind with its superior view. "I keep thinking there ought to be a way to cross over there."

"There is a way."

"What way?" I said, and then I remembered Pinky. "Oh," I said. "I see what you mean."

"Aphrodite was the goddess of the generation of life," Sadassa said, "as well as love. I see it too, Nicholas; I see the door through which we can't go. I see the static landscape we can't reach. There, the source of life exists; it once orbited our sky. This is a residual message already placed in us by the satellite, before its destruction, a goodbye to each of us. To remember — to keep with us. A goodbye and a promise."

I said, "I have never seen anything so beautiful."

Changing the subject, Sadassa said, "What are you going to do about Vivian Kaplan? That's the immediate problem."

"We'll give them a tape," I said, "lacking the subliminal material. That'll satisfy them for a while. Then we'll begin to press the records. I'll have a few records made from a master lacking the subliminal material and turn one over to them. I'll keep more of the clean pressings around my office, so if they break in and steal them, what they get will confirm their tape. Finally we'll take the plunge and start shipping the discs with the subliminal material on them. And then sit back and wait for the police. They'll go from one radio station to the next, and one record store to the next, confiscating the records, but maybe some will survive and some will get played before that happens. And of course when they pick us up, us and our families, they will kill us. There is no doubt of that."

"Yes," Sadassa said.

"What I feel bad about," I said, "is that I know we are in the trap already. They are aware of what we're doing; they know about the record. At least they know there is this record and we are probably planning some political act in connection with it. They want to see the record mastered; they want to see it produced, so they can play it and determine its content. We're doing what they want us to do. Well, maybe not; maybe they're not sure — they're guessing and wondering, playing hunches. The police are so full of lies. Maybe there was no sound engineer who phoned in a tip. Maybe they didn't pick up our conversation at the La Paz Bar. All they may know is that *Let's Play!* is our hottest new album, that we've got a lot of time and effort invested in it, so the naturally suspicious police mind is alerted to come down hard on us, ask for a tape, ask for a copy before distribution, rather than monitoring it the usual way."

"I say they're lying," Sadassa said. "Bluffing. That is certainly a possibility. We should go on."

"If we stop now," I said, "they won't kill us."

"Let's go on," Sadassa said.

"Knowing we have no chance of escape?"

She nodded silently.

"I'm just thinking of Johnny," I said. "Valis had me anoint him and everything . . . even give him a secret name. I guess that name will perish with him, one of these days soon."

"If Valis had you do that, your boy will live on."

"Are you sure?" I said.

"Yes," she said.

"I hope you're right."

"Valis may not be here now," Sadassa said, "but within each of us—"

"I know," I said. "I felt him stir the other day. The new life within me. The second birth . . . the birth from above."

"That is eternal. What more could we hope for? Bonded to that. If your body or my body is destroyed, firebright escapes into the atmosphere and our own spark goes with him. There we will gather, ultimately, as one entity, always together. Until Valis returns. All of us: you, me, the rest. However many."

"Okay," I said. "Sounds good to me."

"Let me ask you," Sadassa said. "Of all that the satellite showed you, what was the . . . I don't know how to say it."

"The final view of things?"

"Yes. The deepest. Penetrating farthest. Because when it overpowers you it shows you so much about the universe."

I said, "For a little while I saw the universe as a living body."

"Yes," she said, nodding somberly.

"And we are in it. The experience was so strange—it's hard to express it. Like a hive of bees, millions of bees, all communicating over vast distances by means of colored light. Patterns of light, exchanged back and forth, and us deep inside. Continual signaling and response from the — well, bees or whatever they were; maybe they were stars or star systems of sentient organisms. Anyhow, this signaling went on all the time, in shifting patterns, and I heard a humming or a bell-like sound, emitted by all the bees in unison."

"The universe is a great group mind," Sadassa said. "I saw that too. The ultimate vision imposed on us, as to how things are in comparison to how they simply appear."

I said, "And all the bees, as they signal across great distances to one another, are in the process of thinking. So the total organism thinks by means of this. And throughout it exerts pressure, also across great distances, to coordinate every part, so it's synchronized into a common purpose."

"It is alive," Sadassa said.

"Yes," I said. "It is alive."

"The bees," Sadassa said, "were described to me as stations. Like transmitting and receiving on a grid. Each lit up as it transmitted. I guess the colors were prearranged different frequencies of the light spectrum. A great universe of transmitting and receiving stations, but, Nicholas, sometimes many of them, differing at different moments, were dark. They were temporarily inactive. But I kept watching lit-up stations receiving transmissions from distances so far off that — I guess we use the word parsecs for distances like that."

"It was beautiful," I said. "The pattern of shifting lights formed by the active stations."

Sadassa said, "But into it, Nicholas, had crept something which snuffed out some of the stations. Abolished them so they never lit up again. And replaced them with itself, like a cloak falling over them here and there."

"But new stations were opened up to replace them," I said. "In unexpected spots."

"This planet does not receive or transmit," Sadassa said, after a moment. "Except for the few of us — a few thousand out of three billion — governed by the satellite. And now we're not. So we've gone dark."

"Until the replacement satellite arrives."

Sadassa said, "Did we see a kind of brain?"

"More like a jungle gym that kids play on," I said, "with colored buttons stuck all over." Her analogy was too heavy for me: the universe as a giant brain, thinking.

"This is a very great thing we were shown," Sadassa said. "To see from that vantage point, the ultimate vantage point. We should always treasure it. Even if the stations in this local region or sector are all overshadowed and don't light up any longer, it is a sight to remember. With this the satellite presented us with its final insight into the nature of things: synapses in a living brain. And the name we give to its functioning, its awareness of itself and its many parts —" She smiled at me. "It's why you saw the figure of Aphrodite. That's what holds all the trillions of stations into harmony."

"Yes," I said, "it was harmonized, and over such distances. There was no coercion, only agreement."

And the coordination of all the transmitting and receiving stations, I thought, we call Valis: Vast Active Living Intelligence System. Our friend who cannot die, who lies on this side of the grave and on the other. His love, I thought, is greater than empires. And unending.

Sadassa cleared her throat. "When do you expect to have a tape?"

"At the end of the month."

"And the master discs?"

"First the mother and then the masters. It won't take long, once we have the tape. I have nothing to do with that. My part will be over when the tape is prepared and authorized."

Sadassa said somberly, "Be prepared for them to show up and seize a stamper at any time. Right in the middle of production."

"Right," I said. "We'll have some clean stampers and some with the subliminal material — maybe they'll get a clean one. Maybe luck will be with us."

"It will all depend," Sadassa said, "on which they seize, one with material or one without it."

She was right. And over that we had no control. Nor did they.

"By the way," Sadassa said. "I want you to wish me luck; I have an appointment the last day of the month to see my doctor. To find out if I'm still in remission."

"I wish you all the luck in the world," I said.

"Thank you. I'm sort of worried. I'm still losing weight ... I just can't seem to eat. I'm down to ninety-two pounds. And now that the satellite no longer exists —" She smiled wanly at me.

I put my arm around her, hugged her against me; she was light and frail, like a mere bird. I kissed her, then, for the first time. At this she laughed a tiny, low laugh deep in her throat, almost a chuckle, and pressed against me.

"They will arrest your friend Phil," Sadassa said. "The one who writes the science fiction."

"I know," I said.

"Is it worth it? To abolish his career along with yours?"

And, I thought, his life ...

PART THREE

PHIL

28

... ALONG WITH MINE, I thought to myself. Nicholas and I are going down the tubes together, if he goes through with this. What a thing to find out.

"You think it's worth it?" I asked him. "To destroy yourself, your family, and your friends?"

"It has got to be done," Nicholas said.

"Why?" I demanded. I was in the middle of writing a new novel, the best yet. "Nicholas," I said, "what's in the material you're putting on the LP?"

We were sitting together in the stands at Anaheim Stadium, watching the Angels play. Nolan Ryan was pitching; it was one hell of a game. Pittsburgh was screwing up badly. My last baseball game, I said to myself bitterly as I drank from my bottle of Falstaff beer.

Nicholas said, "Information that will eventually cause Fremont's fall from power."

"No information could do that," I said. I didn't have that much faith in the written or spoken word; I wasn't that naive. "And in addition," I said, "the police will never let you get the record out. They probably know all about it."

"Admittedly," Nicholas said. "But we have to try. It may be only that one FAPer, that gung-ho Vivian Kaplan; she may have developed this as a personal, private lead to feather her own nest. Her suspicions may not be police policy."

"All suspicions are police policy," I said.

"Our illustrious President," Nicholas said, "has been a sleeper for the Communist Party."

"Is that just a slur," I said, "or can you prove it?"

"We're putting names, dates, and places into the material and God knows what else. Enough to—"

"But you can't prove it," I said. "You have no documents."

"We have the details. Or anyway the person working with me has. They're all going on the record, in subliminal form."

"And then you saturate America."

"Right."

"And everybody wakes up one morning," I said, "singing, 'Fremont is a Red; Fremont is a Red; better a dead Fremont than a Red,' and so forth. Chanting the material in unison."

Nicholas nodded.

"From a million throats," I said. "Fifty million. Two hundred million. 'Better he's dead than red; better—'"

"This is no joke," Nicholas said starkly.

"No," I agreed, "it's not. It means our lives. Our careers and our lives. The government will forge documents to refute you, if they take notice of the smear at all."

"It's the truth," Nicholas said. "Fremont was trained as an agent of Moscow; it's a covert Soviet takeover, bloodless and un-noticed. We have the facts."

"Gee," I said, as it began to sink in. "No wonder there's no criticism of him from the Soviet Union."

"They think he's great," Nicholas said.

"Well," I said, "do it."

Nicholas glanced at me. "You agree? That's why I had to tell you. She said I had to."

"Did you tell Rachel?"

"I'm going to."

"Johnny will have different parents," I said. And, I thought, someone else will have to write the great American science fiction novel. "Do it," I said, "and do it good. Press a million of the damn things. Two million. Mail a copy to every radio station in America, AM and FM. Mail them to Canada and Europe and South America. Sell them for eighty-five cents. Give them away at supermarkets. Start a mail order record club with it as a freebie. Leave them on doorsteps. You have my blessing. I'll stick the material in my new novel, if you want."

"No, we don't want that," Nicholas said.

"Valis told you to do this? He's guiding you?"

Nicholas said, "Valis is gone. An H-warhead got him, got his voice."

"I know," I said. "Do you miss him?"

Nicholas said, "More than I can ever express. I'll never hear the AI operator again, or him again — any of them, as long as I live."

"Good old Moyashka," I said.

"It must be wonderful to be a nation's foremost astrophysicist and shoot things down out of the sky. Things you don't understand. In the name of communicating with them."

"But you have the information on Fremont anyhow."

"We have it," Nicholas said.

"You are now part of Aramchek," I said. I had guessed who the "we" was, what organization.

Nicholas nodded.

"It's a pleasure to know you," I said.

"Thank you," Nicholas said. And then he said, "Vivian came to see me."

"Vivian?" I said, and then I remembered. "What about?"

"The record we're producing."

"Then they do know. They know already."

"I'm providing her a hoked-up sample without the material. We'll see if that does it long enough to get the real thing out."

"They'll come in and take your master stampers."

"Some will be clean."

"They'll grab them all."

"We're banking on their taking a representative one."

"You have no chance," I said.

"Maybe not," Nicholas said; he did not argue it.

"A quixotic attack on the regime," I said. "Nothing more. Well, do it anyhow. What the hell; they're going to get us all anyhow. And who knows? Some FAPer might listen to it and wake up to reality. For a little while. You can never tell about these things ... sometimes an idea catches on and no one can say why. Or it can fail, even if everyone hears it, and no one can say why. You've gone too far anyhow to pull out, haven't you? So do it and do it right; when FAP listens to the record maybe the subliminal material will get into their minds and that alone will do it. They've got to listen to the record to know what you've done; even if it goes no further —"

"I'm glad you don't mind my dragging you down with me," Nicholas said. He put his hand out and we shook hands.

THE ANGELS WON the ball game, and Nicholas and I left the stadium together. We got into his green Maverick and joined the mass of cars maneuvering out onto State College. Presently we were driving toward Placentia.

A large blue car pulled in front of us; at the same time a marked police car flashed its red light at us from behind.

"We're being pulled over," Nicholas said. "What'd I do?"

As we reached the curb and stopped, the blue car's doors opened and uniformed FAP Special Investigative Unit militiamen leaped out; in a moment one of them was in front of the Maverick with us, his gun against Nicholas's head.

"Don't move," the cop said.

"I'm not moving," Nicholas said.

"What's this —" I began, but I fell silent when the muzzle of a police pistol was shoved into my ribs.

A few seconds later Nicholas and I had been hustled into the unmarked blue Ford; the doors shut and were electrically locked. The car moved out into traffic and made a U-turn. We were on our way to Orange County FAP headquarters — I knew it and Nicholas knew it. The cops did not have to tell us.

"What," I said as we drove into the underground garage at FAP headquarters, "have we done?"

"You'll be told," a cop said, indicating for us to get out of the car; they still held their guns, and they looked mad and mean and hateful. In all my life I had never seen faces so twisted up with hate.

Nicholas, as he got from the car, said to me, "I think we were followed to the ball park."

The ball park, I thought in fear. You mean they can tape your conversation at the ball park, in the middle of a baseball game? In that crowd?

Presently we were taken down a damp, dark concrete tunnel, under the offices on the ground floor; we ascended a ramp, reached an elevator, were held there for a time, and then we entered the elevator. A cop pressed a button and a moment later we were in a brightly lit hall with waxed floors, being led into a large office.

Vivian Kaplan and several other FAPers, including one high-ranking police official with stripes and gold braid, sat or stood around, looking grim.

"I'll be honest with you," Vivian Kaplan said, her face pale. "We put a recording device on you, Nicholas, when you two were in line at the ticket window. We recorded your entire conversation during the ball game."

The high police official said hoarsely, "I've already given orders for Progressive Records to be closed down and their property and assets seized. No record will be made or released. It's over, Mr. Brady. And we're in the process of picking up the Aramchek girl."

Both Nicholas and I were silent.

"You intended to put subliminal material in a record," Vivian said, in an incredulous voice, "saying that President Fremont is an agent for the U.S. Communist Party?"

Nicholas said nothing.

"Ugh," she said, shivering. "How insane. How perverted. That miserable satellite of yours — well, it's gone now, gone for good. We caught it shooting down subliminal material into prime-time TV broadcasts, but it only had the power to override small areas at a time. It never said anything like this. It told you this stuff? It said to say this?"

"I've got nothing to say," Nicholas said.

"Take him out and shoot him," Vivian Kaplan said.

In terror I stared at her.

The high-ranking police officer said, "He might be able to tell us —"

"There's nothing we don't know," Vivian said.

"All right." The police officer made a sign; two FAPers took hold of Nicholas and propelled him from the office. He did not speak or look back as he departed. I watched them go, powerless and paralyzed.

"Bring him back," I said to Vivian, "and I'll tell you everything he has told me."

"He's not a human being anymore," Vivian said. "He's controlled by the satellite."

"The satellite is gone!" I said.

"There's an egg been laid in his head," Vivian said. "An alien egg; he's a nest for it — we always kill them when we find them. Before the egg hatches."

"This one too?" A FAPer asked her, pointing a gun at me.

"He's not part of Aramcheck," Vivian said. To me she said, "We will keep you alive, Phil; we will release books under your name which we will write. For several years we have been preparing them; they already exist. Your style is easy to imitate. You will be allowed to speak in public, enough to confirm them as your books. Or shall we shoot you?"

"Shoot me," I said. "You bastards."

"The books will be released," Vivian continued. "In them you will slowly conform to establishment views, book by book, until you reach a point we can approve of. The initial ones will still contain some of your subversive views, but since you are getting old now it won't be unexpected for you to mellow."

I stared at her. "Then you've been planning all this time to pick me up."

"Yes," she said.

"And kill Nicholas."

"We did not plan that; we did not know he was satellite-controlled. Phil, there is no alternative. Your friend is no longer a —"

"Vivian," I said, "Let me talk to Nicholas before you kill him. One final time."

"Will you cooperate afterward? Regarding your books?"

"Yes," I said, although I did not intend to; I was trying to buy time for Nicholas.

Vivian picked up a walkie-talkie, said into it, "Hold up on Nicholas Brady. He's to be taken to a cell instead, for now."

The walkie-talkie sputtered into response. "Sorry, Ms. Kaplan; he's already dead. Wait — just a minute and I'll check." A pause. "Yes, he's dead."

"Okay," Vivian said. "Thanks." To me she said calmly, "Too late, Phil. It's police policy not to delay in—"

I lunged at her, trying to hit her in the face. In my mind a fantasy wiped out reality; in my mind I hit her in the face, right in the mouth, I felt teeth break and fly into bits, I felt her nose and features collapse. But it was a dream, a wish and nothing more; immediately the FAPers were all over me, between me and her, hitting me. A gun butt slammed against my head, and the scene — and the dream — were gone.

29

I RECOVERED CONSCIOUSNESS, NOT in a hospital bed but in a jail cell.

Sitting up, I felt pain everywhere. My hair was matted with blood, I presently discovered. They had given me no medical attention, but I did not care. Nicholas was dead, and by now Rachel and Johnny, who had done nothing, had been rounded up. Progressive Records no longer existed; they had been ground into the dirt, abolished, before their record had even come into existence. So much for the great project, I said to myself. So much for the idea of a handful of people overthrowing a police tyranny.

Even, I thought, with the help of Valis.

My friend is dead, I said to myself. The friend I have had most of my life. There is now no Nicholas Brady to believe crazy things, to listen to, to enjoy.

And it would never be rectified. No force, no superior entity would arrive and make everything right. The tyranny will continue; Ferris Fremont will remain in office; nothing was achieved except for the death of innocent friends.

And I will never write a book again, I realized; they will all be — have been, in fact — written for me, by the authorities. And those who followed my writing and believed what I had to say will be listening to the voice of anonymous flunkies in Washington, D.C., offices, men wearing fashionable ties and modern expensive suits. Men saying they are me but who are not. Creatures rasping like snakes in imitation of my own style and getting away with it.

And I have no recourse, I said to myself. None.

Two cops entered the jail cell. They had been watching on closed-circuit TV; I saw the scanner mounted on the ceiling and realized that they had been waiting for me to regain consciousness.

"Come with us."

I went with them, slowly, painfully, down a corridor, having trouble walking. They led me down hall after hall, until, ahead, I saw a double set of doors marked MORGUE.

"So you can see for yourself," one said, pressing a bell.

A moment later I stood gazing down at the body of Nicholas Brady. There was no doubt that he was dead. They had shot him in the heart, making identification of his features easy.

"All right," one of the cops said. "Back to your cell."

"Why was I shown that?" I asked, on the way back.

Neither cop answered.

As I sat in the cell I realized that I knew why they had shown me Nicholas's body. It told me that it was all true, what they had done to him, what they would do to me, what they were probably doing to the others. It was not fakery to frighten me; it was grim reality. This time the police were not lying.

But, I thought, maybe some of the Aramchek organization still remains. Just because they got Nicholas doesn't mean they got them all.

The death of men, I thought, is a dreadful thing. The death of good men is worse still. The tragedy of the world. Especially when it is needless.

I half dozed for a while, aching and miserable, still in shock from the loss of my friend. Finally I was awakened from my trance state by Vivian Kaplan entering the cell. She carried a glass in her hand, which she held down to me.

"Bourbon," she said. "Jim Beam. Straight."

I drank it. What the hell, I thought. It was the real thing—it smelled and tasted like bourbon. It made me feel better at once.

Vivian seated herself on the cot facing me; she held a handful of papers and she looked pleased.

"You got everyone," I said.

"We got the record company before they even had a tape. We got the material to be inserted, too." Examining a typed sheet of paper she read, "'Join the Party!' No, it's called 'Come to the Party!' They say 'join the party' later on. And here's another: 'A grand chick saved me, put back together my whole world.' The background turns into 'Aramchek saved the world.' Isn't that gross? I mean, really."

"It would have worked," I said.

Vivian said bitingly, "'Is everybody *president* at the party?' I wonder which of them made up this stuff. And they intended to flood the market with this garbage. Maybe it would have influenced people subconsciously. We use this technique too, but not as crudely."

"And not for the same ends," I said.

"You want to see the manuscript for your next book?"

"No," I said.

Vivian said, "I'll have it brought to you. It has to do with an invasion of Earth by alien beings who rape people's minds. *The Mind-Screwers* it's called."

"Christ," I said.

"Do you like the title? As they say, if you liked the title you'll love the book. These hideous things come here from across space and work their way into people's heads like worms. They're really horrible. They come from a planet where it's night all the time, but because they have no eyes they think it's daylight all the time. They eat dirt. They really are worms."

"What's the moral of the book?" I said.

"It's just entertainment. It has no moral. Well, it—never mind."

I foresaw the moral. People should not trust creatures different from themselves: anything alien, from another planet, was vile and disgusting. Man was the one pure species. He stood alone against a hostile universe ... probably led by his glorious Führer.

"Is mankind saved from these blind worms?" I asked.

"Yes. By their Supreme Council, who are genetically higher humans, cloned from one aristocratic —"

"I hate to tell you," I said, "but it's been done. Back in the thirties and forties."

Vivian said, "It shows the virtues of humanity. Despite some of its glaring luridness, it's a good novel; it teaches a valuable message."

"Confidence in leadership," I said. "Is the one aristocrat the Supreme Council is cloned from named Ferris Fremont?"

After a pause Vivian said, "In certain ways they resemble President Fremont, yes."

"This is a nightmare," I said, feeling dizzy. "Is this what you came here to tell me?"

"I came to tell you I'm sorry Nicholas died before you could talk to him. You can talk to the other one, the woman he was conspiring with, Sadassa Aramchek. Do you know her?"

"No," I said. "I don't know her."

"Do you want to talk to her?"

"No," I said. Why would I want to talk with her? I wondered.

"You can tell her how he died," Vivian said.

"Are you going to shoot her?" I said.

Vivian nodded.

"I'll talk to her," I said.

Signaling to a guard, Vivian Kaplan said, "Good. You can tell her better than we can that Nicholas is dead. We haven't told her. And also you can tell her —"

"I'll say what I want to say," I said.

"You can tell her that after you're through talking to her," Vivian continued, unperturbed, "we will shoot her too."

AFTER THE PASSAGE of ten or fifteen minutes — I couldn't be sure; they had taken my watch — the door of the cell opened and the guards let in a small girl with heavy glasses and an Afronatural hairstyle. She looked solemn and unhappy as the door locked after her.

I rose unsteadily. "You're Ms. Aramchek?" I said.

The girl said, "How is Nicholas?"

"Nicholas," I said, "has been killed." I put my hands on her shoulders and felt her sway. But she did not faint and she did not cry; she merely nodded.

"I see," she said faintly.

"Here," I assisted her to the cot and helped her sit down.

"And you're sure it's true."

"I'm sorry," I said. "I saw him. It's true. Do you know who I am?"

"You're the science fiction writer, Phil, Nicholas's longtime friend. He talked about you. Well, I guess I'm next. To be shot. They invariably shoot or poison members of Aramchek. No trial, not even an interrogation anymore. They're afraid of us because they know what's inside us. I'm not scared, not after what I've gone through already. I don't think they'll shoot you, Phil. They'll want you alive to write crappy books for them full of government propaganda."

"That's right," I said.

"Are you going to cooperate with them?"

"I'm not going to be allowed to write the crappy books," I said. "They've got them written already. It'll just be my name on them."

"Good," Sadassa said, nodding. "It means they don't trust you. It's when they trust you that it's bad — bad for you, for your soul. You never want to be on that side. I'm proud of you." She smiled at me then, her eyes alive and warm behind her glasses. Reaching out, she patted my hand. Reassuringly. I took her hand and held it. How small it was, the fingers so thin. Incredibly thin. And lovely.

"*The Mind-Screwers,*" I said. "That's the first title."

Sadassa stared at me, and then, astonishingly, she laughed, a rich, hearty laugh. "No kidding. Well, leave it to a committee. Art in America. Like art in the U.S.S.R. How neat, how really neat. *The Mind-Screwers.* All right."

"There won't be many books by me after that," I said. "Not from the description Vivian Kaplan gave me of it. You should hear the plot. This blind worm, see, migrates from—"

"Clark Ashton Smith," Sadassa said instantly.

"Of course," I said. "His kind of thing. Mixed up with Heinlein's politics."

We were both laughing, now. "A mixture of Clark Ashton Smith and Robert Heinlein," Sadassa said, gasping. "Too much. What a winner! And the next one . . . let me see. I've got it, Phil; it'll be called *The Underground City of the Mind-Screwers,* only this time it'll be in the style of—"

"A series," I broke in. "In the first one, the mind-screwers arrive from outer space; in the next one they bore up from below the surface of Earth; in the third one—"

"*Return to the Underground City of the Mind-Screwers,*" Sadassa said.

I continued. "They slip through from between dimensions,

from another time period. In the fourth one the mind-screwers arrive from an alternate universe. And so forth."

"Maybe there could be a fifth one where some archaeologist finds this ancient tomb and opens a great casket, and all these horrible mind-screwers tumble out and right away gang-bang all the native workmen and then fan out and screw every mind in Cairo, and from there the world." She took off her glasses and wiped her eyes.

"You okay?" I said.

"No," she said. "I'm scared, very scared. I hate the slammer. I was in the slammer for two days one time, because I didn't show up for a traffic ticket. They put out an APB on me. I had mono then; I was just out of the hospital. This time I just went into remission from lymphoma. Oh, well; I'm not going into the slammer this time, evidently."

"I'm sorry," I said, not knowing what else to say or what to do.

"It's okay," Sadassa said. "We are immortal, all of us. Valis conferred that on us, and he will on everyone, someday; we just have it now . . . the first fruits, as it's said. So I don't feel too bad. We put up a good fight; we did a good job. We were always doomed, Phil; we never had a chance, but that's not our fault. All we had was some information that should have done it. But they had us before — you know. Before we could act. And without the satellite . . ." She shrugged, unhappily. "No one to protect us, as in the past."

"Nicholas said —" I began, and then I shut up, because of course the jail cell was bugged, and I didn't want the authorities to know that another satellite, as Nicholas had told me, was on the way. But then I remembered that he had told me at the ball park, so they knew. Still, they might have missed it. So I said nothing.

A guard came to the door. "All right, Miss Aramchek. Time to go."

She smiled at me. "Don't tell them how lousy their books are," she said. "Let them find out the hard way."

I kissed her on the mouth, and she held onto me warmly and tightly for a moment. Then she was gone; the cell door rattled and clanged shut.

30

AFTER THAT THERE is a lot I do not remember. I think
Vivian Kaplan stopped by to inform me that Sadassa Aramchek
had been shot, as Nicholas had been, but I'm not sure; if so, I repressed it and forgot it and did not know it had happened. But
sometimes in the later nights I woke up and saw a FAPer standing pointing a pistol at a small figure, and in those lucid moments I knew she was dead, that I had been told and could not
remember.

Why would I want to remember that? Why would I want to
know it? Enough is enough, I sometimes say, as a sort of cry of
misery, of having entered regions exceeding my capacity to endure, and this was one of them. I had withstood the death of my
friend Nicholas Brady, whom I had known and loved most of
my life, but I could not adjust to the death of a girl I didn't even
know.

The mind is strange, but it has its reasons. The mind sees in
a single glimpse life unlived, hopes unrewarded, emptiness and
silence where there should have been noise and love. . . . Nicholas and I had lived a long time and done much, but Sadassa Aramchek had been sacrificed before any good luck came to her,
any opportunity to live and become. They had taken away part
of Nicholas's life, and part of mine, but they had stolen all of

hers. It was my job now to forget I had met her, to recall that I said no to Vivian Kaplan instead of yes when she asked if I'd talk with Sadassa; my mind had the solemn task of rearranging past reality in order that I could go on, and it was not doing a good job.

Sometime later in the month, I was taken from my cell, brought before a magistrate, and asked how I pled to fifteen charges of treason. I had a court-appointed attorney, who advised me to plead guilty.

I said, "Innocent."

The trial lasted only two days. They had tape recordings in vast boxes, some of them genuine, most of them fake. I sat without protesting, thinking of spring and the slow growth of trees, as Spinoza had put it: the most beautiful thing on earth. At the conclusion of the trial I was found guilty and sentenced to fifty years in prison without possibility of parole. That would mean I would be released after I had been dead some good time.

I was given a choice between imprisonment in a solitary confinement situation or what they called "work therapy." The work therapy consisted of joining a gang of other political prisoners to do manual labor. Our specific job lay in razing old buildings in the slums of Los Angeles. For this we were paid three cents a day. But at least we stayed out in the sun. I chose that; it was better than being cooped up like an animal.

As I worked clearing broken concrete away, I thought, Nicholas and Sadassa are dead and immortal; I am not dead and I would not be immortal. I am different from them. When I die or am killed, nothing eternal in me will live on. I was not granted the privilege of hearing the AI operator's voice, that voice Nicholas spoke of so often, which meant so much to him.

"Phil," a voice called to me suddenly, breaking my reverie. "Knock off work and have lunch; we got half an hour." It was Leon, my buddy who worked beside me, a former plumber

who'd been arrested for passing out some kind of mimeographed handbills he had created himself, a sort of one-man re-
bellion. In my opinion he was braver than any of us, a plumber
working by himself in his basement at a mimeograph machine,
with no divine voices to instruct or guide him, only his human
heart.

Seated together, we shared sandwiches provided us. They
were not bad.

"You used to be a writer," Leon said, his mouth full of bologna and bread and mustard.

"Yep," I said.

"Did you belong to Aramchek?" Leon asked, leaning close to
me.

"No," I said.

"You know anything about it?"

"Two friends of mine belonged to it."

"They're dead?"

"Yes," I said.

"What's Aramchek teach?"

"I don't know if it teaches," I said. "I know a little about what
it believes."

"Tell me," Leon said, eating his sandwich.

"They believe," I said, "that we shouldn't give our loyalty to
human rulers. That there is a supreme father in the sky, above
the stars, who guides us. Our loyalty should be to him and him
alone."

"That's not a political idea," Leon said with disgust. "I
thought Aramchek was a political organization, subversive."

"It is."

"But that's a religious idea. That's the basis of religion. They
been talking about that for five thousand years."

I had to admit he was right. "Well," I said, "that's Aramchek,
an organization guided by the supreme heavenly father."

"You think it's true? You believe that?"

"Yes," I said.

"What church do you belong to?"

"None," I said.

"You're a strange guy," Leon said. "Do the Aramchek people hear this supreme father?"

"They did," I said. "They will again, someday."

"Did you ever hear him?"

"No," I said. "I wish I had."

"The Man says they're subversive. They're trying to overthrow Fremont."

I nodded. "That is true," I said.

"I wish them luck," Leon said, "I might even be willing to run off some mimeographed flyers for them." Speaking in a hoarse, confidential voice, he muttered in my ear, "I got some of my flyers hidden away in my backyard, where I lived. Under a big rhododendron plant, in a coffee can. I espoused justice, truth, and freedom." He eyed me. "You interested?"

"Very much," I said.

"Of course," Leon said, "we got to get out of here first. That's the hard part. But I'm working on that. I'll figure it out. You think Aramchek would take me?"

I said to him, "Yes. I think they have already."

"Because," Leon said, "I really can't get anywhere alone. I need help. You say you think they've taken me already? But I never heard any voice."

"Your own voice," I said, "is that voice. Which they have heard through the ages. And are waiting to hear again."

"Well," Leon said, pleased. "How about that. Nobody ever said that to me before. Thank you."

We ate together in silence for a time.

"Did believing that, about a heavenly father, get them anywhere?" Leon asked presently.

"Not in this world, maybe," I said.

"Then I'm going to tell you something you maybe don't want to hear. If your Aramchek friends were here I'd tell them too. It's not worth it, Phil. It has to be in this world." Leon nodded firmly, his lined face hard. Hard with experience.

"They gained immortality," I said. "It was conferred on them, for what they did or even for what they tried to do and failed to do. They exist now, my friends do. They always will."

"Even though you can't see them."

"Yes," I said. "Right."

Leon said, "There has to be something here first, Phil. The other world is not enough."

I could think of nothing to say; I felt broken and feeble, my arguments used up during all that had happened to me. I was unable to answer.

"Because," Leon continued, "this is where the suffering is. This is where the injustice and imprisonment is. Like us, the two of us. We need it here. Now."

I had no answer.

"It may be fine for them," Leon said, "but what about us?"

"I —" I began. He was right and I knew it.

"I'm sorry," Leon said. "I can see you loved your two friends and you miss them, and maybe they're flying around somewhere in the sky, zipping here and there and being spirits and happy. But you and I and three billion other people are not, and until it changes here it won't be enough, Phil; not enough. Despite the supreme heavenly father. He has to do something for us here, and that's the truth. If you believe in the truth — well, Phil, that's the truth. The harsh, unpleasant truth."

I sat staring down mutely.

"What's this," Leon said, "about the Aramchek people having something resembling a beautiful silver egg placed with care very secretly in each of them? I can even tell you how it enters

— along the optic conduit to the pineal body. By means of radiation, beamed down during the time of the vernal equinox." He chuckled. "The person feels as if he's pregnant, even if it's a man."

Surprised that he knew this, I said, "The egg hatches when they die. It opens and becomes a living plasmatic entity in the atmosphere that never —"

"I know all that," Leon broke in. "And I know it's not really an egg; that's a metaphor. I know more about Aramchek than I admitted. See, Phil, I used to be a preacher."

"Oh," I said.

"That about the beautiful silver egg that's put into each of them that grows and hatches and guarantees immortality — that's in the Bible, Phil. Jesus speaks about it several times in different ways. See, the Master was talking so as to bewilder the multitude; it was only supposed to make sense to his disciples. Or rather, it made sense to everyone, but the real meaning was known only to his disciples. They guarded the secret carefully because of the Romans. The Master himself feared and hated the Romans. Despite their efforts the Romans killed them all anyhow, and the real meaning was lost. In fact, they killed the Master ... but you know that, I guess. The secret was lost for almost two thousand years. But now it's coming back. The young men now, see, are having visions, and the old men, Phil, are dreaming dreams."

"There's nothing about silver eggs in the New Testament," I said.

"The pearl," Leon said emphatically, "of great price. And the treasure which is buried in the field. The man sells everything he has to buy the field. Pearl, treasure, egg, the yeast that leavens the mass all through — code words for what happened to your two friends. And the mustard seed that's so tiny but it grows to become a great tree that birds land on — birds, Phil, in the sky. And in Matthew, the parable about the sower going out to sow . . . some seeds fell on the edge of the path, some fell on patches of rock, some on thorns, but listen to this: Some fell on rich soil and produced their crop. In every case the Master says that's how the kingdom is, the kingdom which is not of this world."

I was interested. "Tell me more, preacher Leon," I said, half kiddingly, half in fascination.

"I'm not a preacher any longer," Leon said, "since it isn't worth anything. I'll tell you one further instance, though, where Jesus talks about it. Your friends that died, they are now a single creature together instead of separate. Did they tell you that before they died?"

"Yes," I said. "Nicholas had told me about their future merging into a composite life form, all of them in Aramchek. The corporate existence that would come."

"That's from John, chapter twelve, verse twenty-four. It goes 'Unless a wheat grain falls on the ground and dies, it remains only a single grain' — for 'single' read 'solitary' —'but if it dies, it yields up a rich harvest' — read 'corporate life' for 'rich harvest.' And —'Anyone who loves his life loses it; anyone who hates his life in this world will keep it for the eternal life.' See? In each case something small — a treasure, a mustard seed which is the smallest seed of all, the sower sowing seeds in rich soil, a grain of wheat — *something is placed in the ground*, which is a secret symbol of the early Christians for the human head, the brain, the mind, and it grows there until it hatches, or sprouts, or is dug up, or it leavens the whole mass, and then it brings eternal life — the kingdom which no one can see. It's what your Aramchek friends were talking about, probably without knowing it, that happened to them, before they died and caused their condition now, after they have died."

"All the parables of Christ have to be decoded, then?" I asked.

"Yes," preacher Leon said. "The Master says he's speaking cryptically so the outsiders won't understand. Matthew thirteen — twelve."

"And you know what he said is true."

"Yes."

Amazed, not understanding, I said, "And yet you still —"

"Still I say," Leon said, "that hating this world and forgetting this world is not enough. The work must be done here. Let me ask you this." He gazed at me intently with ancient but clear eyes. "Where did the Master teach? Where did he do his work?"

"Here in this world," I said.

"You see, then," Leon said, and returned to his bologna sandwich. "These sandwiches get staler every day," he muttered. "We ought to complain. Those red-white-and-blue ladies shouldn't get away with so much; they're getting lazy."

Having finished eating, I got out my sole cigarette and carefully lit up.

"Can I have half of that?" Leon asked.

I tore the cigarette in half and gave one part to my friend. To the only friend I had, now that the others were gone. To the old ex-preacher who had shown me, so compellingly, that all that we had done, Nicholas and I and Sadassa Silvia, was worthless. The man who, as if speaking for Valis himself, had brought me the truth.

"What kind of stuff did you write?" Leon asked me.

"I'm still writing it," I said jokingly. The government forgeries of my work were already beginning to appear. They made it a point — probably Vivian made it a point — to send me a copy of each one.

"How do you do that?"

"It's easy when you know how," I said.

Leon leaned over and nudged me. "Look," he said. "Kids watching us." Sure enough, beyond the rusty cyclone fence inside which we worked, a group of schoolchildren were staring at us with a mixture of fascination and fear. "Hey, kids!" Leon yelled to them. "Don't you ever wind up like us. Do everything you're told, you hear?"

The kids continued to stare.

One of them, an older boy, had a portable transistor radio; Leon and I could hear the raucous rock music blaring from its tiny speaker. The announcer, a local Los Angeles DJ, was babbling on excitedly about the next cut, the latest release, he was saying, already a bullet on the charts, from the rock group Alexander Hamilton, the San Francisco performers who were number one these days.

"Okay, here we go," the announcer dinned, as the gang of kids gazed at us and we gazed timidly back. "It's Alexander Hamilton with Grace Dandridge featured in 'Come to the Party!' All right, Gracie — let us have it!" The music swirled out, and, seated with my bologna sandwich, hunched over and weary, I heard the words stray across to us through the smog-drenched midday air:

> *Evubody present,*
> *Hey hey.*
> *Evubody present,*
> *The people say.*
> *Evubody's president at*
> *PARTY TIME.*
> *Evubody here*
> *Have a good climb.*

Leon turned to stare at me with disgust.

I said, "That's it!"

"That's what?" Leon said.

"He — they — got another record company to press it," I said.

"And it's already out, it's already a hit. So—" I calculated, from what I knew of the record business. It must have been at virtually the same time, I realized. As Progressive was preparing its tape, another company, another group, other members of Aramchek, guided by the satellite, prepared another.

Nicholas's efforts had served as a diversion. Those efforts had fitted into a plan none of us saw or understood. While they were killing him, him and Sadassa, and imprisoning me, Alexander Hamilton, the hottest rock group in the country, was recording the material at Arcane Records. Progressive had nobody to equal Alexander Hamilton in their entire catalog.

Suddenly the music ceased. There was absolute silence. Then another tune began to play, this one instrumental: obviously whatever the station had at hand.

A mistake, I realized. The DJ wasn't supposed to air "Come to the Party!" He forgot his instructions—what the authorities had told him. But the records were pressed, I realized, pressed and shipped, and some of them—for a time at least—played. The government had moved against Arcane Records too late.

"Did you hear that?" I said to Leon.

"That garbage," Leon said. "I never listen to AM radio. At home, before they arrested me, I had a big quad set, worth maybe three thousand dollars. That stuff is for kids—they like it."

The kids continued to stare at us. At the two political prisoners, old men to them, worn and dirty and defeated, eating their lunches, now, in silence. The transistor radio continued to play. Even more loudly. And, in the wind, I could hear others starting up everywhere. By the kids, I thought. The kids.